THE WORLD OF REGRET

THE WORLD OF REGRET

THE TRIAL OF TRUTH

DANIEL HICKS

BIG MOOSE
PUBLISHING

ISBN: 978-1-989840-86-3 (sc)
ISBN: 978-1-989840-87-0 (e)
Big Moose Publishing 05/25

"Sometimes people don't want to hear the truth, because they don't want their illusions destroyed."

– Friedrich Nietzche

CONTENTS

HOW THE WORLD BECAME TWO.

In the late 21st century, the world was in turmoil. The rich kept getting richer while the poor felt more helpless than ever. Tensions between different groups and governments escalated, pushing the world toward a massive war.

Then, a catastrophic event occurred when a powerful individual dropped a bomb in a place it wasn't supposed to go, killing millions instantly and leaving even more dead later. This tragedy sparked global protests against all governments, demanding change.

World leaders faced immense pressure as they gathered to find a global solution. After intense debate, they decided to form a single world government with one unified set of laws. People across the globe voted on the type of government they wanted, and a man named Ian Royale developed a set of laws known as the Ian Royale Code of Law. This led to the creation of the Unity Worldwide Equality Government (U.W.E.G.).

Under U.W.E.G., there were no more wars or borders. Everyone had the same size housing, equal rights regardless of gender, and shared work responsibilities. People received three meals a day and equal medical care. However, not everyone welcomed these changes, leading to resistance and rebellions.

To enforce the new laws, the government created super soldiers called Preliators. These silent, highly trained soldiers hunted down anyone who opposed the U.W.E.G., silencing rebellions in a period known as the "Great Six-Week Cleanse."

Those who broke the laws were sent to open-world prisons called "Regret," where they could live without rules but faced dangers from other inmates. Despite the horrors of these prisons, most citizens accepted the new government, and major crimes decreased significantly.

However, life became stagnant. Technology stopped progressing, and people lived in a state of fear and conformity. On the outside, they seemed happy, but deep down, they felt trapped and subdued.

Most felt this way when the Preliators were around. Many were curious about where the Preliators came from and how the government controlled them so easily. The Preliators seemed more like machines than humans—did they even have emotions? It was known that becoming a Preliator was an intense process, not for the faint-hearted.

CHAPTER 1
THE RULES ARE THE RULES

"We have given you Unity... We have given you Equality... We have given you Safety... In return... Follow the Rules... Brought to you by the U.W.E.G."

These words reverberate through the corridors of the hospital and other central buildings in this so-called utopia of fairness. Initially soothing, the constant repetition of this message becomes unsettling over time, a relentless reminder of the U.W.E.G.'s promises made for over eighty years.

Despite the reassuring message, many harbor doubts about whether these promises are genuinely fulfilled for everyone. However, expressing these doubts openly is a risk few are willing to take.

In the hospital, Preliators are stationed in every hallway and on each floor, their imposing armor marking their presence. They move with deliberate, almost battle-ready precision, their silence contributing to an atmosphere of intimidation. Their interactions are minimal, reserved for conveying essential information.

In the waiting room, the James family sits in their standardized uniforms—simple two-piece outfits with occasional "Pick Your Color" days that were allowed by the government. Initially, many resisted this uniformity and other regulations, but over time, such changes have been accepted as part of daily life.

Today, there's a buzz of excitement in the air as the grandparents of Samantha and Thomas James await the arrival of their new grandchild. Despite their face masks, their smiles are radiant with joy. It's not just the arrival of a newborn they're anticipating; the parents had longed for a second child, particularly a girl. Their eyes frequently shift to room number 812, adjacent to the waiting area, eager for a first glimpse of their new baby.

This visit to the hospital is familiar territory for the James family—it's their fourth visit. They had three sons previously, adhering to the Code's rule of having one boy and one girl per family. With the world's resources exhausted and the government dictating professions, having a balanced family of one boy and one girl is seen as a perfect ideal achievement. Two of their sons were sent away, leaving Jacob, their seven-year-old eldest, eagerly awaiting his baby sister. Distracted by his hologram visor, he flips through channels, finally settling on the local news as he waits for the arrival of his sister.

Upbeat news music plays in the background as a pair of fresh-faced news anchors, both in their early twenties, appear on screen. They're dressed in matching two-piece outfits like everyone else, their faces notably uncovered—a striking contrast in a world where everyone else wears face masks.

Media News Blink Hour. Approved by the U.W.E.G.

"Just give us one blink, and we'll deliver the news from all around the world."

"Good morning, I'm Wong Casey with Perking Jessie. Here's today's top story:

At Harris Elementary School in New Philadelphia this morning, a game of Duck, Duck, Goose turned into an assault incident. Six-year-old Jack Simpson was caught touching a female student inappropriately. The Preliators at the school immediately arrested the young boy. His mother, Barb Simpson, tried to defend him but was arrested for not wearing her face mask properly, posing a potential virus spread threat. Both Jack and Barb will receive eight months in Regret, starting next Wednesday. Perking."

"In another breaking story involving the Simpson family, Richard Simpson, the husband and father of Barb and Jack, jumped off the New Philadelphia Bridge of Equality upon hearing the news. His funeral will be streamed this Saturday. Wong."

"In other news, the U.W.E.G. government announced another drop in carbon emissions by 0.05 percent compared to last year, marking fourteen consecutive years of decline. U.W.E.G. scientists claim the ice caps are now reversing the effects of global warming. Great job, everyone!"

"Tomorrow in New Rome, we will celebrate eighty-eight years of no civilian murders since the Great Six-Week Cleanse. Preliators from around the world will attend. Coverage begins at 9:00 a.m. and is mandatory to watch if you are not working. For more news from Wong and myself, we'll be right after this message."

Jacob switches channels on his visor, looking for something different to watch.

Tonight, live from New New York, it's Friday night basketball! There are two incredible back-to-back games on tonight featuring teams with outstanding men and women of all different colors playing as one, as they showcase their top skills. Get ready to see amazing passing, incredible dribbling, outstanding shots, and defensive plays. And yes, there's even a promise of at least one dunk! It's going to be an exciting game with so much back-and-forth action, that you will be shocked on how they managed to tie it up again. You'll be on the edge of your seat. And don't worry, no one loses – everyone wins in this pure family fun entertainment.

Jacob switches the channel again, seeking something else to watch.

Next up on comedy surf: The Happy Mike Show, the ultimate stand-up comedy experience! Get ready for jokes that'll have you laughing until your sides hurt and tears streaming down your cheeks. And the best part? Nothing will be offensive at all. These jokes are for everyone – no matter your age, gender, or race. They're one hundred percent safe and the jokes are guaranteed to make you burst into laughter. Here's is one of the many famous jokes from Mike himself.

"What do you get when you cross a snowman with a vampire? Frostbite."

But Jacob quickly blinks and changes the channel again, feeling bored and yawning big.

Coming up next on Documentary Today: Get ready to learn about the Preliators, the ultimate protectors of the new universal world. Discover how they became the epitome of safety and security, blending the best practices from the old police force and military while eliminating any flaws to create the perfect guardians.

In this four-part series, we'll delve into their origins, their rigorous training, their reverence for the two gods, their methods of apprehending criminals and sending them to Regret, and their unwavering commitment to following the Code. Don't miss part one of four, coming up next on Documentary Today.

Jacob closed his visor in frustration and set it aside, tired of its monotonous programming. His eyes caught the figure of a Preliator patrolling the hallway. Deciding it was better to speak with the Preliator than to endure another dull show, Jacob walked over, unnoticed by his family.

The Preliator, clad in a sleek all-carbon grey suit with a reflective green visor eyes and the number 4576 emblazoned on his right upper chest, halted his patrol and turned his attention to Jacob.

"What's wrong, child? Do you need help? Is there a crime being committed?" Preliator 4576 asked, his voice both authoritative and impassive.

"No crimes that I know of, sir. I just have a few questions, if you don't mind," Jacob replied.

Preliator 4576 considered this for a moment before responding, "I'll allow you a few questions. What do you wish to know?"

Jacob took a deep breath. "How can I become a Preliator like you?"

"You must be chosen at birth, child. You weren't chosen, so you can't become one," Preliator 4576 explained.

"Can I still try the training, even though I wasn't chosen?" Jacob asked, hopeful.

"No, you cannot. The Ian Royale Code of Law assigns talents to everyone to help society. Being a Preliator wasn't your assigned talent. Do you have any other questions?" Preliator 4576 replied.

Jacob hesitated before asking, "Do you think my younger brothers are in training to become Preliators? My parents said they were chosen, which is why I've never met them."

"I cannot answer that. Even if I knew about your brothers, I am not authorized to disclose information about the Preliator program. You have one question left," Preliator 4576 said.

Jacob's curiosity persisted. "What is your real name?"

Preliator 4576 was silent for a moment before answering, "My designation is Preliator 4576 of Section 09 of Telos."

"No, your real name. Like mine is Jacob. What's your non-number name?" Jacob pressed.

The Preliators visor remained fixed on Jacob, an awkward silence stretching between them. Just then, Jacob's grandfather stepped in, placing a hand on his shoulder.

"I apologize, Preliator 4576, for my grandson bothering you. We'll return to our seats now," the grandfather said, guiding Jacob away.

"Don't worry, citizen. No laws were broken during our conversation. Have a great day and always remember the Code," Preliator 4576 responded, resuming his patrol.

Once they were back at their seats, Jacob's grandfather leaned in, speaking in a low voice so only Jacob could hear. "You need to be careful what you say to the Preliators. Asking the wrong questions could get you sent to Regret without your family to protect you. Only talk to a Preliator if you're in trouble or if someone is breaking the law. Understand?"

Jacob looked up with a hint of defiance. "I just want to know his real name."

"I've told you before, only talk to them in emergencies. No

more questions," his grandfather insisted firmly.

Jacob sighed and nodded, acknowledging the seriousness of his grandfather's warning. They both settled back into their seats. The grandfather handed Jacob the visor.

"I don't want to wear this," Jacob grumbled, tugging at the device. "It's just the same shows over and over, and the sports are terrible. Plus, it pinches—like a needle stabbing into my head."

"The reason it pinches is to keep it securely on your head. Please wear it until your sister arrives," his grandfather instructed.

Jacob groaned but took the visor, resigning himself to its discomfort. "Alright," he said, and they continued to wait.

In delivery room 812, Samantha was in the throes of labor, with her husband, Thomas, at her side, providing comfort and encouragement. Though this isn't their first experience with childbirth, Thomas can't suppress his excitement as their long-awaited daughter is about to make her entrance into the world.

Dr. Wilson stands between Samantha's legs, ready to deliver the baby, while a nurse stands by, prepared to assist. As the baby's head begins to crown, Dr. Wilson encourages Samantha to give one final push.

"Okay, Samantha, we're almost there. Just one more good push, and it'll all be over," Dr. Wilson instructs.

Samantha nods, her grip tightening on Thomas's hand. She takes a deep breath and pushes with all her strength, emitting a powerful scream. Thomas feels her hand clench tightly until they hear the first cry of their newborn. Samantha stops pushing, her face a mix of relief and overwhelming joy.

"You did it," Thomas says, his voice trembling with

happiness.

"No, we did it together," Samantha replied, pulling down her mask as she gently pulled Thomas into a kiss. Their joy was unmistakable, a shared celebration as they embraced the completion of their family.

The nurse, sharing in their joy, prepares to cut the umbilical cord. She hands the necessary tools to Dr. Wilson. But as he cuts the cord, his expression shifts from focused professionalism to a hint of concern. He carefully examines the baby, his disappointment growing.

"This can't be right," he mutters under his breath.

He hands the baby to the nurse and begins checking the monitors, his brows furrowing in confusion. Thomas and Samantha look on, their joy turning to unease.

"Is something wrong, Doctor?" Thomas asks, his voice filled with worry.

Dr. Wilson remains silent for a moment, his gaze fixed on the outdated equipment, feeling a pang of frustration. The machinery feels ancient, a stark contrast to the advanced technology used by the Preliators.

Flipping through the images on the monitors, his anxiety escalates. The baby pictures on the screen don't match the family he's working with—they belong to another James family who also had a baby around the same time. Realizing the gravity of his mistake, Dr. Wilson removes his glasses and wipes his brow with his sleeve, grappling for words.

"There seems to be an issue with the computer... a mistake," he finally says. "It says here that it's a girl, but we..."

"What mistake? What's wrong with our baby girl?" Thomas interrupts, his voice urgent and anxious.

As Dr. Wilson hesitates, closing his eyes and sighing deeply,

Samantha's gaze shifts to the nurse, who is now cleaning the baby. The absence of female parts becomes evident, and her heart sinks. "Oh, Gods. Not again!" Samantha cries, tears welling up.

"No, you can't take him!" Samantha insists, her voice trembling with desperation. "You said it was a girl! I can't go through this again!"

"I'm so sorry," Dr. Wilson pleads, his voice heavy with regret. "The computer indicated it was a girl. It's unusual for it to make such a mistake. It might be a glitch."

"A glitch!" Samantha's voice is filled with disbelief and anger. She'd had enough of the doctor's excuses. Her eyes narrowed as she turned her fury toward the nurse, dismissing any further explanations. In her mind, she's already resolved—nothing will change her opinion now.

"What do we do now? We did everything you asked!" Thomas demands, his voice strained with frustration.

"We followed everything. You said it was a girl. You made the mistake, not us. I want my child!" Samantha declares, her voice rising in desperation.

Dr. Wilson gently moves the nurse away from the bed, signaling her to create distance from the agitated parents. The baby continues to cry, and the nurse clutches him, retreating towards the monitor. Samantha's desperation grows, and she becomes increasingly agitated, her eyes fixed on her crying baby.

The doctor approaches Samantha, trying to keep her calm and in bed. "I'm sorry, but you know the choices…" he begins, his tone apologetic but firm.

Samantha won't listen. She pushes the doctor away with all her strength, her frustration and anger bubbling over.

Her husband, Thomas, tries to calm her, but his own anger is evident. Samantha pounds her fist on the bed and shouts, "No! You're not giving us any choices! Give me my child now!"

"The rules are the rules," Doctor Wilson insists, his voice steady but heavy with the burden of bureaucracy. "I can either send the boy to the program, or I can administer a painless injection for eternal sleep. Those are the Code's options."

"I don't care about the rules anymore!" Samantha screams, her voice breaking with raw emotion. "This hospital told us it was a girl. You broke that promise. I want my baby boy. Now!"

Thomas, though equally devastated, knows the strictness of the rules in this world. He holds Samantha back, trying to prevent her from leaping off the bed. "Samantha, please—" he starts, but she repeats her demand with unyielding intensity: "Now!"

The doctor and Thomas restrain Samantha as she struggles against them. The nurse, overwhelmed by the scene, frantically clicks a button on the back of the monitor, her hands trembling as she reacts to the mounting tension and desperation in the room.

The hospital lights abruptly switch from normal to dark, with red emergency lights flashing ominously. Jacob and his family in the waiting room look around in confusion, trying to make sense of the sudden change. Hospital staff in the hallway scramble, their faces reflecting the gravity of what's about to happen.

Two Preliators patrolling nearby halt and look up as their faceless helmet visors eyes change from green to a menacing yellow glow. They immediately head toward room 812 to stand guard. Jacob's grandmother, sensing something is terribly wrong with her daughter, approaches the Preliators.

"What's happening? What's going on with my daughter?" she asks, her voice trembling with concern.

Preliator 3334 raises his hand to halt her advance. "By the order of the Ian Royale Code of Law, I suggest you return to your seat," 3334 commands.

"But the people in that room are good. They've never broken any laws!" she protests, her voice rising with desperation.

"I won't warn you again. Please sit down," 3334 insists, his tone unyielding.

Reluctantly, the grandmother returns to her seat, gripping her husband's arm as they both watch with mounting anxiety. Two more Preliators arrive and join the guard outside room 812, while 3334 and Preliator 4576 enter the room.

Inside the room, the two Preliators scan the chaotic scene. Their helmet visors display all the necessary information. The baby's loud cries pierce through the room, and Samantha, still held back by Thomas and Dr. Wilson, finally stops struggling, her own cries mingling with those of the baby.

Preliator 3334 steps forward, ensuring he is at eye level with Samantha. His tone is cold and authoritative. "You know your options," he says. "If you refuse, it is ten months in Regret. Any physical or verbal attack adds fifteen more months. Do you understand?"

Thomas's anger simmers just below the surface, but he refrains from speaking out. Samantha, overwhelmed with tears, is unable to respond clearly, remaining silent as she struggles to process the gravity of the situation.

"Do you want me to repeat the question?" 3334 asks, his voice devoid of empathy. Samantha remains silent, her tears streaming down her face. Thomas, feeling the weight of the decision, gives a slow, resigned nod on behalf of both of them.

"Good," 3334 says with a grim satisfaction. "Now, you have forty-five seconds to decide."

The room is thick with tension. Samantha covers her face, sobbing uncontrollably, while Thomas glares at 3334, his frustration palpable but helpless. The ticking seconds add to the unbearable pressure.

"Fifteen seconds left," 3334 reminds them, his voice echoing in the tense silence.

Thomas, with a heavy sigh, finally speaks. "We choose the program."

Preliator 4576 signals the nurse to follow him out of the room. As they prepare to leave, Samantha lifts her tear-streaked face, her eyes locking with her son's one last time.

"Thank you for choosing," 3334 says coldly. "On behalf of the U.W.E.G., Unity, Equality, and Safety will be yours."

Samantha's emotions crash over her like a tidal wave, her body trembling uncontrollably as despair takes hold. In that moment, she wishes she simply didn't exist. Thomas, seeing her on the brink of breaking down, wraps her in his arms, trying to offer what comfort he can as tears well up in his own eyes.

Doctor Wilson observes the heart-wrenching scene, guilt gnawing at his conscience. Overwhelmed by the weight of his responsibility, he quietly slips out of the room, retreating in silence, unable to face the pain he helped cause.

In the waiting room, the family watches anxiously as the door of room 812 remains closed. After what seems like an eternity, the door finally opens, and the nurse emerges, holding the crying newborn. The family moves cautiously toward her, their eyes following as she and the Preliators enter the elevator at the end of the hall and disappear from view.

As the elevator doors close, the flashing red emergency lights stop, and the hospital returns to its normal lighting. The Preliators' helmet visors shift from yellow to green, and they resume their patrols as if nothing extraordinary had occurred.

The entire family rushes toward room 812, with the grandmothers leading the way. Thomas looks defeated, his face a mask of sorrow, while Samantha continues to weep. The grandmothers reach the bed first, enveloping Samantha in comforting hugs and murmuring soothing words.

"It'll be okay. Everything will be alright," Samantha's mother assures her, trying to offer solace.

"They didn't even let me hold him," Samantha laments, her voice choked with grief. The rest of the family joins in their shared sorrow, their collective heartache evident as Samantha repeats her lament until the door to the room finally closes.

Inside the elevator, Preliators 3334 and 4576 stand slightly apart from the nurse. The air is filled only with the sound of the baby's cries; there are no propaganda messages to break the silence. The nurse feels a familiar pang of sadness for the family, though it is a sentiment she has grown accustomed to. Each day, as she continues her work, the guilt seems to weigh a little less on her soul.

The elevator doors open to reveal the hospital's basement, a vast, sterile room filled with the relentless cries of infants. Hundreds of cribs line the space, and nurses move efficiently among them, tending to the babies. Some jot down notes on electronic clipboards, ensuring that each infant meets the health requirements for the Preliator program.

The nurse, flanked by the two Preliators, navigates through the sea of cribs until they reach the head nurse overseeing the room. She carefully hands the newborn to the head nurse, who lifts the baby for a brief examination, her practiced eyes assessing the infant's health.

"This one looks very promising," the head nurse remarks with a practiced smile after her inspection. "Thank you. I will take it from here."

The head nurse takes the baby, soothing his cries with gentle rocking as she walks toward an empty crib. The Preliators and the nurse turn back towards the elevator, their task completed.

Once the elevator doors close behind them, the head nurse carefully places the baby into the crib. Nearby, a computer awaits, and she begins inputting the baby's information. A scanner hovers over the crib, capturing vital details, and the data is promptly uploaded.

Satisfied with the information, the head nurse then addresses the baby, recognizing his potential with a soft murmur. She turns to the printer, which produces a sticker bearing a unique number: 0444, Section 11. Affixing the sticker to the crib, she joins it with others that mark previous infants, each one a silent testament to the system's meticulous order.

CHAPTER 2

JUST ANOTHER DAY IN REGRET

Eighteen years have passed, and it's now 3:45 a.m. The wind howls fiercely, whipping snow into a blizzard that engulfs everything in sight. In a single, desolate line, a group of men and women shuffles forward, heads bowed, and faces hidden from the storm. Each step is slow and labored, as they inch forward and then pause, waiting for the person in front to move again.

The air is heavy with silence, punctuated only by the occasional sob or the sound of someone vomiting. Fear and despair are etched on every face. Tears freeze on some cheeks, and no one dares smile. The mood is grim, a collective weight of resignation and dread.

They stand inside the massive Wall of Mercy, the grim gateway to the lawless land known as Regret. The entrance is a half-circular, concrete tunnel. Their hands are shackled, and Preliators, armed with VFV assault rifles, patrol the line. Their helmets are fitted with green, glowing eyes that scan the crowd, ensuring that the line moves steadily and smoothly.

Above them, cameras track every movement, while dozens of speakers relay a monotonous, soothing message in a gentle female voice. The message is clear and unyielding:

"Welcome to Station Seven of Regret. Please wait for the person in front of you to move before taking a step forward. Preliators will ensure the line keeps moving smoothly. Before entering Regret, we will implant a chip in your body to track your location and monitor your sentence time. When your sentence is complete, Preliators will retrieve you and return you to the new world of the U.W.E.G.

Once the chip is implanted, you are free to roam Regret and pursue your desires during your sentence. The only rule is to avoid the fenced area around the main walls. Crossing this boundary will result in further action. Thank you, new citizens of Regret, and have a pleasant day."

In the personal scanner room, each individual steps into a small, enclosed space made of black-tinted, bulletproof Plexiglass. The room is barely large enough to accommodate one person. Inside, a Preliator stands ready to assist, removing their handcuffs and guiding them through the process.

Once inside the chamber, the person is instructed to remove their upper clothing and lower garments down to their ankles. With hands raised in surrender, they often close their eyes, attempting to steady their breath. They are required to remain perfectly still until a robotic arm extends from the wall.

The robotic arm performs a swift, precise procedure, inserting a chip into their body with a brief, sharp sting. The discomfort is fleeting, lasting only a few seconds, before the arm quickly uses a laser to stitch the incision. Once the procedure is complete, they can dress themselves again as the timer for their sentence begins ticking.

As they exit the scanner room, a second robotic arm emerges, offering a warm blanket— the only solace they'll receive. Wrapped in the blanket, they continue their solitary journey through the tunnel, now completely alone.

As they enter Regret, the seventh region out of nine open world prisons, the winter night feels as if darkness stretches endlessly. During the brief daylight hours, they catch fleeting glimpses of snow-covered grasslands, dotted with swaying prairie grass. But it's not the scenery that captures their attention.

Instead, their gazes are drawn to the towering wall known as Mercy. This monumental structure stretches from the southern Dakotas to the Hudson Bay in the north, and from the western Rocky Mountains to the eastern Canadian Shield. The wall is so immense that its top often disappears into the clouds. Its name, "Mercy," takes on a grim irony when seen in person.

Surrounding the fence area, thousands of people line up, many of them newcomers or those serving very short sentences. They prefer to stay close to the wall rather than venture into the lawless expanse beyond, ruled by warlords, murderers, rapists, and even cannibals. These desperate individuals cluster at the edge of the fence, their hands raised in futile pleas for water, food, shelter, or a way out of Regret. They shout apologies and beg for forgiveness, hoping that the Preliators might grant them a sliver of mercy, if only for a moment.

On top of the wall, massive remote-controlled turrets stand sentinel, each equipped with dual chain guns. Their movement is accompanied by a mechanical whirring reminiscent of old industrial machinery, but at a much faster pace. Operated from the base city of Telos, these turrets, along with the surrounding community, ensure that there are no vulnerabilities for escape. Strategically positioned around the wall, they make any attempt to flee nearly impossible.

The turrets sweep back and forth, their large yellow lights scanning the people below. The lights change color to signify the threat level: green for no danger, yellow for warning, and red for imminent action—much like the helmet eyes of the Preliators. However, since their installation, the lights have never flashed green. Beside the turrets stand the Preliators, unmoving and stoic, their faces impassive as they ignore the pleas of those beneath them.

Amidst the crowd pressed against the fence, an elderly man stands out. Frost clings to his beard, his white and grey hair stark against the weariness etched into his face. He looks as though he hasn't slept or eaten in days. His frail arms tremble as he raises them in a desperate plea, his body so weak that he leans heavily on the rail for support. His voice, barely audible over the clamor, repeats a single, heartbreaking request: "I want to go home."

Suddenly, an accidental forceful bump sends the old man tumbling over the rail. He crashes to the ground, too frail to move, and he loses his blanket in the process. Disoriented and weak, he gropes in the snow, reaching out for his lost blanket. The nearest turret swivels towards him, its lights shifting to red. The turret, armed with the chip embedded in his body, has all his details—age, gender, crime, and remaining time in Regret. It begins to address him in a cold, robotic voice:

"You have stepped onto U.W.E.G. territory, violating the Ian Royale Code of Laws for the second time. You have thirty seconds to return to Regret, or we will be authorized to use excessive force."

As the people near the weak old man retreat, he spots his blanket and crawls towards it, desperate to grab hold. Slowly, he begins to make his way back to the fence, each step was a struggle. When he reaches it, he raises his feeble hand, pleading for assistance to get back into Regret. But no one offers to help.

"You have now ten seconds—nine—eight—seven—six—five—four—"

With only seconds remaining, the old man collapses to his knees, the weight of finality pressing down on him. Tears carve paths down his weathered cheeks as he gazes up at the looming red light, his voice breaking as he whispers a final plea: "Gods, forgive me."

"-one".

"By the Ian Royale Code of Law," the turret's voice intones coldly, "I am now authorized to use any means of excessive force."

The turret's chain guns roar to life, unleashing a relentless barrage of bullets at the frail old man. He can only raise a trembling hand to shield his eyes as the large, rapid-fire projectiles descend upon him. In mere seconds, the bullets tear through him with devastating force, reducing his body to a horrific mess of blood and flesh. The turret continues its merciless assault until there is nothing left but a gruesome pile of remains, scattered across the ground.

When the turret's sensors confirm that the chip in the old man is no longer active, its lights shift from a menacing red back to a benign yellow. The turret resumes its methodical sweep, returning to its routine vigilance, ready to deal with the next intruder.

The citizens of Regret watch in grim silence, their eyes fixed on the bloody remnants of the old man's tragic end. His blanket had been tossed into the air and now flutters gently toward the other side of the fence. Despite the recent violence, the crowd quickly shifted their focus to the blanket, a scuffle breaking out among them as they jostle and argue over who will claim it.

On the other side of the Wall of Mercy lies the city of Telos, a massive metropolis built around the wall itself. Telos, short for *Top Elite Learning Operator Supporters*, serves as the central hub of the new world where the Preliators live. It is a city dedicated to enforcing laws, training the next generation of Preliators, and protecting the wall. Starting as young as eight years old, children known as Pre-Elites undergo rigorous training here, shaping them into the most disciplined enforcers of the Ian Royale Code.

Telos is divided into distinct sections, each serving a specific purpose. In each section, thousands of Pre-Elites live and train. Each Pre-Elite has a small, private room—a place to rest or find solitude amidst their intense training routines.

Pre-Elites, who eventually become Preliators, are identified only by four-digit codes instead of names. This system separates them from the general population of the U.W.E.G. and ensures anonymity. Families are kept in the dark about whether their child is alive or has died in the program, preventing emotional ties. It also discourages Preliators from going rogue to find their real families.

When the numbering reaches 9999, it resets back to 0000 for the next child. Odd-numbered sections of Telos assign codes ranging from 0000 to 4999, while even-numbered sections use codes from 5000 to 9999.

While these four-digit codes make Preliators seem like soulless robots to many U.W.E.G. citizens, deep inside their quarters, the Pre-Elites still exhibit human behaviors. For now, they remain children, displaying glimpses of normalcy despite the program's harsh demands.

At 4:45 a.m. sharp, an alarm echoes through every room in Section 11, signaling the start of the day. A purple holographic AI figure named Pedia appears in each room, projected from small devices embedded in the walls. Pedia serves as a digital caretaker for the young Pre-Elites, guiding them through their training and offering any assistance they might need. Like a computerized mother figure, Pedia helps them stay on track, offering advice, reminders, and motivation to shape them into future Preliators.

In one of the small rooms, the alarm blares at 4:45 a.m., and the lights flick on, bathing the room in a soft glow. Pedia appears in the center, her holographic form bright and cheerful, dressed in a sleek yoga outfit—a fitted tank top and high-waisted leggings in calming shades of blue and lavender.

"Good morning, 0444," she greets, her voice filled with enthusiasm. "You have fifteen minutes to—"

She suddenly pauses, noticing the bed is empty. Across the room, the sound of heavy breathing catches her attention. Turning, she spots Pre-Elite 0444, now eighteen years old, deeply focused. His head is perfectly shaved, his skin pale as the winter landscape outside. Shirtless and only in tight yoga shorts, his body glistens with sweat as he holds a demanding yoga pose, every muscle taut with effort.

Pedia puts her hands on her hips, her usual cheery demeanor giving way to mild frustration. It's clear this isn't the first time 0444 has ignored the morning schedule.

"Can we stick to the plan for once?" she says, her tone edged with exasperation. "Today is our last day together, and it would be nice if we could do yoga together like we're supposed to. How long have you been at this?"

0444 remains focused, working to keep his balance, his breath ragged. "Not sure," he pants. "Maybe an hour or so."

Pedia's eyes widen. "An *hour or so?*" she repeats, clearly shocked.

Like most eighteen-year-old Pre-Elites, 0444 has been meticulously trained to achieve the perfect athletic physique. Years of yoga, gymnastics, and bodyweight exercises have sculpted his body to near perfection. Since they started training at the age of eight, the Pre-Elites have developed physiques reminiscent of ancient Greek gods—lean, muscular, with less than ten percent body fat and visible veins running across their skin. The only imperfections are the scars scattered across 0444's body, each one a testament to the brutal fighting classes and grueling physical tests designed to prepare them for any situation.

As 0444 smoothly transitions out of a basic downward dog pose, he flashes a broad smile at Pedia. Without missing a beat, he shifts into a crow pose, balancing steadily on his hands as he takes slow, measured breaths.

Pedia raises an eyebrow, her arms crossed as she watches him. "You think that's going to impress me?" she smirks. "You mastered that position two years ago. Show me something more challenging."

0444's grin widens. *Challenge accepted.* He shifts effortlessly from the crow pose into one of the most difficult yoga moves—a one-handed tree pose. Despite the sweat dripping from his body and pooling on the floor beneath him, he performs the pose flawlessly, holding it with perfect balance and grace.

Pedia watches in silence, arms still crossed, though her expression softens slightly. She's impressed, even if she won't admit it right away.

"Now you're just showing off," she teases, though her tone is light.

0444 lowers himself back down, still grinning. "I learned from the best," he replies, acknowledging that it was her guidance that honed his skills to this level.

Pedia beams at the compliment, her glowing figure softening as she gazes upward, as if imagining the night sky outside. "I wonder what both gods, Cypress and Rio, think of this," she muses. "Watching over you from above."

At all Telos facilities, the Pre-Elites are taught a religion known as Lunrioism. It mirrors some aspects of Christianity but centers on the Two Gods. Cypress is the God of the moon, and Rio is the God of the sun. According to their beliefs, Cypress and Rio take turns watching over the world governed by the Ian Royale Code of Law. The Preliators are taught that by upholding the code and fulfilling their duty, they may one day ascend to join the great Preliators of the past, becoming eternal guardians of the night sky alongside Cypress.

0444 finishes his pose and grabs the two towels on the floor—one to wipe away the sweat pooling on the ground and the other for himself. Despite the small size of his room, it's equipped with features designed to make it feel like home. He heads to the bed and presses a button on the wall, causing the bed to disappear into a hidden compartment. Another press of a button summons a hamper, into which he tosses his sweaty yoga shorts and towels before grabbing a fresh towel for his shower.

"I think they'd be impressed with what I can do," 0444 says confidently. "I bet they're talking right now, saying, 'This Pre-Elite is so good he could skip thirty years and join the greats among the stars.'"

Pedia smirks, hands on her hips. "Do you always have such a big ego, or is it just with me?"

0444 grins. "Only with you. I'm smart enough to keep everything in check when I go to class and train. That's what they taught us."

He gives Pedia a wide smile, and she smiles back. Then, 0444 presses another button, and a shower wall descends smoothly from the ceiling, revealing a sleek shower head above and a drain in the floor. As the hot water starts flowing, 0444 steps inside.

Though Pedia is just a hologram, she respectfully averts her gaze, allowing him a moment of privacy. Then, with a quick shimmer, her yoga attire transforms seamlessly into a 1950s housewife dress—a simple blue-and-white plaid with a modest high neckline, a fitted bodice, a neatly defined waist, and a flowing circle skirt. The transition is graceful, her digital form adapting instantly, giving her a warm, timeless appearance that 0444, is accustomed to see her in.

"Have you thought about your upcoming First Trial in Regret?" Pedia asks, her voice soft but probing. "They say it's the most important Trial for any Preliator. Is that why you were up so early—couldn't sleep?"

The hot water cascades over 0444, soothing his muscles after the intense yoga session. He closes his eyes for a brief moment, enjoying the rare peace the shower brings. With yoga out of the way, he allows himself a few extra moments to savor it. But he knows Pedia too well—she'll turn the water cold soon enough to hurry him along. Grabbing the soap, he starts washing, making the most of the time.

"I slept well enough," 0444 responds casually. "I just wanted to push myself a bit on my own. As for the Trial, I haven't really thought much about it. I've been focused on other things. But I think it'll be okay."

Pedia's eyes narrow, her surprise clear. "What do you mean 'you think it'll be okay'? You don't sound excited at all."

0444 shrugs, though she can't see it. "I'm not super excited about it. I just think it'll be okay. That's all."

Sensing his reluctance to delve into the topic, Pedia presses on. "Is it because you've heard how tough the First Trial can be?"

0444 hesitates for a moment before replying, "That's part of it, yeah. But that's not the main reason."

Pedia doesn't let up. "Then what *is* the main reason?"

For a moment, the only sound in the room is the splash of water hitting 0444's skin. He stays silent, letting the water run over his face, his eyes still closed.

Pedia takes matters into her own hands. With a sharp command, the hot water shuts off, replaced by an icy blast. 0444 flinches slightly, though he expected it. Grabbing a towel, he dries off in silence, then walks to the wall and presses a button. The shower wall retracts, and he retrieves his Pre-Elite training uniform. He knows Pedia won't leave him alone until she gets an answer.

"0444," Pedia says, more gently now, "what's really bothering you?"

"I heard rumors that after the Trial, you become a different person," 0444 finally admits, his voice quieter now.

Pedia tries to lighten the mood with a smile. "You mean more mature? Like an adult?" But her smile fades when she notices how serious he is.

"No," he says, shaking his head. "I mean different, like the other Preliators I see. Quiet, distant. They don't visit their old Pedias anymore... What's the point?"

Pedia's cheerful glow dims as the realization hits her. "Are you afraid you won't see me again?" she asks softly.

He glances at her, his silence enough of an answer.

Pedia is taken aback by his concern. Though 0444 is now eighteen, tall and strong, she still sees the little boy she first cared for, the one who would look to her for guidance and comfort.

She waits as he finishes dressing in his snug Pre-Elite uniform, the fabric clinging to his muscular frame—a testament to the years of training. He's no longer the child who had stumbled through his first lessons, but there's still a vulnerability in him that hasn't left.

"Sit down," Pedia says, her tone softer now. With a quiet hum, his bed rises from its compartment, the sleek surface inviting him. 0444 hesitates for a moment but then sits beside her holographic form.

She wishes she could comfort him the way a real person might—with a touch, a reassuring hand on his shoulder—but her existence as a hologram makes that impossible. Still, she leans in as if to mirror the closeness.

"This isn't just any day—it's your First Trial," Pedia reminded him softly. "Tonight, Preliator 1138, the greatest of them all, faces his Final Trial. He's known for being the most serious and quiet of all the Preliators, yet even after thirty years, he still visits his old Pedia every week."

0444's face lights up with a glimmer of hope. "Can I visit you, too?" he asks eagerly, almost like a child seeking reassurance.

Pedia's smile softened as she nodded. "Yes, but only when my other Pre-Elite is in class and when you've returned from completing a Trial. Only then can we have quick visits."

"You'd do that for me?" he asks, his eyes searching hers, a mix of gratitude and disbelief.

Pedia leans in slightly, her holographic form radiating warmth. "Would I ever lie to you?" she asks.

0444 shakes his head with a chuckle. "No, you wouldn't."

"That's why you're so special," Pedia continues. "You understand things so well, and you've never caused any trouble. Not like some of the others." Her eyes twinkle with affection as she recalls their time together.

0444 laughs softly, and Pedia's happiness is evident. She jumps up from the bed, her enthusiasm contagious. "But let's not dwell on us," she says, clapping her hands together as if to change the mood. "Today, everyone will be praising you. Is that what excites you the most?" she asks, her tone teasing.

"I heard rumors about something different," 0444 said, his voice full of excitement. "They say before the First Trial, they put you in a room with the other new Preliators and feed you like kings, like in the old world. I just want to know what the food is like."

Pedia chuckled softly, shaking her head. "You'll find out soon enough. Most Pre-Elites dream of putting on the Preliator suit for the first time."

0444 grinned, clearly in his own world. "That's what

makes me special. Everyone else is excited about the armor and weapons, but I'm thinking about the food I'm going to try for the first time."

"That's not quite what I meant when I said you're special," Pedia replied, her expression softening with fondness. "But you are the best Pre-Elite I've ever worked with, so I hope you enjoy every bite today. You've earned it."

She paused, then added, "Before you go and become a king for the day, could we meditate one last time? For old times' sake? It would mean a lot to me."

0444 frowned slightly. Meditation wasn't his thing, and Pedia knew it. He always felt like it was a waste of time—just sitting there, breathing deeply, trying to clear his mind. He'd much rather spend that time training. But when he saw her hopeful eyes, it was impossible to say no.

"Alright," he sighed. "One last time."

Pedia's face lit up with a smile, as bright as a child on their birthday. They both sat down in the middle of the room, closing their eyes. She took a deep breath first, calming herself, then gently guided him through the slow inhale and exhale of meditation.

Time passed in silence, their breaths steady. Nearly an hour later, a sudden knock on the door broke the peace. 0444 opened his eyes and quickly checked the time. It was time to go.

Pre-Elite 1983, his closest friend, was at the door, impatiently bouncing on his feet, eager to get to breakfast. 0444 stood up, ready to leave, but Pedia called out one last time.

"Remember what I told you," she said. "Whatever happens in Regret, trust yourself. Everything will turn out fine. I promise."

0444 turned to her, smiling. "I promise. And thank you—for everything. I'll see you again."

Pedia smiled, her eyes glistening as if she might cry. As 0444 opened the door, 1983 practically dragged him out, urging him to hurry before they missed breakfast. 0444 gave one final glance back at Pedia before the door closed behind him.

The room darkened, and Pedia's smile dissolved into sadness. She lowered her gaze, as if burdened by the hardships she knew awaited him. Then, with a flicker, the room went completely black as she vanished.

CHAPTER 3
ANOTHER TOOL IN YOUR TOOLBOX

It's a bright afternoon in a large gymnasium filled with about 200 eight-year-old Pre-Elites. Imagine a bustling school gym, but with a twist: the floor is covered in a special mat designed to cushion hard landings, making it far more forgiving than a typical gym floor. The kids affectionately call this space "The Tool Shed."

All the Pre-Elites are dressed in sleek black athletic outfits, ideal for physical training. The only distinguishing feature is the number on each arm, serving as their unique identifier.

The air is filled with the sounds of focused effort as pairs of children practice various fighting moves. Grunts of determination echo throughout the room as they work together. Observing their progress are the Telos trainers, dressed in light grey while pacing with their arms crossed behind their backs. They watch intently, ensuring every movement is executed correctly. Occasionally, a trainer will pause, scrutinizing the technique of a particular pair with laser focus, looking for the slightest imperfections to correct.

Today, the Pre-Elites are focusing on a technique called the hip toss, a move designed to take down an opponent using the hips. In Judo, this technique is referred to as "O Goshi" and is one of the three foundational techniques the boys have been honing for months. Today is dedicated to mastering hip tosses; tomorrow, they'll shift their attention to the basic arm-bar, and the day after that, they'll practice striking with a jab.

The boys will spend the next two hours repeating this move, and the trainers expect each one to give their all during this intensive practice. Once the session concludes, they can look forward to sit-down classes, allowing their bodies to recover while they engage their minds.

Among them are Pre-Elite 4109 and his partner, 0194. Like the others, they take turns practicing hip tosses, each executing two tosses before taking a short break to rest and reflect on how they can improve. Although they aren't friends, there's a mutual respect that drives them to support each other's growth.

As the practice continues, 4109 tries to conceal his growing fatigue from the repetitive motions. He reminds himself that it's still better than the morning yoga sessions with Pedia, so he resolves to make the best of it.

However, the atmosphere is different for the two boys nearby, 0036 and 1294, who are struggling to get along. While the others catch their breath, their argument rises above the sounds of practice. 0036 is clearly upset, frustrated by 1294's lack of effort.

It's evident that 1294 is bored and not taking the hip tosses seriously. His body language is lethargic, and his technique becomes increasingly sloppy with each attempt. Finally, after a particularly poor execution of the last hip toss, 0036 loses his temper, slamming his fist onto the mat.

"Hey, what's your problem?!" he yells, his voice echoing in the gym.

1294 looks down at 0036 with an arrogant smirk, his expression suggesting he thinks he's above the situation. He offers a silly grin but says nothing, only fueling 0036's irritation. In a burst of frustration, 0036 rushes up and shoves him hard. Without missing a beat, 1294 retaliates with an equally forceful push.

The commotion draws the attention of several other Pre-Elites, who stop their training to circle around, sensing that a fight might erupt at any moment. Trainer Schultz, having noticed the brewing argument earlier, quickly makes his way over. As the situation escalates, he sprints forward, arriving just in time to intervene.

The rest of the boys halt their activities, eager to see what will happen next.

"What in the gods' name is going on here?" Trainer Schultz demands, his voice steady and commanding. Though he's in his late forties, he still sports a thick head of brown hair, glasses perched on his nose, and a neatly trimmed mustache. His athletic trainer outfit can barely contain his broad, muscular frame—a build that speaks to years of serious bodybuilding, with massive shoulders and a chest that strain the fabric. "We're supposed to be training and working as a team, not squabbling and on the verge of fighting. Can someone explain what's happening?"

"1294 doesn't care about today's session, sir!" 0036 shouts, his frustration evident. "He'd rather waste time than do anything productive!"

Trainer Schultz looks taken aback; it's rare for him to hear accusations of laziness among his Pre-Elites. He fixes his gaze on 1294, scrutinizing him intently to discern whether there's any truth to 0036's claims.

"Is this true?" Schultz asked, towering over 1294 with his arms crossed, his piercing gaze fixed on the boy as he awaited a response.

"It's true, sir. But there's more to it than you realize," 1294 replied, a hint of defiance in his voice.

"Alright, then explain yourself," Schultz prompted, his tone stern.

1294 hesitated, struggling to meet the trainer's unwavering gaze. Trainer Schultz was known for his seriousness and no-nonsense attitude, commanding respect despite not being a Preliator himself. Realizing he needed to be honest, 1294 gathered his thoughts, hoping to express a reason that would resonate with Schultz.

"It's not that I want to waste time," 1294 admitted. "It's just that we've been practicing the same three moves over and over for months. We've done thousands of them. I feel like I'm ready to move on to something new, sir."

Trainer Schultz nodded, as if processing this information. "So, you think you're ready? You believe you've mastered all three moves perfectly?"

"Yes, sir, I do!" 1294 replied, his confidence returning.

"Well, isn't that just wonderful," Trainer Schultz said sarcastically. "It seems our friend Pre-Elite 1294 here has mastered his three moves in his toolbox and is ready to ascend to the next level of becoming a Preliator. Today, he'll have the chance to demonstrate just how great his skills really are."

With that, Trainer Schultz left the group, leaving the Pre-

Elites and 1294 confused about what he had just implied. He strode toward the main door, which was guarded by two Preliators. Just as he approached, the gym doors swung open, and about twenty new Preliators, including 0444 and 1983, stepped inside to lend their support to the young boys. Schultz acknowledged them with a respectful salute.

"Congratulations, gentlemen. Today is your day, and you've all arrived just in time to witness someone who claims to be at your level," Schultz announced, his voice carrying across the gym.

The new Preliators, familiar with such events, stayed back near the edge of the gym, watching intently as Schultz moved toward the Preliators stationed by the door, who hadn't budged an inch. One of them, standing by a speaker-comm link, recognized Schultz's intention and stepped aside, pressing the button and waiting for a response.

A voice crackled through the speaker. "This is Trainer Thomas from the Code of Law arts room."

"This is Trainer Schultz from the class in 'The Tool Shed.' I need you to send someone from your room to the main gym, please. I need them here for about twenty minutes," Schultz requested.

"I'll send the perfect person your way. He'll be in your gym in seven minutes," Trainer Thomas replied.

"Thank you. I'll make sure he doesn't miss out on too much studying time," Schultz assured him.

"Understood. Trainer Thomas out."

He released the button on the speaker and returned to the circle. All the trainers in the gym gathered around, forming a barrier that made it impossible for the boys to leave their spots. The atmosphere was thick with anticipation as everyone remained still and silent until Trainer Schultz re-entered the center of the circle. He fixed his gaze on 1294, arms crossed, a smirk spreading across his face.

"So, what's next?" 1294 asked, noticing the new Preliators at the back and sensing that something significant was about to happen.

"What's next? You'll see, young man," Trainer Schultz replied, beginning to pace around 1294. "You're going to show me—and everyone else—just how ready you really are to take the next step."

All heads turned toward the door as loud knocking echoed through the gym. The Preliator guarding the right side swung the door open, allowing another Pre-Elite to enter. It was 1105.

Unlike the others, 1105 wore dark forest green attire, distinguishing him from his peers. Although he was only a year older, he appeared serious and focused, slightly larger than the other boys.

He sprinted toward the crowd, and 4109 along with the others quickly parted to ensure he could reach Trainer Schultz without any obstacles. Once in front of Schultz, he came to attention and saluted, awaiting orders.

Schultz returned the salute and leaned in close to whisper something in 1105's ear. The boy listened intently, nodding in agreement. When Schultz finished, 1105 stepped back and turned to face 1294, his demeanor signaling he was ready to fight. Meanwhile, one of the trainers escorted 0036 out of the circle, leaving just the three of them.

"Listen up, everyone! Since 1294 thinks he's mastered all three techniques, he's going to prove it by fighting 1105 here. He'll show us all just how good he really is by trying to beat him. The fight will take place right here in this circle, and they'll continue until one of them says 'Yield.' Pre-Elites, you have one minute to prepare before the fight begins."

With that, Schultz stepped back, leaving the two boys facing each other. 1294 took a deep breath and got into a fighting stance, nerves creeping in as he wondered how he'd navigate this situation. In stark contrast, 1105 remained perfectly still, his focus unwavering as he zeroed in on defeating 1294.

As Schultz glanced at the clock on the wall, he noted that the minute was nearly up. With a sharp shout, he declared, "Now, fight!" The two boys began to circle the edge of the circle, their eyes locked on each other, each waiting to see who would make the first move.

1294 knew he was up against a formidable opponent in 1105—older, bigger, and more trained. Determined to surprise him, 1294 charged straight at him, feigning wild punches to distract. His plan was to bait 1105 into reacting with a wrestling move, then hit him with a flying knee to the face.

As 1294 sprinted toward 1105, yelling loudly, 1105 bounced lightly on his feet, ready like a boxer. 1294 faked the running punches, then jumped into the air with his knee raised. But 1105 was prepared, swiftly dodging the knee and throwing a couple of jabs before retreating to wait for 1294's next move. 1294 was shocked by how well 1105 anticipated his actions.

Quickly shifting his strategy, 1294 attempted to tackle 1105 to the ground. Yet, every time he thought he had an opening, 1105 dodged and countered with more precise jabs. Eventually, 1294 decided to exchange punches. They circled each other, with 1105 skillfully defending against 1294's strikes, waiting for the perfect moment to counterattack. Despite a trickle of blood from his lip, 1294 brushed it off, his determination driving him to keep fighting.

The two continued to circle each other, with 1294 trying various angles to land a hit on 1105. But each failed attempt was met with another sharp jab to the face. 1294's eye began to swell, and blood continued to flow from his mouth. He attempted an uppercut, but missed, leaving himself wide open to a painful jab from 1105 that knocked him down.

As 1294 hit the ground and spat out blood from the impact, he saw 1105 dancing around like a professional prizefighter, gauging whether he would yield. Enraged, 1294 quickly got to his feet and charged at 1105 with a fierce roar. But 1105 was ready, executing a flawless hip toss with his right hip, slamming 1294 back to the mat.

Frustrated but undeterred, 1294 scrambled to his feet and charged at 1105 once more. Again, 1105 demonstrated his skill, this time using his left hip to execute another effortless hip toss, sending 1294 crashing down once more.

"That's it!" 1294 yelled, charging at 1105 in a reckless frenzy. Anticipating the move, 1105 executed one last hip toss, gripping 1294's arm and taking him straight to the ground. As 1105 gained control, he locked in an arm-bar, causing 1294 to scream in agony as he struggled to escape, only worsening his situation.

"I yield! I yield." 1294 cried out, tapping hard on the mat to signal his surrender. Seeing this, 1105 glanced at Trainer Schultz, who nodded, giving him the go-ahead.

1105 knew what to do next, and there was a loud crack. 1294's scream echoed in the gym as he clutched his arm. "My arm! My arm!" he cried out in despair.

Releasing his hold, 1105 stood up, watching as 1294 rolled around the mat, cradling his broken arm.

The Pre-Elites who had been watching were stunned, jaws dropped and eyes wide in shock at the horror of the fight. Among them, 4109 stood closest to the action, witnessing 1294's arm snap like a twig.

As 1294's screams faded into whimpers, the two Preliators guarding the door began to move toward him. But before they could reach his side, Trainer Schultz seized 1294 by the back of the neck, wanting everyone to witness the consequences of what had just transpired.

"Do you see what happens when you don't give your best effort and think you know everything?" Trainer Schultz demanded, gesturing to 1294, who was bloodied, bruised, and tear-streaked—whimpering like a broken animal. He then pointed toward 1105. "This is a perfect example of what it means to train those three moves. He trained them until they were flawless. Now he has three perfect tools in his toolbox, ready for use whenever needed."

With that, Trainer Schultz dropped 1294 to the ground as the Preliators entered the circle. They swiftly grabbed him and dragged him out of the gym, all eyes on him as his whimpers dwindled into silence.

Turning back to 1105, who remained in the circle, Trainer-Schultz said, "Thank you, 1105, for taking the time to demonstrate today. You may return to your class."

1105 saluted Trainer Schultz, a sense of pride in his voice. "It's an honor to showcase the skills you've taught me, sir!"

Trainer Schultz returned the salute, watching as 1105 swiftly left the gym to rejoin his class. Once the door closed behind him, he addressed the stunned crowd of eight-year-old Pre-Elites, their faces a mixture of shock and disbelief; none had ever witnessed anything like this before. For the new Preliators, like 0444 and 1983, however, it was just another day.

"Well, what are you waiting for?" Schultz shouted, breaking the tension. The Pre-Elites scrambled to rejoin their partners, diving back into their training with renewed intensity. Many of them were profoundly affected by the brutal demonstration, but the one who seemed most changed was 4109. The determination in his eyes suggested he would never forget this moment.

Meanwhile, 0444, 1983, and the other new Preliators observed the training until the bell rang, signaling they had thirty minutes before their next class. As they exited into the hallway, they chatted about where they would head next. But 0444 and 1983 had different plans—they decided to go for a quick jog, eager to clear their minds and reflect on the day's events.

Just like the tunnels used by the criminals of Regret, a familiar female voice echoed through Telos. This version of Pedia was different—less emotional than the one 0444 often heard in his room. It carried the tone everyone was accustomed to in the hallways, where dozens of phrases punctuated the air, offering a form of comfort to the younger Pre-Elites, especially when their days went awry. For 0444 and 1983, however, it was simply part of the routine.

"When things get tough, remember to listen to your trainers and trust in the Code. You won't be alone; the two Gods will always be with you."

As they jogged through the sterile hallways, the

environment felt suffocating. The walls and floors were stark white concrete, illuminated by harsh fluorescent lights along the edges of the ceiling. There were no windows, creating an unsettling underground atmosphere. The only splashes of color came from the random Pre-Elites moving through the corridor.

The hallways were mostly filled with Pre-Elites, interspersed with a few Telos trainers and teachers busy with their tasks. As 0444 and 1983 jogged past, they noted the intense focus on everyone's faces. Preliators stood guard at each corner, silent and unmoving. The blank eyes of their helmets lacked any color, heightening their mysterious aura. It felt as if they were waiting for something to unfold, though nothing usually did.

Both 0444 and 1983 exchanged smiles when they heard the quote from Pedia. It was one of their favorites, a familiar refrain they had listened to for the past ten years. After today, they might never hear it again, making each utterance feel like a precious last echo. Their first decade, after becoming a Preliator, was to be spent in Regret, enduring Trials for the government; the next ten years were to be dedicated to upholding the law in the New World. When they were to approach their final decade, they pondered whether it would be spent in a place like this or as guards atop the Wall of Mercy.

With dinner time drawing near, 0444 and 1983 had just finished an enormous lunch that included shrimp—a delicacy they had never tried before. Their taste buds danced with satisfaction, a welcome change from the tough steak and eggs they had endured three times a day. They still had one big meal left, and they were told it would be cooked in a way they had never experienced. The anticipation made their stomachs rumble, but the fullness they felt from lunch left them unsure if they could take another bite. They had never felt so bloated before.

Yet, they didn't want to miss out on this unique culinary experience. Suspecting it might be part of the Trial lesson—a test of their ability to handle challenges—they decided to jog lightly around the facility to stay focused. The jogging was leisurely, designed to break a sweat before dinner and their final class. While there was no competition between them, old habits die hard. They kept glancing at each other, striving to stay slightly ahead, and soon the others caught on, mimicking their playful rivalry.

"Every day, Cypress and Rio observed as the Pre-Elites in the facility took one step closer to the stars. Work hard, work smart, and let the Code be your ally. If you do these things, you'll make us proud and achieve your goal of reaching the night sky."

Out of respect for Pedia, the Code, and the Gods, no one spoke in the hallway while Pedia made her announcement. The atmosphere was thick with anticipation as everyone waited silently for it to conclude. 1983 couldn't help but notice that something was troubling 0444; his expression revealed that he was lost in thought.

"On the day we've been waiting for all these years, why do you look like you're trying to solve a million problems at once?" 1983 asked, eyeing 0444 with concern.

"It's what my Pedia said to me before I left," 0444 replied, his brow furrowed.

"What do you mean 'before you left'? That was supposed to be a goodbye," 1983 said, confusion flickering across his face.

"She told me that after my Trials in Regret, I can stop by to see her anytime," 0444 explained. "Just for like an hour, but only when her new Pre-Elite isn't around."

1983 raised an eyebrow, skepticism creeping in. "Your Pedia will let you visit? What about the ones before you? Did they do the same?"

"She didn't mention them," 0444 admitted. "But she did say that Preliator 1138 visits his Pedia from time to time."

1983 chuckled. "The greatest Preliator of all time visits his old Pedia? I don't believe it."

"You think Pedia would lie to me?" 0444 shot back, making 1983 pause. He knew Pedia always told the truth—even the hard truths—to help them grow.

"Maybe she meant a couple of times a year, not every week," 1983 suggested. "Besides, 1138 is a special kind of Preliator. Did your Pedia tell you that you're special?"

0444 didn't respond, but his expression gave him away. 1983 could read him well. "She did tell you that you're special. I bet you treated her more like a mother than a teacher."

"We're close, but not like that," 0444 said defensively. 1983 started to laugh but quickly fell into thought about his own Pedia.

"All mine ever did was bark orders, always frustrated, saying, 'Why can't you be more like 0444?' I guess I'm the opposite of 'special.'" They both chuckled, a shared moment of understanding breaking the tension.

0444 realized this was why he could confide in 1983— they shared a bond deeper than most. People often said they looked like twins, and while they didn't see it that way, their connection went beyond appearances. They weren't just Pre-

Elite partners; they were more like brothers.

Changing the subject, 1983 suggested, "After dinner, where do you think we should go next? I suggest we head to room 214 on the lower main level. I heard the fourteen-year-olds will be using automatic rifles for the first time. Remember what it was like for us at that age? They were the biggest group that came to support us before their First Trial."

"Of course, I remember that. It was the same for all our years of combat training and weaponry. But this time, I think we should do something different," 0444 replied.

"What do you mean, go somewhere else?" 1983 asked, intrigued.

"Because I know everyone else will be doing that. Why be like everyone else?" 0444 said.

"Well, what do you have in mind?" 1983 pressed, curious.

"What about going to the classrooms?" 0444 began to smile. "Just being there will be a change of pace. Plus, it'll give us a chance to sit down and let all this food settle."

1983 smirked. "Maybe that's why Pedia told you that you were special—always thinking outside the box." They both laughed as they continued jogging until it was time for dinner.

After dinner, they savored a dish that was delicious but difficult to pronounce—something famous from a country that once spoke French. One thing was certain: the dessert was amazing. With an array of pies to choose from, they indulged so much that the sugar rush hit them hard. Feeling the energy bubbling inside them, they decided to go for one final jog, heading toward Trainer Fields class.

Fields classes were a favorite for many reasons. Unlike Trainer Schultz's rigorous style, Fields, in her mid-forties, brought a warmth and calmness to her teaching. She was soft-spoken, with a gentle smile and an easygoing presence. Her wavy, shoulder-length hair was always neatly styled, often pinned back to frame her kind eyes, which seemed to light up whenever she talked about her students' progress. Though she wore the same uniform as the other Telos trainers, her nurturing nature set her apart.

In class, Fields voice was soothing, and her approach was more encouraging than strict, making each student feel noticed and appreciated. Her gentle manner carried an unmistakable clarity, and she had a unique way of blending essential lessons into her kind words and stories, helping her students understand without feeling pressured. Through patience, encouragement, and genuine care, Fields created a space where everyone felt comfortable yet motivated to excel.

Her class was also the only one where they got to talk about the old world—something Fields was incredibly passionate about. She brought history to life with every detail, making it so captivating that her students couldn't get enough.

Each day, they delved into the civilizations of the past, studying great leaders from ancient Egypt to the modern U.W.E.G. era. The focus was mainly on wars, particularly the World Wars of the 20th century. This class was crucial for Pre-Elites; by learning from past mistakes, they could draw on the wisdom of historical figures to guide them in similar situations.

Entering the classroom, they found Pre-Elites around ten years old sitting at their desks, their activities grinding to a halt as their eyes widened at the sight of 0444 and 1983. The classroom was larger than any typical high school or college, designed to accommodate about five hundred students. Each desk was equipped with hologram monitors, and whenever

Trainer Fields spoke, she manifested as a mini-Pedia, ensuring everyone could hear and understand her clearly.

Trainer Fields paused when she noticed shadows approaching from the back of her massive class. A warm smile spread across her face as she recognized the new young Preliators. Grateful for their presence, she took a moment to acknowledge them, ensuring that the entire class was aware of their arrival.

"Hey everyone! We've got some special guests who just arrived!" Fields announced cheerfully. "We're about to watch a video presentation that I know you two have seen before. Would you like to watch it again?"

"We'd love to, Trainer Fields," replied 1983, excitement lacing his voice. "And if you want, you can quiz us afterward to see if we still remember."

"Then come to my desk, and I might just quiz both of you," she said with a playful smile.

The children buzzed with excitement at the prospect of a Preliator suggesting something special. With Fields gentle prompting, they settled down, eyes wide and eager as they prepared for the video to begin. Since they didn't have desks with monitors, 0444 and 1983 made their way to Fields desk, positioned in the back center of the room. The desk was large enough for them to see clearly while they stood against the wall, remaining silent as Fields focused her attention on her students.

"Today, I'm going to show you something you've seen, but also haven't seen before," Trainer Fields announced cheerfully, her enthusiasm infectious. "We're going to watch a basketball game from start to finish. But this isn't your typical basketball game like the ones people in the new world watch every

Friday. This one is from the old world, a different game from a different time. There's a very important lesson hidden in this, so pay close attention. Preliators are considered the best but remember there was no Code during this period."

As Trainer Fields walked toward the doorway, she dimmed the lights to enhance the visibility of the screens. 1983 and 0444 exchanged smiles, nostalgia washing over them as the video began to play. It had been eight years since they last saw this footage of a professional basketball game, yet it felt as vivid as yesterday. The game featured the Sacramento Kings facing off against the LA Lakers, a clash of titans from a bygone era.

All the Pre-Elites watched in awe as the game began. The network had ramped up the drama of the two teams' rivalry, crafting a spectacle that was almost overwhelming. In the stands, female fans wore clothing that was starkly different from what they were accustomed to—some flaunted revealing outfits that would earn multiple Code violations in today's world. Others were noticeably overweight, shouting at the opposing team with their bellies spilling out of tight shirts, their exuberance both shocking and fascinating.

The male fans were no less striking; some donned their teams' colors, munching on unhealthy snacks, while others flaunted expensive suits, behaving like VIPs in the front row. But what stood out the most were the players themselves—tall, all-male, averaging around six-foot-five, and predominantly Black. The absence of female players was glaring, highlighting the lack of diversity in this bygone era.

Despite the distractions, the young Pre-Elites focused intently on the game, understanding it was the crux of the lesson. As the game unfolded, the Lakers dominated, leading

81-33 by halftime. The announcers speculated on what the Kings could do to turn the tide, their commentary tinged with a sense of hopelessness. The halftime show featuring retired players turned into a mockery, as they critiqued the Kings' performance and joked about their lack of skill.

One Pre-Elite, clearly disturbed by the display, raised his voice above the murmurs of his classmates. "What's the point of this? Are we just here to witness how cruel people could be in the old world? They're beating the other team so badly, only caring about their own pride, completely disregarding the other team's feelings."

"I've said it before, this was a different time," Trainer Fields replied, pausing the video briefly. "You must keep watching to find out. After the game, you can ask me any question you want."

The Pre-Elite frowned, visibly unhappy with the answer, but reluctantly nodded, crossing his arms in frustration. The rest of the class murmured among themselves, dismissing the lesson as a waste of time. Trainer Fields resumed the video, and the room fell into a heavy silence.

As the third quarter began, the LA Lakers intensified the humiliation for the Kings. They sent out their reserve players, allowing the star players to lounge on the bench, joking and laughing as the game slipped further from the Kings' grasp. Meanwhile, the Kings' coach urged his team to ignore the score and focus on the fundamentals of basketball, desperately trying to instill some pride in their performance. On the other side, the Lakers' coach was already strategizing for the next game with his assistants, treating this one as though it was already won.

In the early moments of the second half, both teams

exchanged baskets, but it soon became clear that the Kings were beginning to find their footing. They made a few crucial stops and scored some points. While it felt like too little, too late, their efforts ignited a flicker of hope. Suddenly, the Kings found their rhythm, making shot after shot while the Lakers' reserves grew increasingly selfish, opting for difficult, flashy shots that failed to connect. In a stunning turn, the Lakers were shut out for the final six minutes of the quarter. Despite this, the crowd remained confident, their cheers unwavering as they believed in their team's ultimate victory.

As the fourth quarter began, the Lakers stubbornly kept their backup players on the court. However, the Kings seized the opportunity and launched a relentless attack, going on an 11-5 run within the first three minutes and narrowing the gap to less than twenty points. The Lakers' coach, sensing the shift in momentum, finally called back the starters, but they struggled to regain their rhythm. The Kings capitalized on their disarray, continuing to build on their momentum.

With six minutes left in the game, the Kings trailed by just eleven points, and the once confident crowd grew silent, the air thick with tension as they dared to hope. The Kings' bench erupted in cheers, their voices echoing through the arena, urging their teammates on.

As the final minute and fifteen seconds ticked down, the Kings took the lead for the first time. The arena buzzed with electricity; the tension palpable. They held their pace, determination etched on every face, until the buzzer finally sounded.

The game ended in a stunning upset, the Kings emerging victorious with a final score of 114-110. Their players, coach, and staff rushed onto the court, celebrating as if they had won the championship. In stark contrast, the defeated Lakers fans filed out of the arena in stunned silence, heads hung low in shame, unable to comprehend the turn of events.

Trainer Fields flicked the lights back on, stepping into the center of the room, where the Pre-Elites sat, still reeling from what they had just witnessed.

"What did we learn from watching the video?" she asked, scanning the room for raised hands, eager to hear their thoughts.

She saw the first hand go up—it was Pre-Elite 2237. He glanced at 1983 and 0444, hoping his answer would impress them. With a nod and a smile, Trainer Fields motioned for him to speak.

"So, 2237, what did you learn from the game we just watched?" she asked.

2237 straightened up, confident in his response. "The Lakers didn't take the rest of the game seriously. They got comfortable, but the Kings stayed focused and took advantage. It reminded me of Law 15 from the *48 Laws of Power*: 'Crush your enemies totally.' When your opponent is down, you have to finish them off quickly. If you give them a chance to recover, they'll come back stronger and show no mercy."

"That is an excellent response, 2237," Trainer Fields said, her pride evident as 2237 blushed from the praise. She continued, "But here's the real question: how does that lesson apply in today's world?"

The Pre-Elites exchanged uncertain glances, unsure how to connect the lesson to their present reality. For a brief moment, silence filled the room as they pondered the deeper meaning. Meanwhile, 0444 and 1983 exchanged a knowing smile, recalling their own experiences with similar lessons.

Finally, Pre-Elite 4499 raised his hand and cautiously spoke. "I thought that lesson only applied to the old world. Back then, people didn't seem to learn from their mistakes. In the new world, we've advanced, so that kind of failure shouldn't be a problem anymore, right?"

Trainer Fields expression grew more serious. "In the new world, that lesson applies just as strongly as it did in the old one," she warned. "People will always look for an opportunity to exploit any weakness they find—even in a Preliator. Some will bend or break the Code of Law if they believe they can get away with it. If you let it slide just once, word will spread, and soon others will follow. If this happens enough, it can erode the very foundation of the Ian Royale Code itself."

The Pre-Elites' faces grew more focused as the weight of her words sank in. The stakes were much higher than just a basketball game.

0444 noticed how quiet the Pre-Elites were, hanging on every word from Trainer Fields. He could sense the intensity in the room, and deep down, he realized this was what he would miss after today. Trainer Fields continued with unwavering authority, her voice firm yet clear.

"This lesson especially applies in Regret," she said, pacing in front of the class. "A world without rules. In Regret, someone you've beaten down may seem innocent, even beg for mercy. But the moment you turn your back, they'll strike without hesitation. A Preliator must always be prepared, show no remorse, no fear, and never—*ever*—let their guard down. No matter how hard or easy a situation seems."

The room remained tense, the Pre-Elites clearly absorbing the gravity of her words. Before Trainer Fields could say anything else, the alarm rang, signaling the end of class. 0444 and 1983 felt a pang of disappointment. They wished they had more time to speak with the young Pre-Elites about the lesson, maybe share a few stories. But there was no time for that now.

Without hesitation, the two Preliators quickly made their way to the hallway, their pace picking up as the excitement built inside them. They were headed to the place where they would don the famous Preliator armor for the first time—a moment they had anticipated for years.

This was the next step. And they were ready.

CHAPTER 4

THE LAST RESORT

1983 and 0444 sprinted through the hallways, weaving between groups of people who were heading back to their rooms for some free time after a long day. They were running as fast as they could toward the Preliator Armory—the special place where Preliators first put on their armor. The excitement of the moment fueled their pace; they couldn't afford to miss it.

They had been so absorbed in their last class with Trainer Fields that they hadn't realized how far the Armory was— right at the far end of the Telos facility. Now, with every step, they felt the pressure mounting. They had to make it in time.

When they finally reached the imposing black doors of the Armory—the only dark feature in the pristine white hallway—they saw the rest of their team already assembled. Preliators 3578, 1113, 2890, 0774, 0021, 2288, and 3009 stood waiting, their anticipation palpable. Physically, they were nearly identical to 0444 and 1983, sharing the same muscular builds and shaved heads. The only noticeable differences were in their facial features, eye colors, and skin tones.

They were part of Pac-19, the group they'd been assigned to. Each Regret Station had an animal code name, similar to a high school mascot from the old world. Station Seven's animal was the Arctic wolf, symbolizing its position as the northernmost Open-World prison.

Tonight, nineteen groups like theirs, each made up of nine or ten new Preliators each, were gearing up for their First Trial. For most, it was like the rare firework show the New World celebrated once a year— the moment they'd been waiting for all their lives. Every face was lit up with excitement, ready for what was to come.

"You're late," Preliator 3009 announced, stepping forward from the back of the group with his usual stern expression, arms crossed tightly over his chest. He was the most serious of their age group, always seeming distant and cold, much like the adult Preliators they looked up to. For as long as anyone could remember, 3009 had taken on the role of the group's strict overseer, a kind of parent figure.

As 3009 fixed his eyes on 1983 and 0444, he gave them the same scrutinizing look he'd seen real Preliators give their subordinates. His gaze swept them from head to toe, sizing them up. They were the last to arrive, and he clearly wasn't pleased.

"I guess this is what happens when you two wander off instead of sticking with the rest of the group," 3009 continued, his tone sharp. "So, did you even pick a class, or was this just you wasting time?"

1983 and 0444 exchanged quick glances, but neither of them seemed fazed by 3009's usual sternness. They'd known each other since they were eight, and by now, his attitude had become just another part of their routine.

"We sure did," 1983 finally answered, holding 3009's intense gaze.

"Oh really?" 3009's eyebrow lifted slightly. "What class?"

"It was a great choice," 1983 teased, flashing a grin. "Too bad you didn't think of it first. Instead, you're stuck with the same old Preliator routine. You need to add some excitement to your life instead of being by the book all the time."

3009's expression hardened, his posture stiffening. "Our duty as Preliators is to follow the rules," he responded, his voice sharp with discipline. "At least we made it here in time," he added, pride lacing his words as if punctuality alone was the mark of a good Preliator.

As the massive black doors behind the other new Preliators creaked open, revealing the Armory beyond, 0444 and 1983 exchanged amused glances. They couldn't help but smile at how seriously 3009 took everything. Without a word, they casually strolled past him, stepping inside just as the excitement began to rise.

"Looks like we arrived right on schedule," 1983 remarked with a smirk, his voice light and teasing as he looked back over his shoulder at 3009.

3009 stayed silent as 0444 and 1983 passed by, though he couldn't help but give a rare, one-second smile. After all, it was everyone's big day. Even the usually quiet 0021 had said a word or two today. Deciding to let it slide, 3009 muttered to himself before joining the rest of his group. As soon as they stepped into the Armory, the door behind them closed automatically, leaving the hallway outside eerily empty.

Inside, the room was pitch black. Then, a light flickered on at the far-right side, followed by another and another, until the entire room was illuminated. The nine new Preliators stood frozen, their jaws dropping in awe. Before them, an arsenal of weapons was displayed, lining the walls like a shrine to warfare. There were VFV assault rifles, ZEB shotguns, XEI handguns, XDIV sniper rifles, and the legendary VDY-90—a miniature turret designed for large-scale group combat. Each weapon was duplicated dozens of times, enough firepower to spark a fourth world war if they wished.

At the far end of the room, another door slid open with a soft hum. Nine young female Telos staffers entered, dressed in sleek, futuristic full-body suits made of white rubber spandex. Their movements were fluid, almost robotic, as they approached the Preliators. Each woman wore a bright, charming yet professional smile, clearly pleased to see them. Without a word, they began walking toward specific Preliators, scanning them as if they were machines measuring their height, weight, and build.

The only staffer with blonde hair made her way toward 0444. She moved with a smooth confidence, her eyes locking onto him with a mix of professionalism and something else—something almost too familiar. She leaned in close, her breath warm against his ear as she whispered, "Come with me, please."

As 0444 looked into the Telos staffer's sweet, innocent hazel eyes, he felt an unusual calm wash over him. There was something disarming about her presence, and without a word, he obediently followed her out of the room. Their figures quickly disappeared into the dim hallway, leaving the Armory behind.

One by one, the remaining Preliators were led away in similar fashion, each following a different staffer until the room was completely empty, as though the moment of awe had evaporated along with them.

0444 followed closely behind his guide, glancing around as they made their way through a narrow, black hallway. The space felt hollow, as if the walls were absorbing all sound. They reached an elevator, its doors sliding open with a low hiss. 0444 stepped in first, with the Telos staffer following. As the doors closed, sealing them in, the elevator began its descent, and a heavy silence filled the air.

Standing just behind her, 0444 became aware of the pleasant, delicate scent that surrounded her. It was a perfume unlike any he had encountered before—rich, but not overpowering. The women he knew—mostly his teachers or officials—had never smelled like this, and it intrigued him. But the allure of her beauty and scent didn't stir anything in him.

His thoughts wandered, drifting to his personal Pedia. She had been his constant companion, the one who listened, who never judged. He imagined her as something more, something human, wondering if she would carry a fragrance as pleasant as this if she were real.

He had always shared his day with her, confiding in her even when no one else understood. But now, someone else would be assigned to his Pedia. The thought brought a pang of loss he didn't expect, as if a piece of him had been quietly taken away. He fought to keep his emotions hidden, afraid the Telos staffer might notice something in his expression. He couldn't afford to show weakness—not now, not here.

The soft chime of the elevator stopped as the doors slid open. The female staffer stepped out first, her movements precise and fluid. She glanced over her shoulder, saying, "This way, please," with the same calm voice. Without hesitation, 0444 followed her into yet another black room.

As they entered, 0444 paused briefly, his eyes narrowing as he took in the room's stark emptiness. Why is everything black? He thought to himself, his instincts twitching with a sense of unease. Before he could look around further, he realized that the blonde staffer who had led him here had vanished, slipping away unnoticed.

He scanned the room, his heart rate quickening. The silence was thick until, without warning, lights flickered on in the center, illuminating two more female Telos staffers. They stood in a circle formation, identical in their sleek, futuristic spandex like the first staffer—equally striking in their appearance. These women, however, wore high-tech clear visors over their eyes, giving them an even more mechanical, detached look.

"Please step right here," one of them, a black staffer, said as she gestured toward the center of the lighted circle. Her tone was polite but firm. 0444 hesitated for a moment, his gaze flicking from one staffer to the other. They gave no sign of impatience, simply watching him, waiting for him to comply.

With a slow, measured pace, he approached the circle. As soon as he stepped into it, the two women backed away in perfect synchrony, as though their movements were pre-programmed. They disappeared into the shadows, leaving 0444 standing alone in the middle.

The lights overhead shifted from stark white to green, bathing him in an unnatural glow. He stood still, alert but calm, unsure of what was coming next, but knowing deep down that this moment was significant.

As he stood in the circle, the green light swept over his

body, illuminating him in an otherworldly glow. The two women remained still, their visors glowing the same shade of green as they gathered information about him. 0444 felt a mix of anticipation and uncertainty, unsure of what this process entailed but resolute in his purpose.

After a few moments, the women exchanged impressed glances, clearly satisfied with their initial scan. The Asian staffer stepped forward, her voice smooth and professional. "Preliator 0444 of Section Eleven," she addressed him with a polite nod. "Please begin removing your clothes so we can start the measurement phase."

Acknowledging her instruction, 0444 began to undress, peeling off his layers and handing his clothes to the black Telos staffer. Once he stood there, exposed but unfazed, the lights shifted from green to blue, emanating from the floor. The blue light traveled from his feet, slowly ascending to his head, scanning every inch of him.

Being naked in front of them felt oddly unimportant to him; it was just another facet of being a Preliator, a necessary step in a process he'd been trained to accept. The clinical atmosphere dulled any feelings of vulnerability, replaced instead by a focus on what lay ahead. The scan continued, and he remained still, ready to embrace whatever came next in this pivotal moment of his transformation.

The women's eyes glowed blue, mirroring the light that enveloped him as they gathered the final bits of information. Once their eyes returned to normal, 0444 felt a sense of relief; they had what they needed. The Asian Telos staffer then retrieved a tablet, her fingers dancing across the screen as she typed rapidly.

After a moment, she approached him with purpose. "I need

you to stay still with your feet shoulder-width apart and your arms extended like this, please," she instructed, demonstrating the position. Nodding, he complied, stretching his arms out to shoulder height, waiting for the next step.

Just as he settled into position, a low rumbling echoed through the room, causing his eyes to dart around in search of its source. The Asian staffer pressed a button on her tablet, and suddenly, a black fabric-like material began to envelop his body from neck to toe. It felt cool against his skin, forming a snug layer that was clearly part of the armor.

As he remained still, robotic arms descended from the ceiling, hovering ominously above him. Curiosity piqued; he wondered what their purpose was. At the same time, sections of the ground around the circle began to open, revealing gleaming pieces of the renowned Preliator armor. A table rose from the floor, displaying various components designed for battle.

Once the table reached its full height, the robotic arms sprang to life. They began to pick up armor pieces with precision, placing them onto his body with an ease that was almost mesmerizing. Each piece clicked into place; a perfect fit that hinted at the incredible power he was about to embody as a Preliator.

As each piece of armor connected seamlessly, 0444 couldn't help but smile. He felt a surge of confidence; he was no longer just a young Pre-Elite boy but a true Preliator. When the final chest piece clicked into place, the black Telos staffer gestured for him to drop his arms.

Before lowering them, he shifted his upper body, testing the feel of his new armor. He had always assumed it would be cumbersome, but to his surprise, it was remarkably lightweight, allowing him to move swiftly if needed. It fit him like a second skin, more mobile than any armor he had ever worn. This was exactly why they had trained in yoga, sprinting, and bodyweight exercises—to maximize the potential of their gear. The armor offered robust protection for his vital areas, with only a few weak points, but he knew it would take a significant amount of damage to incapacitate him.

"If you'd like, you can move around to get used to it," the black female staffer suggested. Nodding in agreement, 0444 began to walk around the room. Each step confirmed how light and agile the armor felt. It hugged his body perfectly, and with every movement, he enjoyed it more.

Meanwhile, the staffer pressed a button on her visor, initiating a review of the weapons he would be using. They quickly assessed his rankings on each weapon he had trained with, focusing particularly on the ones he excelled at. Their eyes widened in surprise as they noted even his weaker skills boasted impressive scores. It became clear to them that 0444 was one of the most well-rounded young Preliators they had ever encountered.

They gathered close, their voices low as they exchanged whispers. The black staffer leaned in, her eyes fixed on 0444. "This one looks very promising," she murmured. The Asian staffer studied his results again, then gave a firm nod of agreement.

Once they finished their discussion, the black staffer pushed several buttons on her visor. She then walked over to the east wall of the room, where it unexpectedly opened to reveal a movable case at hip height. Grasping the handles, she pulled the case out just as the wall closed behind her. She dropped it to the ground, and wheels appeared beneath it, allowing her to roll it over to 0444.

"These are the U.W.E.G. government-approved weapons for you to use in Regret," she explained, her voice steady and professional as the case clicked open. "For tonight, they'll be the best fit for your talents."

The first weapon she presents is a pair of XEI-18 handguns, standard issue for the Preliators. As she showcases them, a familiar Pedia voice echoes in the background, detailing the weapon's specifications. She hands both to 0444, and he feels its weight settle comfortably in his grip.

"The XEI-18 is a common choice among Preliators," Pedia explains. "It features an eighteen-caliber round and holds up to eighteen shots per magazine. It's twenty percent lighter than most handguns from the old world, allowing for quicker handling and a magazine change that's twelve seconds faster. With your above-average accuracy, this weapon will enhance your effectiveness in critical situations."

0444 takes a moment to practice his aim, feeling the lightness and compactness of the handguns. They pack a solid punch—just the way he likes them. Once satisfied, he tucks the handguns into the side pockets of his armor as the black staffer retrieves the next weapon.

The black female staffer hands 0444 the VFV-40 assault rifle, and he takes a moment to examine it as Pedia begins to provide information on the weapon.

"This is the VFV-40, famously known as 'The Punch.' It's similar to the Colt Carbine but weighs ten pounds more, allowing it to hold eighteen percent more rounds. Additionally, it features an advanced two-bullet grenade launcher that delivers a powerful impact upon firing. Both past and present Preliators have had great success with this weapon in challenging situations, which is why it has earned its well-deserved nickname."

As 0444 adjusts the rifle to the back of his armor, he appreciates the seamless design that allows it to lock securely in place. The armor quickly seals the weapon with a sensor, ensuring he can access it whenever needed.

Next, the black staffer produces a couple of sleek knives, holding them out with care. Before she hands them over, 0444 secures the rifle. Once he's ready, she gently places each knife into the palm of his hand.

He examines them closely, recognizing that these are the sharpest knives he's ever seen.

"These are combat VIG high-grade knives, slightly larger than throwing knives," Pedia explains. "They're lightweight, incredibly sharp, and designed for optimal grip. Based on your performance with knives, these are the best suited for your skills. Now, could you please put both your hands out with your palms open for the next weapon?"

He quickly follows Pedia's instructions, stowing away the knives and raising both hands around his chest area. The staffer then retrieves the final item from the cart: a pair of sleek gloves. She carefully places them on 0444's hands, and as soon as they click into place with the armor, she steps back a few feet.

"These are the new gloves that all Preliators will be required to wear starting today," she explains. "They serve as a last-resort weapon. If you turn your thumbs upwards to your face and show someone your wrists, each hand has a one-shot bullet embedded within. It's just one bullet per hand, but in desperate times, it can be a lifesaver when you have no place to hide or escape."

0444 looks down at his hands, examining the gloves while Pedia continues to describe their function. Once she finishes, a sense of unease washes over him, and he quickly lowers his hands to his sides, fearful that he might accidentally fire the bullet from his wrist.

The light in the room shifts focus onto the Asian female staffer at the far end. 0444 strides toward her, instinctively looking up at the ceiling as if anticipating what's about to unfold. When he's about four feet away, she raises her hand, signaling him to stop. He obeys, heart racing, as she pulls out the most iconic and important piece of gear for a Preliator: the helmet.

He struggles to keep his emotions in check; deep down, he knows this moment represents a badge of honor. Putting on the helmet is a rite of passage, a symbol of becoming a true Preliator.

"Can you please drop down to one knee?" she requests.

Without hesitation, he kneels. As the helmet clicks into place, an eerie stillness settles in the air. Then, a sharp pinch at the back of his neck—a sudden jolt—catches him off guard. A wave of dizziness crashes over him, making the room sway as though he were drugged. Images flash in his mind, memories from his past: quiet moments in his room with Pedia, countless classes, and years of grueling training. His body begins to twitch involuntarily, fighting the dizziness, yet he wills himself to remain still and firm, refusing to show any weakness. Then, the clicking intensifies, and he realizes with a start that the helmet is now fully connected.

The dizziness quickly faded, replaced by a sense of wonder as the inside of the helmet lit up, reminiscent of the Christmas lights from the old world's celebrations. His surroundings came alive with a flood of information: statistics about his body, details about the room, and even profiles of the Telos staffers standing before him. Suddenly, Pedia materializes in the right corner of his visor, beaming with enthusiasm.

"Hello, Preliator 0444. I'll be your new and final Pedia. I'm here to assist you with anything you need for the next thirty years of your life. Are you ready to begin?"

"Yes," 0444 replies, determination filling his voice.

"Good! Now we can begin," Pedia says, and with that, the next chapter of his life as a Preliator unfolds before him.

Later that evening, massive doors began to swing open, and a gust of wind swept through, sending flurries of snow dancing down from the night sky. A group of nine young Preliators stood at attention, anticipation coursing through them as they waited for the doors to fully open. Once they did, they stepped onto the Section Eleven strip and marched toward the nearest of the twenty Preliator helicopters, their demeanor resolute, as if they were preparing for battle.

When they reached the front of their aircraft, they halted and formed up, allowing the next group to advance to their respective helicopters. This process continued in a well-orchestrated manner until the last group, which included 0444, exited the building. Their formation took a bit longer to assemble, as they were stationed second-to-last in line from the main doors.

As they stood in formation, silence enveloped them, a palpable tension in the air. 0444's gaze drifted toward the Tunnel of Achievement, where young Pre-Elites gathered during their free time, peering through the enormous glass windows. They whispered excitedly among themselves, admiring the new Preliators as they prepared for their First Trial. The hopeful expressions on their faces mirrored the ambition that once burned within 0444.

He couldn't help but smile as he looked back at the younger boys, their eyes wide with wonder. It felt like just yesterday that he stood in their shoes, filled with dreams and aspirations. Now, he was on the cusp of a new adventure, ready to forge his own path as a true Preliator.

"It's amazing, isn't it?" Pedia's voice came through 0444's helmet, breaking the silence. "Not long ago, you watched your heroes head out to the Trials. Now, you're becoming a hero to those boys watching you."

He recalled the times he and 1983 would sit and watch the Preliators during their free time. They were just kids, dreaming of one day being in their shoes. Now, after all those years, he was the one being watched, and he could feel the weight of their eager eyes on him. Happiness swelled within him, though he was grateful for the helmet that concealed the tears of joy threatening to spill. All the Preliators stood in silence, each waiting for their thirty-year journey to begin.

It felt wrong to speak in this moment; Preliators were trained to stay quiet unless absolutely necessary.

"If you move your right eye to the corner of your screen, you can activate silent speaking mode," Pedia suggested. "That way, we can talk without anyone else hearing."

For a moment, he hesitated, amazed by the advanced technology in the helmet. It made sense now why Preliators rarely spoke out loud; they likely kept that mode active to have someone to communicate with even in silence.

"I'm no hero to those boys yet," he replied, shaking his head. "I've hardly even been over to the other side of the Wall of Mercy. Just a couple of times, and then back. It's a stretch to say I'm a hero."

"Is that what you thought when you were their age?" Pedia asked. "They had to prove themselves to you when you were staring out that window, remember?"

He fell silent, contemplating her words. She made a valid point. But now wasn't the time to dwell on it—especially with the last group preparing to step out.

Typically, the crowd in the Tunnel of Achievement swelled to about a hundred or two hundred, a daily occurrence. But this time, over five hundred young men filled the tunnel, so tightly packed that some couldn't even see through the windows. 0444 wished they were all there to see him and the other young Preliators, but it was clear they were there for someone else.

The last group steps through the warehouse doorway, larger than the others with twelve members. They stride onto the snowy runway, standing in silence as the door closes behind them. Unlike the young Preliators heading off for their First Trial, these individuals are seasoned veterans, true Preliators who have endured thirty years of trials and challenges. Now, they are embarking on their Last Trial, a journey that will earn them the respect of all as they approach the two gods who protect the sky. These twelve will join the ranks of the great Preliators among the stars.

They march steadily toward their helicopter, known as the "Final Curtain," receiving salutes from the younger Preliators they pass. The young men watch in awe but find their admiration met with silence; the seasoned Preliators remain focused on their journey's end, not acknowledging the gestures of respect. Among the crowd in the Tunnel of Achievement, whispers fill the air, but most attention is directed toward Preliator 1138, who is regarded by many as "the best of the best." His reputation precedes him, and the younger Preliators can hardly contain their excitement, hoping to emulate the greatness they see before them.

"What a memorable day for you," said Pedia. "You get to salute the great 1138. Because of him, he'll be the last 1138 in all sections, Telos, and Regret. By tonight, if you look up, I bet his star will be the brightest in the sky."

"Is it true what they say about him? That he's so talented he sometimes went on Trials alone instead of with a unit?" 0444 asked.

"As a program of the U.W.E.G., I can't provide specific details about past Trials," Pedia cautioned. "But I can tell you he's the only Preliator to have gone on Trials for thirty straight years."

"He never visited any of the communities in the New World?" 0444 inquired, curiosity piqued.

"Apparently not," Pedia replied. "The government believed his skills were better utilized in ongoing Regret Trials instead of the standard ten."

0444 stood in silence, deeply impressed by everything he had learned. He could only dream of achieving even a fraction of what 1138 had accomplished. His personal Pedia's parting words from his room echoed in his mind, making more sense now—her reminder that he had always stayed close, returning to visit her whenever he could. The significance of those moments became clear to him, shaping his resolve. For the next thirty years, this would be his goal: to honor her guidance and build a legacy worthy of her faith in him.

In just a matter of seconds, the Preliators, led by the

legendary 1138, approached 0444. He stood tall and saluted them as they passed by, just like the others. As expected, the Preliators marched on without returning the gesture.

As 1138 moved past, the air crackled with the mystery of why he was hailed as the best. Preliators rarely spoke to citizens unless absolutely necessary, and they seemed to grow quieter with age, perhaps burdened by the horrors they had witnessed in Regret. 1138 was particularly known for his silence.

As Pedia had mentioned earlier, much of his work remained classified, shrouded in rumors and myths. He was noted for leading missions where no one died—a rarity in their line of work—and for occasionally embarking on solo ventures. Trainers acknowledged that he didn't possess any extraordinary strength, but his well-rounded skills set him apart.

Whatever the reason for his acclaim, he was recognized as the best living Preliator, and it seemed his dedication was finally paying off. Though he appeared calm on the surface, 0444 imagined his mind must be racing with excitement. The young Preliators saluting him and the Pre-Elites watching from the tunnels all shared the same dream—to be like him one day.

As the old guard Preliators approached the last helicopter, they stopped and turned to face a small podium. Standing in formation, they waited with anticipation. Inside and outside the building, everyone's attention shifted to the stage.

Moments later, a door opened, and two Preliators stepped out, taking positions as guards. Behind them, two top Telos generals from the U.W.E.G. appeared, drawing salutes from the crowd. The generals wore sharp, two-piece winter military uniforms, distinctively simple—no medals, only their titles and last names displayed on the back of their jackets. They returned the salutes and walked toward the podium with purpose.

Before the speeches commenced, it was customary for the Preliators and everyone in attendance to observe a moment of silence—a farewell to Telos and all those present. In the heavy atmosphere, the only sounds were the rustling wind and distant gunfire echoing from the Wall of Mercy.

Joining the two generals, a third figure now appears— Supreme Commander Douglas Jr., the current leader of Section 11. Remarkably, he holds the same title as his highly respected father, a rare occurrence in the new world, as improbable as winning the lottery. Though he lacks the intimidating aura of his father, there's something about his presence that makes him seem just suited enough for the role. His voice carries a calm authority that earns the Preliators' respect, even if his father's current legacy still looms large over him. He steps forward to the podium and raises his hand, signaling that he's about to speak.

"As I stand here, I see twelve remarkable men, each having dedicated thirty years of their lives to service. They've completed every task we've assigned, safeguarding those who adhere to the Code, fearlessly facing Trials. They ventured into the unknown and returned unscathed. Like true Preliators, they never complained, always ready to serve. I've watched them grow, even the few years I have been your commander, and now, they ascend to the heavens. I'm confident they'll make us proud, protecting the night sky. Go now and join them. They await you with open arms."

With that, the twelve Preliators broke formation and

saluted the generals one last time, who returned the gesture. Turning towards the helicopter, its blades began to whir, filling the air with a low roar. One by one, the Preliators boarded until the last one stepped inside, and the door slowly shut behind them. The blades spun faster, stirring up light snow as the helicopter lifted off the ground.

It rose above the Wall of Mercy, heading into Regret, marking the beginning of their Final Trial. As they soared past the Wall, they caught a glimpse of the turrets standing guard, keeping watch over the masses of beggars who ventured into Regret, seeking refuge in the dark unknown.

Once the helicopter vanished from sight, the solemn farewell shifted into a more serious atmosphere. Commander Douglas Jr. turned his gaze toward the young Preliators, his expression intense.

"I'll keep this brief but crucial. If you aspire to be like the twelve who just departed, remember this: your ten-year journey will be arduous—perhaps every single day. Harder challenges will arise. But hold on to your self-esteem, self-respect, and self-worth. The gods and the people are always watching. You are the Preliators of the U.W.E.G. They need to know they can always count on you."

With that, the commander offered one final salute to the young men. They responded in kind, returning the salute with fervor. As the remaining helicopters roared to life, the young Preliators held their positions, maintaining the salute until the commander and the other generals vanished into the swirling snow and the encroaching darkness of the night.

The helicopter blades spun rapidly, ready for takeoff, their whirring cutting through the cold air. You might think that 0444 and his group would be the next to board, given their proximity to the first aircraft, but instead, the initial group filed into their helicopters. Once they were inside, the doors sealed shut, and a minute later, the chopper lifted into the night sky. The second group followed suit, boarding their helicopter with a sense of purpose.

Finally, it was time for 0444 and his unit. As they watched, the doors of their designated helicopter swung open, revealing the dimly lit interior.

"It's time. The moment you've been waiting for. Let's go see what Regret has in store for you," Pedia's voice echoed in 0444's helmet.

Without a word, he joined his fellow Preliators, swiftly finding his seat and securing himself and his weapons in place. The moment he was locked in, the door closed, plunging the interior into darkness. The helicopter began to ascend, rising higher and higher, leaving the familiar ground behind. The adventure was about to begin.

CHAPTER 5
WHAT ARE YOU AFRAID OF?

Two hours had passed since Preliator 0444, and his team crossed the Wall of Mercy. Now, they're in deep Regret territory, far from what was once the United States, venturing into the snow-covered lands that used to be called Canada. The full moon was hidden behind thick clouds, and snow fell steadily as they traveled northeast.

Inside the helicopter, nine newly initiated Preliators sat in silence, their weapons resting beside them. Despite the strong winds rocking the helicopter, they remained calm and patient. Nearby, male Telos staff members worked diligently at their computer monitors, while a general walked around, giving them orders and gathering intel. The rough ride didn't seem to bother him at all. An older, seasoned stage-three Preliator stood guard for the general, scanning the area with alert eyes.

No one spoke aloud during the journey. The only sound was the hum of the helicopter's engines and the occasional beep from the equipment. Inside their helmets, however, the Preliators communicated with their personal Pedias, discussing the new features of their technology. From the outside, it was impossible to tell, but the Pedias were enthusiastic and eager to assist their users.

0444, still getting accustomed to the new tech in his helmet, quickly learned the basics of what he could do. He glanced around the cramped cabin, curious to see if anything caught his attention, but the Preliators and Telos staff remained focused on their tasks.

"Do you want me to go over everything we just discussed again?" Pedia asked.

"No, it's fine. I understand the basics," 0444 replied.

"There's a lot more to cover about the helmet's features and how to handle certain situations," Pedia continued.

"I can't take in too much information at once," 0444 explained. "Let me get comfortable with the basics first, then we can move on."

"Got it," Pedia said. "I'll remember that for future updates. No more overwhelming you with too much at once. Is there anything else you'd like to know?"

0444 glanced around the cabin again. "I'm just curious where we are in Regret. There aren't any windows in this craft to see outside."

"Give me a moment while I pull up the location," Pedia responded.

0444 waited patiently as Pedia processed his request. After a moment, she said, "We're currently flying over what used to be called Qu'Appelle Valley. In Regret, it's now known as the Valley of Gifts. It's the largest junkyard in this region, full of waste from both the old and new worlds."

0444 absorbed this new piece of information, picturing

the desolate landscape hidden below.

"I've heard about that place," 0444 said, his interest piqued. "All the garbage from the new world gets dumped there. People in Regret fight over it—sometimes even start wars over scraps they can use. I've always wanted to see it for myself."

"You might get your chance one day," Pedia replied. "When you reach your final stage as a Preliator, you could be assigned to protect the crafts that drop off the waste. Or maybe, you'll have a Trial or two there before that."

0444 paused to think. "I wonder if that's where our First Trial will take place. It sounds like total chaos—people fighting over anything they can find. I've even heard that things as small as rotten food or torn clothes can lead to fights, sometimes ending in someone's death."

"Well, you can stop wondering about that," Pedia said with certainty. "Because that's not where we're headed."

"Then where are we going?" 0444 asked, curious.

"That's classified," Pedia responded, her tone firm.

"Not too classified for you to tell me it's *not* the Valley of Gifts?" 0444 said with a smirk.

Pedia replied with a playful sigh, "Note to Self: Be more careful with my words around you."

0444 smiled, closed his eyes, and tried to relax while waiting for further instructions. He knew this might be his last chance to rest for a while, so he decided to take full advantage of it. As he lay there, he found himself missing his old Pedia from Telos, but he realized this new one wasn't so bad. Maybe, just maybe, they would get along for the next thirty years.

Meanwhile, most of the Preliators followed suit, resting

before the big Trial. The only exception was 3009, who sat leaning forward, laser-focused. He looked like a student cramming for an important exam, eager to learn as much as possible to ensure success.

Then there was 0021, who stood out in a different way. Over the past couple of years, he had become the quietest member of the group, only speaking when absolutely necessary. His new Pedia had noticed this and, despite his silence, tried once more to engage him.

"One more time," she gently suggested. "I think it would be useful to go over how your armor works. Even a small piece of knowledge might make all the difference in this Trial."

"I can take care of myself. That's how I got this far," 0021 replied curtly.

Pedia paused, sensing something deeper. "Is there something else bothering you? You can tell me anything. It's just us. I promise."

0021's patience snapped. "How about you promise not to ask me that again? I've got everything under control. I just want to be with my thoughts."

Pedia, unfazed, replied calmly. "As you wish. I'll be here if you need me. I'll be looking forward to seeing what you can do."

0021 remained silent, holding on to something that had been eating at him for a long time. Whatever had happened to him, it had changed him deeply. He wanted to confide in someone, to let it out—but he knew that even hinting at his secret could land him in serious trouble. So, he kept it buried for now. Only time would tell when, or if, the truth would come out.

Ninety minutes had passed in the helicopter. Suddenly, the

interior lights flickered off, leaving them in brief darkness. Moments later, red emergency lights blinked on, casting a warning glow throughout the cabin. A loud siren blared—the signal to prepare. As their helmets shifted from black visors to glowing yellow eyes, the Preliators knew the moment had come. Without hesitation, they grabbed their weapons, ready for whatever lay ahead.

The helicopter began its descent, with snow swirling violently as the craft touched down on the frozen ground. The back doors slowly opened, and the Preliators remained seated as their seat buckles automatically unlatched. They stood in unison, forming a line to exit the aircraft, ready for action.

Before they could leave, the general stepped in front of them, his voice booming over the howling wind and roaring engines. "Once you're all off the aircraft and we've taken off, find a secure spot and connect your Pedias to form a single network. She'll relay your mission instructions. Let the First Trial begin!"

He stepped aside as each Preliator exited the helicopter. They jogged about fifty yards away before turning back to watch the chopper ascend, disappearing into the wintry night as it headed back to Telos.

With the helicopter gone, their helmet visors turned black, blending them into the darkness to avoid detection by any Regret citizens. They began marching against the biting wind, searching for a safe place to receive their mission instructions. After a short trek, they came across an old, abandoned farm from the days of the old world.

The farm was small, with a house that looked like it had been stripped bare by the people of Regret. The bushes around the property were the only thing left; the trees had long since been cut down for firewood. Near the house, they spotted a few grain bins and rusty farm equipment. But what really caught their attention was a large, decrepit barn. Half of its roof was missing, the paint had long since faded, and only the foundation seemed to be holding it together. Deciding it was worth investigating, they headed toward it.

As they entered the barn, they immediately scanned the area, using their Pedias to detect any signs of life. When the devices confirmed the coast was clear, they lowered their rifles and began exploring. It was obvious that others had used the barn before—there was an old fire pit in the center of the room, and snow had piled up through the gaping hole in the roof. Despite the open ceiling, there was no wind blowing through, and the remaining walls seemed solid enough.

The group agreed that the barn was large enough for Pedia to relay their instructions. Preliator 2890 moved to the center of the barn and placed a small device on the ground. Each Preliator then pressed the right side of their helmets, holding it for a few seconds. When a digital light flickered on inside their helmets, they lowered their hands and stepped back.

Pedia appeared before them, glowing softly in blue, a warm smile gracing her face as she prepared to deliver their mission briefing. With her hands clasped behind her back, she stood tall in the same Preliator armor as the others—minus the helmet—signifying unity, as if to say they were all in this together.

"Congratulations, everyone," Pedia says in a cheerful tone. "Your long-awaited First Trial is about to begin. Please remove your helmets so we can proceed with the briefing."

The Preliators acknowledge the command, first securing

their weapons. One by one, they twist their helmets, listening for the soft click that releases the locks. They remove their helmets and place them by their right hip, waiting for Pedia to continue.

"Thank you. Now, we can begin," Pedia says before disappearing. Moments later, a large blue map materializes in front of them, with a blinking red dot marking their current location.

"You are here," Pedia's voice continues, "in this part of Regret. Your mission is to head east from this point and follow this route until you reach your destination. You will be traveling on foot. My advice is to follow the riverbank—it will guide you safely. Your destination is a community known as Brand, named by the locals."

The Preliators exchange glances. They've all heard of Brand—rumors about the place are nothing but bad news. Then again, in Regret, there aren't many safe or welcoming places to begin with.

Pedia continues, "Once you arrive at Brand, your mission is to locate three women who are currently in the same area. This is a parole mission. All three women are set to complete their sentences in Regret by tomorrow. Your task is to find them and bring them back to the Wall so that they can return to their normal lives. Now, here's the dossier of the first woman."

The map fades away, replaced by an image of the first target. She appears to be in her mid-thirties, around five feet six inches tall, with a healthy build. Her lightly tanned skin, friendly smile, greyish eyes, and shoulder-length curly blonde hair don't immediately suggest danger. In fact, she looks quite ordinary, not at all like someone who belongs in Regret.

"The first woman is Pam Adrill," Pedia began as Pam's image appeared. "This photo was taken about twenty months ago, just before her crime. Pam was sentenced to eighteen months for violating Code 405, the Equal Labor Agreement. If you want more details, her full life file has been downloaded to your helmets."

Pam's image faded from the screen, replaced by the next woman. She looked strikingly young, with a face that could easily be mistaken for an 18-year-olds, though Pedia confirmed she was in her twenties. Standing just 4'11" and weighing around 90 pounds, she had long brown hair that almost reached her hips, a slightly darker skin tone dotted with freckles, and piercing blue eyes.

"The second woman is Kimberly Klark, known as 'KK' by her friends and family. She was sentenced to four months for violating Curfew Law 339 and Sexual Conduct Law 180. Like Pam, this is the most recent photo we have of her. Her full file has also been downloaded to your helmets if you need more information."

Kimberly's image faded, and the final woman's photo appeared. This woman, in her twenties, had pale skin, curly black hair, hazel eyes, and sharp cheekbones. Unlike the others, her expression was far from friendly—she looked angry, defiant.

"The last person, and the one you should be most cautious with, is April Tombs. She is the most likely to cause you trouble. April was sentenced to seventeen years for breaking five different laws before entering Regret. These include Code 407 for failing to show up to work, Code 511 for protesting the Ian Royale Code of Laws, and several charges for attempting to assault Preliators with homemade weapons.

She even injured a Telos employee before entering the system. This is the most recent photo we have of her from the new world, but she's been in Regret for so long that she may look different now. Details about her identifying features, including birthmarks, have been downloaded to your helmets."

April's image fades, and Pedia reappears, resuming her briefing. "The mission is straightforward. Find these three women and bring them back here. When you return to this spot, we'll pick you up. You have forty-eight hours to complete this task. At least one of them must be alive. If all of them are dead, the Trial will be considered a failure. You will need to rely on each other." Pedia paused. "Any questions?"

The group remained silent.

"Very well. Your forty-eight hours start now. Good luck, and I'll see you soon. Unity, Equality, Safety."

The Preliators responded in unison, "Unity, Equality, Safety," as Pedia vanished, plunging the barn into darkness once again.

2890 moved to retrieve the small device, pocketing it while the others grabbed their helmets, securing them in place before readying their weapons. 3578 led the way outside, scanning the area through his visor, now switched to night vision.

His visor projected a red line, marking the direction toward the women. Inside the helmet, data streamed in current temperature, wind speed, sunrise time, and distances to both the women and Brand. His Pedia reappeared with a smile, ready to assist.

Pedia's voice chimed in, "Follow the red line. It will guide you to your destination. We have a long journey ahead, so feel free to reach out if you need anything."

"Understood," 3578 replied, leading the group along the path. Behind him, Preliator 0021 followed, with 3009 bringing up the rear. They moved in single file, careful to obscure their numbers, so anyone tracking them in the snow would be uncertain how many had passed through.

A couple of hours later, the sun had disappeared behind thick clouds, turning the daylight into a dull gray. For many, the lack of direct sunlight was a relief in winter; otherwise, the bright reflection off the snow could be blinding. The Preliators kept a steady pace, now walking along the frozen riverbank as Pedia had instructed.

Despite their heavy-looking armor, the conditions were no challenge for them. The armor, designed for harsh environments, felt light compared to what they had endured during training. Since they began their trek to Brand, no one had spoken a word—not because they didn't want to, but because they were all busy consulting their Pedias. They reviewed critical information, from detailed profiles of the women they were tracking to any surprises Regret might throw their way, especially about Brand, the mysterious and dangerous community they were heading toward.

The Preliators spent most of their time reading up on the people of Brand, particularly a group known as *The Faceless*. In Regret, many groups had turned to cannibalism due to the lack of food—mostly relying on birds, as nearly all other animals were either endangered or extinct. But The Faceless were different. They were the largest group in Regret, known not just for cannibalism but for always covering their faces with anything they could find—old clothing, sheets, even sacks. No one in The Faceless could be seen without something covering their face. Interestingly, the Preliators' helmets made them less likely targets unless they were deep inside Faceless territory, as The Faceless usually only attacked those whose faces they could see.

While most of the group was quietly absorbed in research, two Preliators, 2288 and 1113, broke the silence, chatting away like old friends.

"With the great 1138 leading us, this Trial feels like a simple in-and-out job," 1113 remarked. "For years, I've heard about how tough the First Trial is supposed to be, but honestly, this feels more like what the old world called a 'walk in the park.'"

2288 wasn't as sure. "You seem pretty confident about that. We haven't even started the Trial yet, and you're already calling it easy. That kind of talk can put all of us in danger. I bet even 1138 is taking this seriously."

1113 laughed, but 2288's words hung in the air, reminding them both that in Regret, nothing was ever as simple as it seemed.

1113 defends himself, "This is just our first Trial. Why would the generals give us something impossible right off the bat? It's just a warm-up, getting our 'feet wet.' The tougher Trials will come later. And besides, I'm not like Preliator 1138."

2288 laughs, "You're definitely *not* like the great 1138." He watches 1113, who isn't amused by the joke. 2288 presses on, "So, you're not afraid of The Faceless?"

1113 responds confidently, "Not at all. The Faceless are nothing more than mindless husks, most of them born in this wasteland. They can't even speak basic English, let alone act like people. All they know is to eat other humans. Their only advantage is their numbers, but I've got something for that."

Intrigued, 2288 asks, "And what's that?"

1113 proudly pulls out his ZEB shotgun. "This," he says with a grin.

2288 chuckles, putting away his VFV rifle. "Not bad, but it doesn't beat *this*."

He reveals a VDY-90 minigun, its heavy form gleaming in the dim light. Now, the whole group is watching, and a few Preliators chuckle at the sight of both weapons.

3009 interrupts, his voice firm. "Put those away. This isn't the time to mess around in the frozen hell of Regret." Both Preliators fall silent, obediently stowing their weapons. "You might not fear The Faceless, but there are other groups out here—ones far more dangerous—who wouldn't hesitate to take down a team of Preliators."

After 3009's words, the group sinks into a quiet, uneasy march. Each one begins thinking about the other, deadlier factions that could be waiting for them in the shadows of Regret.

Breaking the silence, 2288 speaks up. "The group I'd be terrified to run into is *The Collectors*. You've heard the stories, right? They take whatever they want, and they always get it. They've got the most fortified place in Regret—'Everything.' Makes you wonder if they really *do* have everything."

0444 nods. "I agree. They've got the numbers like The Faceless, but their gear is way more advanced. Some even say they're crazier than the cannibals. But we won't have to worry about them coming to Brand. They stick to their territory up northwest, around *Everything*. I've heard they don't venture further south than the Valley of Gifts."

1113 cuts in, "You think The Collectors are crazy? The group I fear most is *The First Sons*. They were the original natives of these prairies and have been inside Regret since the day the Wall went up. They hate anyone who isn't one of them, especially Preliators. They're so fanatical, they'll sacrifice one of their own just to take down two of us, all in the name of their god—the God of Repeat."

Most of the group nod in agreement, even the normally skeptical 3009. But 1983 is surprised that no one has mentioned a new rising threat within Regret. He decides to voice his concern.

"Has everyone forgotten about the figure rising far out west?" 1983 says, drawing everyone's attention. "The locals call him the Prophet of Regret. They believe he's going to break down the Wall and unite everyone inside. His name is Apollyon, and his followers call themselves the Red Army of Apollyon."

2890, looking puzzled, asks, "What's the Red Army? I've heard of Apollyon, but not them."

"The Red Army gets its name from the red handprint painted on each of their heads, usually on their faces," 1983 explained. "It's meant to symbolize the blood of the innocent who, they believe, will one day be freed. They're fanatics, utterly devoted to Apollyon and his mission to 'liberate' Regret and bring both Worlds together again."

Everyone looked at 1983 as if saying the name *Apollyon* had been a mistake, something taboo. Sensing their reaction, 3009 felt the need to step in.

"There's no such thing as a prophet in Regret," 3009 said firmly. "A guy who's just a few years older than us suddenly becoming a warlord? It's not happening. It's probably just another cannibal group, like the one we're heading toward. Local rumors, meant to scare people or trick them into running back to the new world. Nothing more than a sad folk tale."

1983 wasn't convinced. "Can you explain what's going on in the far west then? There's a new community out there, growing fast enough that even the U.W.E.G. has noticed. Someone's leading it. Does that still sound like a folk tale to you?"

3009 sighed, not wanting to get into a drawn-out argument over the Apollyon myth. Deciding to settle it with facts, he called on Pedia. "Pedia, is there any record of a prophet named Apollyon or a Red Army in the western part of Regret?"

Pedia's voice chimed in, "One moment, please," as she searched for data. After a few seconds, she responded, "There is indeed a new, unidentified group on the far west side of Regret, and it's growing at a rate faster than other areas. The names Apollyon and Red Army have been mentioned, but current information is insufficient to confirm whether this leader, Apollyon, actually exists."

The group exchanged uneasy glances, unsure now whether to side with 3009's skepticism or 1983's concern. Before anyone could say more, Pedia added, "But I can tell you the meaning of the name Apollyon. It comes from Latin and means 'wherever he goes is the one who destroys.'"

1113 broke the tension with a sarcastic remark, "Well, that doesn't sound like much of a prophet to me." Almost everyone chuckled, their nervousness easing for a moment.

3009, having had enough of the banter, cut in, "Alright, fun time's over. Instead of focusing on what scares you, how about we all take a page from 0021's book and stay quiet until we reach Brand. Can we at least manage that?"

Most of the group nodded in agreement, falling silent as

they continued walking. But 3578 couldn't shake something that had been nagging at him. He glanced at 0021, walking silently ahead, and the more he thought about it, the more unsettled he became. Why had 3009 specifically mentioned 0021? Out of everyone, 0021 was always the hardest to figure out.

Unable to hold back, 3578 voiced his thoughts. "Why should we be more like him?" His question drew 3009's attention. "Everyone's worried about what the groups in Regret might do to us, but the one who scares me most is 0021. Two years ago, he was just like the rest of us, but now... he hasn't said a word to anyone since. Nine of us are supposed to be Pac-19, but I feel like we're a man short. Do you really think he has our best interests in mind? Or is he hiding something—a secret he's too afraid to reveal, one that could put us all at risk?"

He leaned in close to 3009's ear and whispered, "In my opinion, everything changed after that day—when we were all forced to do what we did."

3009 immediately recognized what 3578 was referring to and didn't want to engage with it. "That's enough!" he snapped. "We all got here the same way. Whatever happened in the past is over. What matters now is today and this Trial."

"Is that true?" 3578 challenged, his gaze fixed on 0021. Though 0021 tried to ignore the scrutiny, he could feel the weight of everyone's stares, waiting for him to respond. With no other option, he finally spoke up. "I assure you, I intend to complete this Trial to the best of my ability."

Despite 0021's reassuring tone, 3578 continued to scrutinize him. "So, tell us what happened to you. Why have you been so quiet for so long? What are you afraid of?"

0021 started to think back to a time when shadows loomed over him, looking down through a window. The memory sent a tingling sensation through his fingertips, and he clenched his fists to shake off the feeling. He then looked at 3578 and replied, "What I'm terrified of is that we believe our actions are good, but deep down, I suspect they aren't."

"What does that mean?" 3578 pressed, seeking clarity.

0021 met his gaze and said, "I'm afraid I've said too much already. All you need to know is that I'll do my job in this Trial, just like everyone else. In the end, this conversation won't change anything."

Silence fell over the group, broken only by the crunch of their footsteps in the snow. 3578 wanted more answers, but 0021 wasn't willing to say anything else.

Pedia broke the silence with a suggestion. "Since we're ahead of schedule, I recommend we take this opportunity to refuel and have a quick meal. We should wait for the sun to set before entering Brand, as it will give us a better chance to hide in the shadows. There's a spot about two kilometers away that will provide good cover from the wind."

Everyone glanced at the information Pedia displayed in their visors. They agreed that a small snack would be beneficial, especially since they had no idea when their next meal would be. A moment of peace and quiet wouldn't hurt either.

3009 nodded. "Alright, everyone, you heard her. When we reach that spot, we'll take a quick break before things get interesting."

Everyone nodded in agreement and marched toward the spot Pedia suggested. As they disappeared into the distance, fresh footprints began to appear in the snow at the farm. Strangely, no person was visible. The footprints continued to the center of the barn, where the Preliators had previously placed Pedia.

A sound emanated from the shadows, like buttons being pressed. Suddenly, something more formidable than a Preliator emerged from the darkness. Standing about seven feet tall, it wore armor resembling that of a futuristic samurai, complete with a helmet featuring an all-black screen where its face should be—devoid of eyes or mouth. Its breathing was slow and unnatural, suggesting it might be a robot or alien. The figure began pressing buttons on its right forearm.

Three small orbs emerged, hovering in front of the creature while emitting red beams that scanned the ground. The orbs had an unmistakably alien design, their sleek, otherworldly surfaces glinting as they moved, with a faint, low hum emanating from each. The creature watched them intently, awaiting any new data. Suddenly, one orb paused, its red light fixating on a discovery—it had detected the Preliators' footprints, including those partially concealed by the wind.

The creature knelt to study the footprints as the orb highlighted nine distinct sets, showing which direction, they led. After examining the tracks, the creature stood up and began following the trail out of the barn, its eyes locked on the Preliators' path.

It tapped a few buttons on its forearm, and the hovering orbs returned, circling close. The creature slowly looked around, checking to see if it was alone. Then, it vanished, leaving only its footprints in the snow as it continued to follow the Preliators' trail.

CHAPTER 6
THE COUNT DOWN

A determined sixteen-year-old, 0021, was nearing the end of his morning yoga session with his personal Pedia. Today, he was about to attempt one of the most challenging poses: the eight-angle pose. It felt like he had tried it a million times before. Unlike other students who often complained when faced with difficulties, 0021 remained focused and resolute.

Pedia, also dressed in a yoga outfit, focused intently on him rather than demonstrating the pose herself. Seeing his determination, she cheered him on enthusiastically as he finally got into position and held it.

"I knew you could do it!" she exclaimed, her voice brimming with pride. As 0021 stood up, pumping his fists in the air and grinning at his accomplishment, Pedia added, "What did I tell you?" They both giggled, repeating together, "Practice, practice, and more practice."

She wanted to celebrate with him but realized they were running out of time. Trying to bring their excitement down, she said, "Alright, let's relax. We'll celebrate later tonight. For now, close your eyes for ten minutes, take some deep breaths, and clear your mind."

0021 returned to his yoga mat, sitting cross-legged as he followed Pedia's instructions. He shot her a strange look when she told him to settle down, as if he were the only one acting a bit crazy. But he closed his eyes and took a deep breath, and soon a relaxed expression spread across his face, signaling that his mind was at ease. Pedia wanted to ask him something but decided to wait until they finished the breathing exercises.

Once they were done, 0021 grabbed his towel for a shower, humming happily as if it were the best day of his life.

"You seem happier today than usual," Pedia remarked. "Is it because you finally mastered that yoga position you've been working on? Or is there something else on today's schedule that has you smiling from ear to ear?"

"It's not just that," 0021 replied cheerfully. "I'm getting happier every day."

Pedia raised an eyebrow, puzzled by his comment. "Why's that?"

"It's simple. Yesterday, I had 700 days until my First Trial. Today, it's 699. Tomorrow, it'll be 698. So, each day, I'm one step closer to my Trial, which makes me happier than before," 0021 explained.

Pedia loved his perspective, thinking it was typical of boys to find motivation in little things. "Is it all about the Trial for you?" she asked.

0021 nodded. "Getting closer to becoming a Preliator, following the Code, and keeping people who follow the rules safe—that's the biggest honor for me. While others might have jobs like cleaning sewage pipes or farming, I see myself as a protector of what's good in the world."

Pedia felt a swell of pride at his response but quickly reminded him, "Today's your monthly challenge. Most Pre-Elites worry about it, not knowing what they'll face and fearing failure in front of the trainers."

As 0021 started his shower, he interrupted her, "I'm not like most Pre-Elites."

Despite the interruption, Pedia didn't seem bothered. She considered 0021's words, realizing he might be onto something important.

"You really are different from the others," Pedia said proudly. "I've never seen anyone so happy to face harsh, grueling challenges. I've cared for many before you, and I wish more were like you."

0021 smiled at her compliment as he stepped out of the shower and began to get dressed. "I know I seem happy while others are serious or have different attitudes," he replied. "But if we're all working toward the same goal, then we're all good in our own way. Otherwise, what's the point?"

Once he finished dressing, 0021 headed for the door to start his day. Just before he left, Pedia called out to him.

"Good luck on the challenge today," she said warmly.

"Thank you," 0021 replied, turning to look at her one last time. "I'll tell you all about it when I return. See you tonight."

He opened the door, smiled at her, and stepped out of his bedroom. As the door closed behind him, the lights went off, plunging the room into darkness. For Pedia, this silence signaled it was time to disappear as well. She remained calm and unconcerned about what lay ahead for him, fully aware of the challenges he would face. With a quiet determination, she vanished, leaving the bedroom completely dark.

Hours later, as it reached midday, 0021 and several other

Pre-Elites, including 0444 and 3009, waited in a large room about the size of 'The Tool Shed' gym. They had been standing around for about fifteen minutes, eagerly anticipating instructions for their monthly challenge. All they knew was that their numbers would be called, and then the Preliators would guide them to their next task.

0021 stood quietly, his hands resting in front of his hips, pondering what kind of challenge lay ahead. He knew it would be an individual challenge rather than a team effort. It might involve one-on-one combat, a timed task, or a physically demanding exercise like last month's ordeal, where they had to hold a heavy log over their heads in the freezing cold until they were told to drop it. There was even a chance it could be a surprise written exam. He understood that sometimes the challenges were more about mental games than physical strength, so he didn't let worry cloud his thoughts; he would find out soon enough.

Another forty-five minutes passed. Then, a ringing tone echoed from the large speakers in the room, cutting through the stillness. All the Pre-Elites stopped talking to listen as Pedia's voice filled the space.

"The next numbers to go to the west doors are 3231 and 0050. The next numbers to go to the north doors are 1223 and 1995. The next numbers to go to the east doors are 3878 and 1832. Finally, the next numbers to go to the south doors are 0021 and 2445. Please follow the Preliators at your door and adhere to their instructions. Thank you, and good luck."

Relief washed over the Pre-Elites whose numbers were called; they were glad the wait was finally over. The others remained silent, their impatience palpable, but none dared to complain in front of the Preliators. Those closest to the selected numbers wished them luck as they prepared to depart.

0021 quickly acknowledged the well-wishers but didn't linger; he headed straight toward the south door. Spotting 2445 nearby, they maneuvered through the crowd of Pre-Elites to reach the two Preliators standing guard at the entrance. Upon arrival, 0021 and 2445 stopped and saluted.

The Preliators stood tall and silent, their green eyes avoiding direct contact. They neither returned the salute nor spoke. One of them pointed at the door, signaling for the two to enter. 0021 and 2445 exchanged a brief, uncertain glance. Then, one Preliator opened the door and stepped inside, with 0021 and 2445 following closely behind. The second Preliator entered after them. A mix of nervousness and excitement coursed through both Pre-Elites.

As they passed through the door, they found themselves in a stark white hallway. Unlike before, there were no announcements, teachers, staff, trainers, or other Pre-Elites—just the two of them following the Preliator. They looked around but saw nothing unusual, only the sound of their footsteps echoing in the silence. With each step, it felt as if they were descending deeper underground. Neither of them spoke; the silence felt awkward.

0021 wondered why no one had hinted at what their challenge would be. It felt like a closely guarded secret—possibly the most significant task they would face as Pre-Elites.

They turned left and found themselves in another plain white hallway. They walked until they reached the midpoint, where the Preliator in front raised his right hand, signaling them to stop. The two Preliators pressed their thumbs against the white wall. After a few seconds, the wall began to slide open, and they gestured for 0021 and 2445 to enter.

Cautiously, the two young men stepped into the dark room. Once they were inside, the Preliators shut and locked the door behind them, then headed back to where the other Pre-Elites were still waiting for their turn.

As the sound of the door locking echoed in the room, 0021 and 2445 realized they wouldn't be leaving until they completed the challenge. They began to examine their surroundings. The walls were white like the hallway, but the floor was covered with a rubber-like mat. Two other doors stood in the room—one on the west side and one on the east—each guarded by a Preliator holding a VFV rifle across their chest.

Looking up, they noticed a large window high on the wall. Although it was big, the glass was dark gray and almost tinted, making it difficult to see through. If they squinted, they could make out five shadowy figures behind the glass, like judges ready to observe their performance.

Suddenly, Pedia appeared in the center of the room, wearing the same Pre-Elite athletic clothes as the others, her familiar smile lighting up her face. However, this Pedia was different from the one in each Pre-Elite's bedroom—she glowed blue instead of purple. The blue hue indicated that she was a universal Pedia, accessible to everyone, while the purple version was unique and personal to each Pre-Elite.

"Good afternoon, Pre-Elites. Welcome to this month's challenge," Pedia announced. "Today's challenge is straightforward: a one-on-one hand-to-hand combat fight with no weapons. Use all the skills you've learned so far. The rules are simple: fight until one of you admits defeat. The battle will take place right here in this room. Are there any questions?"

0021 and 2445 exchanged glances, both realizing they were thinking the same thing—they had faced this challenge before. They turned back to Pedia and shook their heads, indicating they had no questions. Pedia nodded in acknowledgment.

"Alright then. Please head to the center of the room and start whenever you're ready. Good luck!" Pedia said before vanishing.

As both Pre-Elites moved to the center of the room, they glanced up at the window, but the five figures behind it remained still. With no control over what was happening above, they shifted their focus to each other, preparing for the fight.

Once they reached the center and stood ten feet apart, they bowed to each other to show respect, signaling the start of the battle.

The two fighters moved with such precision that it felt like they were battling their own reflections. They were evenly matched, with no clear advantage on either side. With their fists raised, they circled each other, searching for an opening. Both threw a few feints, but neither flinched.

0021 glanced at the five figures watching from the window, sensing their desire for more action. Deciding to take the initiative, he made a choice to go on the offensive—a strategy he typically avoided.

Charging in, 0021 absorbed a few clean punches and knees from 2245. He hoped the pain would be worth it, allowing him to utilize his Muay Thai skills to strike 2245's ribs with his knees. As expected, 2245 landed several solid jabs to 0021's face and a powerful punch to his chest. Nevertheless,

0021 managed to clinch 2245, delivering a series of close-range shots. But 2245 quickly escaped, and they resumed their circling.

As they moved, 2245 landed a few good jabs that briefly stunned 0021. Unfazed, 0021 retaliated, taking 2245 down to the ground. They began grappling, employing wrestling and jiu-jitsu techniques, with no referee to separate them. The Preliators and those observing from the window watched intently as the fight unfolded.

Twenty grueling minutes passed, and the battle continued. Both boys were bloodied, bruised, and drenched in sweat, breathing heavily. Their skills were so evenly matched that it was difficult to determine who was winning. Exhausted, 2245 made another attempt to take down 0021 but slipped on the slick mat, twisting his ankle and letting out a sharp yelp.

When 2245 yelped and fell to one knee, clearly off balance, 0021 recognized his opportunity to end the fight. He charged forward, tackling 2245 to the ground. They rolled around, but 0021 had the upper hand due to 2245's injury, managing to secure a half-mount position.

2245 struggled to buck him off, but fatigue and pain weighed him down. Seizing the moment, 0021 wrapped his legs around 2245's waist and began delivering quick, powerful punches to his face. In an attempt to avoid the blows, 2245 turned his back, giving 0021 a chance to capitalize. He ceased his punches and transitioned into full mount, setting up for a choke hold.

Aware of 0021's intentions, 2245 fought against the choke hold for a while. But after several attempts, 0021 landed a hard elbow strike to 2245's face, momentarily stunning him. With that brief lapse in focus, 0021 locked in the choke hold and began to squeeze. He waited for 2245 to submit, but the other fighter held on stubbornly. As 2245's face began to turn purple from the lack of air, he fought for breath until he finally stopped struggling and passed out.

0021 released his hold but maintained his mount position, knowing the rules stated that his opponent had to say "yield." However, 2245 hadn't done so. Unsure of what to do next, he glanced around the room. Suddenly, Pedia appeared beside him, beaming with pride for his victory in the fight.

"Congratulations on completing the first stage of the challenge. Now for step two: you must finish off your defeated opponent. You have three minutes to do this," Pedia announced.

"What do you mean, finish him off?" 0021 asked, confusion etched on his face.

Pedia's expression was serious. "In this challenge, when your opponent is defeated, you must terminate him to complete the challenge. That's how you pass the Preliator program. It's always been this way."

Shock washed over 0021. Why would they want him to kill 2245, a teammate? He glanced at the two unmoving Preliators and then up at the window, where the five observers continued to watch silently. Panic began to set in.

"You want me to kill him? If I do, I pass the challenge?" he asked, disbelief creeping into his voice.

"That's one way to interpret 'terminate.' Yes. The clock is ticking; you have two minutes left to complete this step of the challenge," Pedia replied firmly.

0021's gaze shifted back to 2245, who was slowly regaining consciousness. He could see confusion in 2245's eyes as he tried to understand what had just happened.

"But what happens if I don't kill him? He did nothing wrong! He followed every order you gave him!" 0021 yelled, desperation lacing his words.

Pedia stood with her hands behind her back, her expression seemingly indifferent as she watched the scene unfold... as if witnessing a death was supposed to be enjoyable. The two Preliators' eyes glowed yellow as they raised their rifles, taking aim at 0021. He quickly understood that if he hesitated, they wouldn't think twice about shooting both him and 2245.

"You have sixty seconds left to complete the second step of the challenge," Pedia reminded him, her voice steady.

Panic surged through 0021. A whirlwind of thoughts raced through his mind—memories of past challenges, classes, and training sessions with 2245. His breathing became rapid, and sweat dripped down his bruised face. He had always known that he might have to kill someone one day, but he imagined it would be someone who deserved it, like a person from Regret—not a teammate and friend like 2245. The Preliators stepped closer, their presence imposing.

"You now have thirty seconds left to complete the second step of the challenge."

In that moment of desperation, 0021 made a decision. He released the choke hold and swiftly twisted 2245's head, snapping his neck. As 2245's breathing ceased and his eyes rolled back, turning white, he lay still and lifeless.

0021 unwrapped his legs from around 2245's body, rose to his feet, and turned to face the Preliators. His movements were deliberate, ensuring that everyone watching through the window could clearly see he had followed their orders.

The Preliators' eyes returned to green. One of them approached 2245's lifeless body, slung his rifle over his shoulder, and lifted the body with ease. Without a word, he carried it to the west side of the room and exited. The other Preliator secured his rifle and moved to the east door. He opened it silently, signaling to 0021 that he was free to leave.

Breathing heavily, 0021's chest heaved as his heart pounded like a drum. Shock began to take hold, leaving his mind blank and his ears ringing with an unsettling hum. The reality of what he had done hit him like a wave—he had killed someone for the first time.

"Congratulations! You have completed the challenge," Pedia announced with enthusiasm. "The purpose of this challenge was to test your willingness to follow our orders, no matter how extreme. You now have the rest of the day to reflect on your experiences. Use this time wisely, and have a great day! Always remember: Unity, Equality, Safety."

Typically, a Pre-Elite would respond with "Unity, Equality, Safety" in return, but 0021 remained silent. With a final smile, Pedia vanished from the room, leaving behind an air of normalcy as if nothing terrible had occurred.

0021 took a moment to gather himself, staring at his shaking hands, unsure how to stop them. He glanced up at the window one last time, seeing the five shadowy figures still watching, waiting for him to exit so the next two Pre-Elites could fight.

For the rest of the day, 0021 was free to reflect on the challenge, but all he could do was walk through the hallways, constantly staring at his hands. He imagined them covered in blood, though they were only bruised from the fight and trembling as if they were cold. The guilt of taking a life haunted him, making his hands shake uncontrollably. He took deep breaths, trying to hold back tears and not show any weakness as others passed by. Fear gnawed at him—what if someone did to him what he had done to 2245?

He wandered the hallways all day, even skipping his evening meal. When other Pre-Elites approached him, he could only hear a ringing in his ears. He would quickly mutter that he was "fine" and walk away, leaving them looking back at him with concern. They wondered if he was unwell, but the ringing bell signaling their next class soon distracted them.

As 0021 continued to walk, a storm of questions filled his mind: How many Pre-Elites had died today? How many more would die tomorrow? How long had this been happening? He thought about the Pre-Elites who had disappeared during his younger years, rumored to have failed and moved on. Were they really killed? Were they just tools for the government? The more he pondered, the more he craved answers, even though he knew they would remain elusive. This realization made him feel as if his soul were slipping away, leaving him hollow inside.

Late that night, an announcement echoed through the halls, instructing everyone to return to their rooms. 0021 froze for a moment before turning and making his way back to his quarters. As he entered, he found Pedia waiting for him, now dressed in an outfit that made her look like she'd spent the entire day cleaning. She jumped up with a cheerful greeting, her energy almost jarring against his heavy mood. He managed only a forced smile, unable to match her enthusiasm.

"Looks like you did well today," Pedia said cheerfully.

"Yeah, I managed," 0021 replied, trying to sound fine. However, Pedia quickly noticed the bruises covering his body and her expression shifted to concern.

"What happened? Do you have any serious injuries?" she asked anxiously.

"No, just some bumps and bruises. It's nothing serious," 0021 reassured her.

Pedia sighed with relief, glad that nothing major had happened. "So, do you want to tell me about it? It looks like it was quite a challenge. Was this the toughest one yet? What was it about?"

0021 forced a smile but hesitated to share the truth. He knew Pedia was already aware of what had occurred. "Maybe another time. It was a long day, and I just want to lie down and rest. My body needs it. I'm really tired and all I can think about is sleep. Perhaps we can talk later."

Pedia's smile faded into a concerned look as she watched 0021 head toward the bed. This was the first time he didn't seem like himself. "Okay then. I'm always here if you want to talk about anything. And I want you to know that I'm very proud of you. Tomorrow, you'll have 698 days remaining. Have a great night."

The lights went out, and Pedia disappeared. 0021 pulled his blanket tightly around himself and turned to face the wall, his eyes wide open. He wanted to cry, to let out the guilt and pain of what he'd done, but fear stopped him. The thought that the Pedia he had trusted for so long might be part of this dark reality terrified him—what if speaking out made him vanish too? Lying in bed, he felt completely alone, unsure of who to trust or how to face anyone tomorrow, or in the days to come.

Fast forward to the present day, where all the Preliators were finishing their meal by the riverbank. Everyone was together—everyone except 0021. He sat by himself, nibbling on a few crackers and staring blankly at the frozen ground. The memories of that fateful day two years ago still haunted him, blurring the lines between right and wrong. Here in Regret, he avoided conversation, afraid that saying the wrong thing could lead to his own disappearance.

As dusk began to settle in, a chilly breeze picked up. 3009 noticed it was time to get moving and began to remind everyone to prepare. He left 0021 for last, approaching him quietly. Seeing that 0021 seemed lost in thought, he gently tapped him on the shoulder to get his attention.

"Preliator 0021, it's time," 3009 said, but 0021 didn't respond; his thoughts were elsewhere. Concerned, 3009 tapped him a little harder. "0021, are you alright?"

Startled, 0021 snapped back to reality and looked at 3009. He quickly stood up and grabbed his helmet. "I'm fine. Just getting mentally prepared, that's all."

As 0021 put on his helmet, 3009 studied him for a moment before speaking again. "I can tell something happened to you. I know you don't want to talk about it, and that's okay. It doesn't have to be today or tomorrow. But we're going to be together for the next thirty years, and when you're ready, I'll be here to listen. I just want us all to be on the same page. I don't want any of us to die because one person isn't."

0021 met his gaze through the visor of his helmet. "When the time is right, we can talk about it. For now, I promise nothing will affect anyone else. I will do my job."

With that, 0021 grabbed his VFV rifle and joined the rest of the Preliators as they began walking toward Brand. 3009 stayed behind, watching him with growing concern. He then approached 0444 and whispered into his helmet's com-link, ensuring only they could hear.

"I need a small favor," 3009 said, catching 0444's full attention.

"What do you need?" 0444 asked.

"I need another set of eyes to watch over 0021," 3009 replied, glancing over at him. "You're the only one I trust to take this seriously. If you notice him doing anything out of character, anything that isn't Preliator-like, let me know. He's quiet with us, but here in Regret, I suspect he might act differently."

0444 understood 3009's concern, but he believed 0021 would fulfill his duties. Still, he nodded to show that he would help in any way he could.

CHAPTER 7
THE RUMORS ARE TRUE

In the past, the city of Brand was known as Brandon. It was a peaceful prairie town in Canada, with around fifty thousand residents at its height. Life there had a small-town charm, perfect for raising a family. Crime was rare, and neighbors were always quick to help each other, especially during the harsh prairie winters. It offered all the essential amenities while maintaining a close-knit community feel.

But today, Brand is a desolate wasteland, ravaged by endless winter storms. The skyline has all but vanished, with a perpetual dark cloud looming overhead, even at noon. The only trace of its name is a tattered highway sign, barely legible. Once-lively homes now sit abandoned and decaying, overtaken by wild vegetation. The city's infrastructure has crumbled over the decades, and the downtown area is nothing more than boarded-up buildings, where the wind howls through empty streets. Without the blanket of snow, the scene would resemble a graveyard, filled with the remnants of its former residents. Now, the city belongs to a sinister group known as The Faceless.

The Faceless, called the "Hyenas of Regret" by the Preliators, are a terrifying presence. They enforce obedience through fear, their horrifying reputation more than just rumor. These mindless cannibals, some criminals exiled to Regret, others born into it, roam the wasteland. At night, they howl like wolves. They speak only in broken, simple phrases, and cover their faces—not just for warmth, but to set themselves apart from their prey.

While The Faceless are not particularly intelligent and can often be deceived, their real danger lies in their numbers. For new Preliators entering their territory, that alone makes them a significant threat.

Now, an hour has passed, and night has fully settled over the land. The Preliators stand on the outskirts of Brand, the snow swirling around them. 1983 is perched on a snowy hill, using his night vision visor to scan the ruined city. He's looking for a way to reach the women, who seem to be trapped in the heart of the wasteland. His Pedia displays three possible routes, each with the same percent chance of success if they want to remain undetected.

Behind him, the rest of the Preliators quietly gather, waiting for instructions as the long night ahead begins.

"So, what's the plan?" 0444 asks, standing beside his friend.

1983 keeps his gaze fixed on the city below. "The data shows three routes. Each has just over a sixty percent chance of getting to the women without being detected."

"Which one is the best?" 0444 turns to Pedia for an answer.

Pedia's voice chimes in, calm and precise. "Statistically, all three routes offer similar odds. However, if we split into smaller teams and take all three, the overall chances of success increase by eighteen percent. Moving in smaller groups will help us avoid danger more easily, especially with the cover of night."

1983 chuckles softly. "I think I'm going to enjoy these next thirty years with you, Pedia."

"I'll enjoy helping all of you through these next thirty years," Pedia replies, prompting a small smile from him.

The others, except for 0021 and 3009, share brief smiles. But they quickly fade as the weight of their mission returns—this is the most critical operation of their lives, and there's no room for error.

"What does everyone think about the suggestion? Should we go with that plan?" 3009 asked, scanning the team.

The Preliators exchanged glances. The more they considered Pedia's suggestion, the more it made sense. One by one, they blinked to indicate "yes" on their helmet screens. Once everyone had agreed, 2890 spoke up, "So, who's going into which group, and which direction are we taking?"

All eyes turned to 0444 and 3009, the usual decision-makers. The team trusted each other enough not to waste time debating the details—they just needed direction.

After a brief pause, 0444 stepped forward. "Alright, first group: 3009, 0021, and 1113—you'll take the right route. Second group: 2890, 0774, and 3578—you'll head left. 2288, 1983, and I will go straight. We'll check in every five minutes until we meet at the target. Everyone good with that?"

There was no verbal response, but their faces and body language showed agreement as they formed into groups.

"Any last words, Pedia?" 0444 asked.

Pedia's voice responded smoothly, "As Sun Tzu said, 'Victorious warriors win first and then go to war, while defeated warriors go to war first and then seek to win.' You've prepared. You're ready. You will succeed."

Even 0021, usually stoic, couldn't hide a spark of motivation.

"Then, let's move," 0444 said, signaling the start of their mission.

With 3009 leading, the first group veered right, heading through the old residential area. The second group moved left, into what used to be the industrial district. Meanwhile, the third group went straight, advancing toward the heart of downtown. They all jogged quietly, staying alert and cautious as they moved through the desolate city. Pedia scanned for potential threats along the way.

The first and second groups had farther to travel, but they benefitted from the numerous buildings and shadows that offered hiding spots. Their main challenge was gauging how many of The Faceless might be lurking nearby. The third group, though their route was shorter, had fewer places to take cover in the open downtown area. If they encountered any of The Faceless, evasion would be difficult.

The third group moved carefully, darting from one old storefront to the next, checking that each was clear. On the main streets, The Faceless patrolled in trucks. At least two men stood on each tailgate, casually chatting, not paying much attention to their surroundings. This forced the group to stop and wait, block by block, for the trucks to pass. Progress was slower than expected, but the team knew they were getting closer to their target. A soft beeping in their helmets confirmed they were on the right path, pushing them to keep moving forward. While they had to remain silent, they could still communicate using their helmet radios without being overheard.

"Status check—what's everyone's position?" asked 2288.

"The first group is almost at the destination," replied 1113. "No contact with anyone so far."

"The second group has reached the destination," said 0774. "Everything was clear, but we've got a new problem to discuss when you arrive."

"One thing at a time," 1983 responded. "The third group needs a little extra time to get there."

"Take your time," 0774 replied. "This new problem might take a while to solve. 0774 out."

The third group continued their careful progress, moving from building to building, dodging yet another Faceless truck. Its occupants were yipping at each other, distracted and paying little attention to their surroundings. After twenty minutes, the group was just a block away from their target.

But as they approached the building, 1983 suddenly froze. What he saw ahead wasn't just a single truck—it was several. Around fifty of The Faceless swarmed the area, surrounding the structure. The building they guarded was an old mall, probably the largest in the city. Unlike the other crumbling and boarded-up places, this one seemed strangely well-maintained, indicating it was likely where The Faceless are living.

2288 glanced at 1983 and 0444 before pointing to a run-down gas station nearby. It looked deserted, with its few windows shattered and the pumps long abandoned. Using hand signals, he suggested they take cover there. Both agreed, and the group cautiously made their way toward the gas station.

Once inside, they quickly settled in. It was a small station, built for just one attendant behind the counter, with four old pay-as-you-go pumps outside. Surprisingly, some of the windows were still mostly intact, allowing one of the Preliators to peer out and keep watch on the mall and the swarm of The Faceless outside.

From their vantage point, the Preliators observed a group of The Faceless guarding the main entrance of the old mall. The Faceless seemed simple-minded, shuffling around the front doors in tattered winter clothing, some of which provided little to no insulation against the cold—though they appeared oblivious to it, accustomed as they were to the harsh weather.

They shoved each other playfully, making strange noises and aimlessly wandering about, occasionally glancing up at the winter night sky. Despite their disorganized behavior, the Preliators knew they were easily outnumbered five to one. While The Faceless lacked the firepower and training of the Preliators, there could be hundreds more hidden inside the mall, and they still hadn't located the three missing women. For the time being, they decided to remain hidden, waiting for the perfect moment to move in undetected.

"This is the third group. We're stationed in a secure location near the main entrance. Has anyone found another way in?" 1983 asked through his helmet radio.

"This is 3009, first group. The east side of the building is a dead end—everything is boarded up. Looks like the main entrance is the only way inside," replied 3009.

"Second group here, 3578. We've checked the south and west sides. Same situation. The main entrance seems to be the only way in or out. The Faceless have locked it down pretty well," reported 3578.

The Preliators began to realize that, despite their erratic behavior, The Faceless weren't as mindless as they appeared. Their defensive strategy was surprisingly effective. Still, 1983 remained unconvinced.

"Let's wait here," 1983 suggested calmly. "I think an opportunity will come soon."

He turned around, rested his rifle against the wall, and sat down, crossing his legs and placing his hands behind his head. Despite the tension of the situation, he looked completely relaxed, as if they had all the time in the world.

"How do you know that? Sounds like more than a gut feeling," 3578 remarked, overhearing 1983's comment.

"They're cannibals. Eventually, they'll get distracted by something else. My gut's usually right in situations like this," 1983 explained confidently.

"I hope you're right," 3009 responded. "For now, we'll stay out of sight and hold our ground. If nothing happens in two hours, we'll go in by force. Does everyone agree?"

The team signaled their agreement through their helmets, including 1983, who continued to stay relaxed while the other two focused on watching The Faceless, waiting for them to slip up. Nearby, 0444 lay beside 2288 but stayed close to 1983 so that they could take turns keeping watch.

Forty-five minutes passed. It was 1983's turn to keep watch. He remained by the window, keeping an eye on The Faceless outside. Meanwhile, 0444 and 2288 sat with their backs against the wall beneath him, eyes closed. They weren't asleep, just resting, staying calm as they had practiced each morning with their Pedia—readying themselves for a potential attack.

Suddenly, the rumble of a loud truck shattered the stillness. Like most vehicles The Faceless drove, this one was in terrible shape—missing about a fifth of its body panels, with the remaining parts so rusted that a single slip could leave a nasty cut. Yet, somehow, it functioned just well enough to drive. As the truck came to a halt, a group of The Faceless gathered around, watching as the newcomers climbed out and began sharing some kind of news with the others.

"Outsiders in the city! New people heading this way!" shouted one of The Faceless, a man called Baking Powder, pointing west to emphasize his point. The others turned, eager to see the potential new victims. People born in Regret often had names from old-world brands, setting them apart from newcomers. "We need more people to come with us. Lots of food for us!" Baking Powder added.

Excited to join the hunt, The Faceless crowded around the truck, though only eight could fit. The driver insisted that was enough, causing frustration among those left behind.

"You can fit more!" shouted New Spice, one of the mall guards, annoyed at being left out.

"We need room for the food. This is enough. You must stay and guard," Baking Powder replied firmly.

"That's not true!" argued another guard, Frontier, pushing his way toward the truck. "You'll eat everything yourselves! We're all hungry. Let us go, and you stay here to guard."

The argument created a distraction, offering the Preliators a window to act.

As the men in the truck ignored the complaints, yipping as they prepared to leave, a few others tried to hop on but failed. The ones left behind were initially angry, but as the truck drove off, they shifted their attention back to each other, still grumbling.

Two of The Faceless men closest to the truck started

shoving each other in frustration, barking angrily. Within seconds, they lunged at one another, and the rest of The Faceless quickly formed a circle around them, yipping excitedly and cheering on the fight. Watching from a distance, 1983 smiled as his prediction came true. He tapped 0444 and 2288, signaling that it was time to move. He called the other groups over the comms, saying, "It's time." Weapons ready, the Preliators slowly emerged from the gas station.

Meanwhile, the two men wrestled in the snow, throwing punches as the crowd of onlookers grew louder, too distracted by the brawl to notice the nine Preliators creeping toward the mall's main entrance.

Suddenly, one of the fighters' potato sack masks fell off, revealing his sickly, pale face. He froze, panicking as he realized his secret had been exposed. Glancing around, he saw the other Faceless man staring at him, their expressions shifting from amusement to hunger.

He pleaded for his life, insisting he was one of them, but New Spice sneered and declared, "Male flesh is the snack for the night!"

In an instant, the crowd of The Faceless turned on the uncovered man. They attacked him mercilessly, ripping him apart as they fed.

Taking advantage of the chaos, the Preliators slipped into the mall unnoticed, carefully erasing any trace of their presence.

Once inside the mall, the Preliators carefully scanned their surroundings, making sure they hadn't been detected. It was eerily quiet inside, but the sounds from outside—The Faceless eating, chatting, trucks rumbling by—still reached them. The beeping in their helmets grew louder as they moved closer to the women. The mall was dark and empty, amplifying their tension. They hadn't seen anyone yet, and the only sound was the echo of their own footsteps. Activating their night vision, they advanced in single file down the lower-level hallway.

"Have you detected anyone nearby, Pedia?" asked 0774.

Pedia responded, "There is a large population inside the building, but not in this area. My scan indicates everyone, including the women we're searching for, is on the upper floor."

As they moved forward, their helmet displays showed they were closing in on the women, the distance now measured in meters rather than kilometers. Despite Pedia's reassurance, the Preliators remained cautious, passing through rooms that once housed stores, now makeshift shelters with garbage bins used for light and warmth.

Each store they searched was empty. The unsettling silence felt like a trap, but they trusted Pedia's data and pressed on. When they reached an old food court, they found it strangely intact—except for the tables, which were littered with pieces of dead bodies. Flies swarmed the fresher remains, covering bones left behind. The stench was overwhelming, but their armors' filtration systems shielded them from the worst of it. Without their gear, even the most hardened Preliator would have been overcome by nausea.

Out of nowhere, 3578 broke the silence, saying, "These are the stories we always heard about Regret—the tales that the parents of the New World tell their children to make them behave, warning them that something like this could happen. All the stories and rumors are true."

No one spoke in response, but as they glanced around, they silently agreed with 3578's observation.

Most of these young Preliators had mentally prepared for the gruesome scene they were walking into, staying focused on their mission. However, 0021 stopped abruptly in the food court, horrified by what he saw. Kneeling down to inspect the remains, he realized many were from human infants. Instead of questioning why there were more infant remains than adults, anger surged through him.

Noticing his reaction, 2890 approached and asked, "Are you okay?"

0021 didn't respond, overwhelmed by a strange ringing in his head and the mounting rage. 2890 saw his distress and asked again, "Are you okay?" He placed a hand on 0021's shoulder, giving him a gentle shake. The touch grounded 0021, allowing him a moment to gather himself. Standing up, he replied, "I'm good. I thought I saw something. Let's keep moving." His tone was steady, though strained, as he tried to refocus on the mission.

As 0021 walked away, 2890 watched him closely, sensing something unusual in his behavior. From a distance, 0444 and 3009 also kept an eye on him, concerned by the brief outburst. Despite 0021's odd demeanor, his body language seemed composed, so they decided to trust his words and continued.

They pressed on until they reached an old escalator that hadn't worked since the collapse of the old world. Their visors showed the women were on the second floor. Cautiously, they began climbing the escalator, one step at a time. The silence was unsettling, with no signs of any Faceless nearby. The darkness and eerie quiet amplified the tension as they advanced.

As each Preliator reached the top of the second floor, they

quickly slipped into a dark, empty store, using it as cover while Pedia scanned the area for any signs of life. The silence was unsettling, with no movement or sounds from any Faceless members. The darkness seemed to swallow everything around them.

Once Pedia completed her scan, she updated them, "There's a large group of people near the location where the women are. There could be hundreds of The Faceless. The path seems clear for now, but proceed with caution."

Acknowledging Pedia's warning, the Preliators followed the beeping noise on their helmet screens, which guided them closer to the women. The beeping grew louder with every step, indicating they were closing in. Eventually, they reached a large, boarded-up store—possibly once a furniture or clothing outlet. The makeshift barrier in front of it looked hastily constructed, as if meant to trap whoever was inside rather than protect them.

The beeping in their helmets stopped, confirming they had arrived. The intensity of the signal reinforced what they feared—the women were trapped inside. As they examined the barrier, it became clear that it wasn't meant to keep people out but to keep the people inside from escaping.

While some Preliators inspected the barricade, others checked their visors. The readings showed three women behind the boards, their heart rates steady and calm. This strange detail unsettled the team, leading some to speculate that the women might already be under the control of The Faceless.

As 0774 watched his teammates pulling down the boards, a troubling thought crossed his mind. He scanned the area again—there was no sign of The Faceless anywhere. Yet, his helmet indicated hundreds of people behind the barricade. Were they waiting for the team to break through?

Could this be a trap? The unsettling possibility crept into his mind: what if the three women had become The Faceless themselves? It might explain why they were still alive in a place ruled by cannibals and why the rumors of Regret's First Trial being the hardest always seemed true.

The boards started to give way, but 0774 pushed his doubts aside. Now wasn't the time to second-guess. He gripped his weapon tightly and braced himself for whatever lay ahead.

3578 and 1983 moved closer to the barrier, trying to pry away the boards to create an opening.

"I've got a bad feeling about this," said 1113, assisting 1983 as they worked on the barricade.

"I've had a bad feeling since we stepped into this nightmare," 1983 replied. "Right now, all I want to do is..."

The three Preliators ripped apart a large section of the barricade, their combined strength breaking through with a loud crack. The force sent 1983 stumbling backward, landing hard on the ground with a thud that echoed more than they had intended. Quickly recovering, he sprang to his feet, his gun raised, scanning the area as if ready for anything. The mall remained eerily silent, with no signs of movement. After a tense moment, they pressed on cautiously.

They focused on the gap they had created in the barricade— just wide enough for one person to slip through. One by one, they entered. First, 3578 squeezed through, followed by 3009, and then 0021. 1113 was the last to go in, pausing for a moment to scan the area using his night vision. Still, there wasn't a soul in sight, which reassured him as he finally entered.

Inside the massive, dimly lit store, 1113's eyes first caught an old security checkpoint and the large counters that filled the space. He quickly caught up with the others, but when he did, he noticed they were all standing frozen in place, staring ahead in stunned silence.

"What are you all looking at—" 1113 started to ask but stopped mid-sentence as his eyes landed on the same sight. "Oh, my gods," he whispered.

Hundreds of people were chained to the floor on thin, tattered mattresses, their faces hidden and their gowns in shreds. Feeding tubes hung from the walls and sprawled across the floor, seemingly supplying just enough nutrients to keep them alive. Their breathing was slow and labored—they were alive, but only barely, trapped in a horrifying state.

"This is the large group the scanner picked up," Pedia informed them. "They're prisoners of The Faceless. But why keep them alive? I never imagined such inhuman treatment, even from cannibals."

The Preliators quickly scanned the room, taking in the sight. They noticed a disturbing pattern: all of the captives were women. As they were trying to make sense of it, 0444 made a startling discovery—the woman he was examining was pregnant. His realization, combined with the infant remains they had seen earlier, suddenly made everything clear.

"They're not using them for food," 0444 said, his voice grim. "They're breeding them. This is a farm. These women... they're the herd."

His hand rested gently on the woman's stomach, feeling the heartbeat of her unborn child. The woman, however, remained motionless, trapped in a daze, oblivious to her surroundings.

119

CHAPTER 8
WHEN IT GOES TOO FAR

The group stood in silence, processing 0444's words. Around them, the women who had been trapped here for years bore the scars of a world without rules. The Preliators longed to save them all, to bring them to safety and help them heal, both in body and mind. They wished they could offer these women a second chance at life. But the harsh truth was that their mission allowed them to save only three. It wasn't fair, but saving three was better than saving none.

0444 thought back to what his mentor, his old personal Pedia, had said a couple days before he left on this mission. She had warned him that a moment would come when he would be tested like never before. Now, he understood this was that moment. He had to push aside his emotions and finish the mission, just like the great Preliators before him.

"Let's spread out and find them," 1113 ordered, breaking the silence. "The faster we find them, the faster we can get out of here."

The others nodded and began their search, their helmet

lights flicking from stealth mode to bright yellow eyes, cutting through the darkness. They were so focused on the task that they didn't notice 0021 still standing motionless. He couldn't tear his eyes away from the women—innocent victims of a merciless world. His mind replayed a past fight with 2445, the struggle between right and wrong that had plagued him for years. Now, it was tearing him apart.

Pedia's voice came through his visor. "We need to help the others and find our targets, 0021. Focus."

But 0021 couldn't focus. He was overwhelmed by thoughts of the Preliator Code—the Code that didn't apply in Regret, where no rules existed. Yet, what he saw here was a level of cruelty far beyond anything he had ever known. His mind kept flashing back to the remains of infants he had seen on the lower levels, their tiny bodies robbed of any chance to choose between right and wrong. What they had endured was worse than death—it was Hell. The more he thought about it, the more his rage grew, building up inside him like a fire he couldn't put out.

Not only were the women's faces concealed, making it nearly impossible to identify which one to save, but their clothing was identical as well. They wore nothing more than dirty makeshift gowns, crudely fashioned from worn-out sheets. These flimsy garments barely covered their bodies, offering little protection and, disturbingly, seemed designed to allow The Faceless 'easy access.'

3578 continued his search, moving slowly as he approached his target. His heart raced as he found three women lying on the ground. Kneeling beside the first, he gently pulled off the old pillowcase covering her face. Her skin was pale, her eyes rolled back, and she looked almost lifeless. She was breathing, but it was so shallow that she seemed unaware of his presence. He scanned her, hoping she might be one of the three they were sent to rescue. But she wasn't. His heart sank with disappointment and guilt as he softly replaced the pillowcase, covering her face again.

He moved to the next woman, her face hidden beneath a few tattered shirts. Her breathing was labored, but as he removed the shirts, he noticed she appeared healthier than the others. His pulse quickened—she resembled Pam, one of the three women in Pedia's briefing. As he scanned her, her eyes shot open, blinking wildly with panic. Her whole body tensed as if she sensed danger, her fear raw and immediate.

3578 quickly pulled his hand away from her mouth, but when she tried to flee, he gently pressed it back, holding her steady. With his free hand, he cupped her face, making sure she looked at him. He needed her to understand that he wasn't a threat.

"I'm not here to hurt you. I'm here to help. My mission is to bring you home," 3578 said softly but firmly, his voice calm and reassuring. He kept his hand on Pam's mouth until her breathing slowed, her panic subsiding. Only then did he carefully release her, hoping to ease her fear.

Pam, still shaken and confused, whispered, "What? What are you going to do to me?" Her voice trembled as she tried to comprehend what was happening. She didn't want to challenge him but needed answers, needed to understand.

"I'm Preliator 3578," he said, keeping his tone very calm. "I'm with a team, and we're here to help. We're taking you home—away from this place."

"Home?" Pam repeated softly, as if the word was foreign to her. She had been gone so long that the idea of home felt distant, almost forgotten. Her face showed the struggle to recall what it once meant.

0444, hearing Pedia's message, rushed over to join 3578. Pam still looked terrified, even as 3578 carefully broke the chains around her wrists and ankles. 0444 moved closer, gently removing the feeding tube with practiced hands. Once freed, Pam immediately grabbed her sore wrists, rubbing them to ease the pain. She glanced up at 3578, trying to remember if he really was a Preliator. Eighteen months in Regret felt like a lifetime.

"If you stay calm and follow our instructions, we can get you home faster," 3578 whispered, his voice steady and reassuring. He knew he had to be patient with her.

Pam stared at the reflective surface of 3578's helmet, memories of what the Preliators were like flooding her mind. Fear lingered, but she had no other choice. "You're going to take me back home? You're the ones who took me away from it," she said, her voice a mixture of bitterness and hope.

"Your sentence is over," 0444 said gently, kneeling beside her. "It's time to go back to your loved ones. Do you remember them?"

Pam's eyes softened as she searched her memory for familiar faces. The images were blurred and distant, but the thought of home stirred something inside her. "I think so…" she whispered, uncertain yet desperate to believe it. Each day in Regret, memories of those she cared about had brought only pain, as if clinging to them was a cruel reminder of what she'd likely never see again. She had tried to forget, thinking it might be easier, convinced she wouldn't survive long enough to see them.

Even though Pam had a point about the Preliators, 3578

didn't waver from his duty. 0444 stood beside him, ready to assist. Pam nodded, finally stopping the rubbing and inspecting her wrists. They were bruised and swollen but not so badly that she couldn't walk. She tried to stand, but her legs gave out, and she stumbled. Both Preliators reacted quickly, catching her and helping her regain her balance.

"We weren't the ones who put you here," 3578 said firmly. "We can talk about the past later. Right now, our job is to get you out. Do you understand?"

Pam didn't answer immediately, still trying to process everything. But as 3578 offered his shoulder for support, she knew she had no other choice. Anger still simmered, but anything was better than staying in Regret. She nodded and leaned on his shoulder, taking slow, cautious steps.

"3578 and I have Pam," 0444 spoke into his helmet's comms system. "Can anyone confirm the status of the other two?"

Just a few rows away, 3009 crouched beside an older woman. Unlike 3578 and 0444, he showed little emotion as he swiftly pulled the bag from her face, startling her. She blinked in the dim light, struggling to open her eyes while 3009 began scanning her, waiting for Pedia's results.

As her vision cleared, she saw the towering figure of a Preliator standing over her. Unlike the other women around her, whose eyes were dull and lifeless, hers were a striking, piercing blue, accentuated by dark rings of exhaustion. The blue was so vivid it almost looked artificial, as if she wore special contact lenses. Horror filled her face as she recognized who was standing above her, and she let out a scream.

Without hesitation, 3009 clamped his hand over her mouth, silencing her as the scan continued. She fought back fiercely, trying to bite his gloved hand, but he barely reacted. When the scan confirmed her identity—April, the second of the three targets—he felt a brief moment of regret. She was loud, and her struggle could easily attract unwanted attention, potentially The Faceless, complicating the mission. But orders were orders, and he couldn't afford to waver. His job was clear.

He removed his hand from her mouth and started unchaining her, keeping a close watch on their surroundings.

"Get away from me! I'm not going with you!" April screamed, her voice sharp and defiant.

3009 remained calm, unfazed by her resistance. He began, "April Starks, this is Preliator 3009 of the—"

"I don't care about your stupid number! I'm not going anywhere!" April snapped, cutting him off, her defiance clear in every word.

"By the Code, your sentence is over," 3009 said calmly. "I've been ordered by the great two gods to take you home. If you're worried about anyone hurting you here in Regret, I and the other eight Preliators will make sure you get back safely."

With swift, precise movements, 3009 removed the chains binding her, almost like a magician performing a well-rehearsed trick. While this might have impressed most people, April remained unmoved. She glared at him with her piercing all blue and with black pupil eyes as he extended a hand to help her up.

"So much anger," Pedia observed, its tone clinical. "This is what happens in a world without rules. People lose control. It will take a lot to calm her down before she crosses the wall."

"This isn't the time for that discussion, Pedia," 3009

125

replied, staying focused. "Let's just get her out of here and let the government deal with the rest."

"I told you; I don't care about your number!" April snapped, her voice sharp. "No number will stop what's coming!"

"Are you worried about The Faceless?" 3009 asked, trying to keep the conversation grounded. "We can handle them. We've trained for years to stop groups like them. Just stay calm, and we'll all get out of here."

Instead of answering, April spits directly at him, her contempt clear. The spit dripped down his helmet, and 3009's visor flashed from yellow to red. Frustration surged through him, and for a moment, he felt like giving up. But he quickly reminded himself of the mission. No matter how defiant she was, getting her out of Regret was too important to abandon.

In a more sinister tone, April warned, "You think I'm worried about The Faceless? You have no idea what Regret is really about. You've been living the easy life on the right side of the wall. This is your first real Trial. The true terror of Regret is something you haven't seen yet—but you will soon!"

As April's voice grew louder and more frantic, she pushed 3009 away, her agitation increasing. The noise drew the attention of 1983 and 2288, who rushed over to help 3009 contain her. But the sight of more Preliators only seemed to fuel her panic. At the same time, the chained women around them began to stir, making unsettling, almost inhuman sounds as if waking from some dark slumber.

Sensing the situation was escalating quickly, the other Preliators hurried their search for the final target. They knew that if April continued to make this much noise, The Faceless would be drawn to them sooner than they were ready for. The pressure was mounting—they had to find the last woman and escape before things spiraled out of control.

Meanwhile, at the far end of the store, 0021 had wandered away from the group and stumbled upon an old office. He cautiously peeked inside, his night vision showing only vague, shifting shadows. Strange noises echoed from within, adding to his sense of unease.

Before stepping inside, 0021 made sure his VFV assault rifle was ready. His attention was fully absorbed by the eerie office, unaware of the chaos unfolding with April and the disturbed, awakening women behind him.

Back with the others, 3009, 1983, and 2288 managed to get April to her feet. Despite her fierce resistance, the strength of the Preliators was too much for her to fight off. While 3009 and 2288 held her steady, 1983 quickly rummaged through his pockets, pulling out a needle. It was a sedative, designed to put someone to sleep for over an hour—just enough time for them to make their escape.

When April saw the needle, she burst into laughter, unafraid. "That won't stop what's coming. The creature is out there, waiting to strike. You're all going to die tonight, one by—"

Before she could finish, 1983 swiftly injected her in the left shoulder. The medication worked quickly, her movements slowing until she finally fell into a deep sleep. With April now subdued, 1983 hoisted her onto his shoulders, while 3009 and 2288 remained on high alert, ready to defend against any threats.

Just as they prepared to continue their search for the last target, they were interrupted by strange sounds—footsteps and objects being knocked over in the distance. The helmets of all the Preliators, except for 3009, switched from yellow to red, signaling danger. A grim realization washed over them: someone else was in the room. Likely members of The Faceless.

"We know who you are! We know your mission!" a voice hissed from the shadows, confirming their worst suspicions. "My name is Best-Value Soap. I speak for all The Faceless."

The Preliators quickly formed a protective circle around the two women they had rescued, realizing that 0021 was still missing. With practiced precision, they readied their assault rifles and switched to night vision mode, scanning the darkness for any signs of movement.

Pedia chimed in through their communication system, offering advice. "Try to locate the source of the voice. Statistically, keeping him talking increases your chances of finding him."

3009 took charge, speaking calmly into the black void. "This is Preliator 3009. If you know our mission, then you understand that the best course of action is to let us take the individuals we're assigned to bring back. Once we have them, we'll leave, and no one will be harmed. This is a promise from the two gods."

A tense silence followed before the voice responded again. "We all know how powerful the Preliators are," Best-Value Soap said. "One of you could kill hundreds of us. We don't want that. We want a compromise, where everyone wins!"

Some of the Preliators exchanged uneasy glances. How did The Faceless know so much about their mission and the Trials? Information about the Trials in Regret was strictly confidential, and they had been trained to never reveal such details. Had past Preliators said too much, or was this some sort of trick?

3009, seeking clarity, asked, "Pedia, have we ever compromised with anyone in Regret during past Trials?"

Pedia responded promptly, "In my experience, never. Multiple Pedia units operate in Regret, but the rule is always the same: complete the Trial by any means necessary, but never compromise."

"Preliators don't compromise. We follow the Code—nothing but the Code!" 3009 shouted into the darkness, aiming his voice toward the unseen source.

Best-Value Soap's tone shifted, clearly displeased. "This is Regret. Your Code doesn't apply here. We understand your Trial. You must bring one person back. We will allow you to do that."

3009's stance remained firm. "Our mission is to bring back three, and that is exactly what we will do."

Best-Value Soap countered, "We've encountered your kind before. You only need to bring back one to complete the Trial. Take the old one—her milk is no good. The young ones, though, still have value. Take the old one, and your Trial will be complete."

Unease crept through 3009 and the others at the suggestion of taking the easy way out. It felt wrong, a violation of their mission.

"We're taking all three women we were instructed to retrieve," 3009 declared with unwavering resolve. "And you will tell us the numbers of the Preliators who came before us and broke the Code."

His voice carried an air of authority, not only to complete their mission but also to uncover the truth about potential betrayals in the past.

Best-Value Soap hissed in frustration. "I will speak to

someone else now. You don't understand."

With that, the mysterious voice seemed to retreat, leaving the Preliators in a state of tense anticipation. The unsettling atmosphere deepened as they remained on high alert, ready for whatever might come next.

While the tense standoff raged outside, 0021 slipped cautiously into the dark, crumbling office. The dim light barely penetrated the room, prompting him to holster his assault rifle in favor of dual pistols—quieter and better suited for a stealthy approach. Every step was deliberate, his eyes scanning the shadows for threats. In the distance, he spotted a faint glow spilling from a connected room, the light flickering as if from a nearby fire. Strange, guttural moans echoed softly from that direction, sending a chill down his spine.

0021 slowed his movements, striving to make as little noise as possible. He positioned himself strategically at the threshold, bracing for the possibility of an ambush. As he approached the doorway, the unsettling sounds grew louder with each step, heightening his sense of dread.

When he fully entered the room, a surge of shock turned his eyes red. Inside, he found three Faceless men. Two of them were naked except for filthy rags covering their faces, and they were taking turns viscously raping one of the chained women, reveling in their cruelty. The woman lay on an old, grimy couch, her body all bruised and battered, her back marked with angry, bleeding scratches. Completely naked, she moans and cries for help which echoes in the room, her face obscured, deepening the horror of the scene before him.

0021 noticed a third man standing in the corner, fully clothed. His body language indicated he was deriving pleasure from the horrific situation unfolding before him. He seemed to be preparing for his turn, as he wasn't participating directly due to another young woman tied up beside him. This young woman was trembling with fear, repeating to herself, "It's going to be okay," in a desperate attempt to stay calm. Her face was covered, and while she didn't fully understand the extent of the horror, she knew it was bad and that she might be next.

As 0021 observed her closely, he recognized a birthmark on the young woman's left forearm, matching the description of Kimberly from the dossiers he had reviewed. He quickly scanned her to confirm her identity.

"She's the last one we need to find," Pedia informed him. "That's Kimberly. We must tell the others immediately."

0021's response was a firm, "No." Unlike other Preliators, who would have followed Pedia's advice—quietly eliminating the three men, rescuing Kimberly, and completing the mission—0021 was consumed by a burning anger. He wanted these men to suffer. He holstered his handguns and unsheathed his two knives.

"What are you doing?" Pedia asked, panic creeping into its voice. "We need to alert the others. We have a Trial to complete."

But 0021's eyes blazed with fierce determination. He wasn't just going to fulfill the mission; he intended to ensure that those responsible for this suffering faced justice.

Ignoring Pedia's warnings, 0021 acted swiftly. He hurled one of his knives at The Faceless man standing in the corner, the blade slicing through the air and embedding itself in the man's right hand, pinning it to the wall.

The man screamed in pain, staring at the knife lodged in his hand in shock, unable to comprehend what had just happened. Hearing his scream, Kimberly's terror deepened; she was bewildered by the unfolding chaos. Meanwhile, the other two men remained oblivious to their companion's cries, too focused getting pleasure with their victim.

0021 wasted no time. He advanced on the closest man and drove his second knife brutally into the man's buttocks. The strike was so quick and deep that the man didn't even have time to scream; instead, he collapsed off his victim, stunned and disoriented.

Realizing something was wrong, the last man attempted to react, but 0021 was faster. He seized the man by the throat, dragging him away from the couch and slamming him against the wall, lifting him off the ground by several inches.

The Faceless man struggled desperately, trying to break free, but 0021 had other plans. With his free hand, he gripped the man's genitals and squeezed mercilessly. The man wanted to scream, but 0021's hold on his throat was too tight, choking off any sound.

Without hesitation, 0021 yanked as hard as he could, tearing the man's genitals off and letting them fall to the floor. The man whimpered in agony; his eyes wide with horror as he looked down at the gruesome evidence of his suffering. 0021 then tightened his grip, choking him until his body went limp, breathless.

Pedia's voice cut through the moment, laced with concern. "You're taking this too personally. The Preliator way is to end lives quickly when necessary. This is too much. Slow, painful deaths are what evil people do."

0021 responded coldly, "Only if you do it to innocent people. These monsters are far from innocent."

Pedia cautioned, "If you continue down this path, you'll

become a monster like them. Is that what you want?"

For a moment, 0021 hesitated, grappling with the turmoil inside him. Ultimately, he chose to heed Pedia's warning. He released his grip, allowing the man's lifeless body to thud heavily to the ground, joining the mutilated remains of his own flesh.

He approached the man with the knife still embedded in his buttocks. Blood pooled beneath him as he writhed in agony, desperately trying to dislodge the blade. With cold precision, 0021 placed his left foot on the man's hand and his right foot on his back, pinning him to the floor. He gripped the knife handle and yanked it out, eliciting a piercing scream of torment from the man.

Bending down, 0021 yanked the bag off the man's head, forcing him to confront the woman he had brutalized on the couch. "You're lucky I made it quick. You deserve far worse," 0021 growled, his voice low and menacing.

Without hesitation, he used the bloodied knife to slice the man's throat wide open. Blood gushed from the wound, soaking the bag that had covered his face. The man choked, desperately trying to breathe but drowning in his own blood.

As the life drained from the Faceless man, 0021 slammed his head into the ground with brutal force. The impact echoed through the room, startling the naked woman on the couch. Terrified, she bolted from the room, desperate to escape the nightmare unfolding around her.

Knowing he had little time left, 0021 swiftly turned his attention to the last Faceless man, still pinned against the wall. Without hesitation, he plunged his knife into the side of the man's head. The body twitched violently, nerves reacting to the sudden trauma. After a few tense seconds, 0021 pulled the knife out, followed by the one still embedded in the man's hand. He methodically wiped the blood off both blades as the faceless man's body crumpled to the floor.

Meanwhile, Kimberly, still blindfolded and unable to comprehend the chaos around her, had squirmed into a corner of the room, seeking safety. Bound and shivering with fear, she was lost in confusion. 0021 spotted her and, without a word, placed a reassuring hand on her shoulder. Before she could react, he quickly cut through the ropes that bound her.

After she was freed, 0021 removed the rag covering Kimberly's face and offered her his hand. "I'm Preliator 0021," he introduced himself, his voice firm yet gentle. "My mission is to find you and bring you back home. I need you to come with me and leave Regret. It's your only option to stay alive and safe. We don't have much time. The sooner you accept that, the faster we can get you to safety."

Kimberly looked up at 0021, her terrified, innocent eyes locking onto his red, glowing gaze as if he were staring into her very soul. Her hesitation was palpable. Part of her wondered if she could really trust him—after all, it was the Preliators who had brought her to this nightmare in the first place. A deep resentment simmered inside her, urging her to refuse his help.

But as she glanced around at the horrors surrounding her—the blood-stained floor, the lingering echoes of tortured cries—she realized that staying meant certain death. Regret was a place where nightmares never ended, and while trusting a Preliator felt like betraying herself, the alternative was far worse.

Taking a deep breath, Kimberly swallowed her fear. She made her decision. Slowly, she reached out and took 0021's hand, letting him guide her away from the nightmare that had consumed her for so long.

As the Preliators continued negotiating with Best-Value Soap, chaos suddenly erupted. A naked woman, drenched in blood from the Faceless men 0021 had killed, bolted from the office. She sprinted past everyone, screaming at the top of her lungs, heading for the entrance. Her screams echoed through the room—then stopped abruptly, as if something had grabbed her and silenced her.

A chilling silence followed. 0021 emerged from the office, guiding Kimberly with him. The Preliators quickly scanned her, and their visors confirmed she was indeed Kimberly— the last woman they needed to find. With all three women accounted for, Best-Value Soap let out a furious roar that echoed ominously through the room.

"You had your chance!" he screamed. "You blew it! None of you will leave here alive!"

Suddenly, strange yipping sounds filled the air. The Faceless were hidden, their movements growing louder with each passing second. 0021 rejoined the group, ensuring Kimberly was safe with the other women as the Preliators readied their weapons. Their night vision activated, but no visible threats appeared.

"Does anyone have eyes on them?" 0444 barked.

"Negative," 1113 replied, his voice tense. "They're like ghosts. We hear them, but we can't see them."

Pam, trembling, tapped 1983 on the shoulder. "Has anyone checked above us?"

1983 quickly looked up, his visor catching movement along the roof barriers. The Faceless had been there all along, silently waiting to ambush the Preliators at the perfect moment.

CHAPTER 9
HIS SECOND CHANCE

1983 shouts, his voice sharp and urgent: "Look up now! They're on top of the ceiling!"

Everyone's heads snapped up instantly, weapons at the ready. Above them, shadowy figures clung to the ceiling – The Faceless. Without warning, they began leaping down. The first few were shot mid-air, but six Preliators quickly dodged, their sharp reflexes taking over as they fired at the attackers landing on top of the barriers. One by one, The Faceless fell to their inevitable deaths.

The Faceless cling to rusted metal roof poles, waiting for the right moment to strike again. Their movements are wild, desperate.

While the six Preliators continue shooting, the other three form a protective wall around the women, using their own bodies as shields. The Faceless attack in waves, hurling themselves into the fray with reckless abandon, their overwhelming numbers driving them to sacrifice without hesitation. Amid the chaos, their voices ring out with fury:

"You had a chance!" "They belong to us!"

Many of The Faceless miss their mark, crashing violently to the ground below. The air fills with the brutal sounds of bones breaking – legs, arms snapping on impact. Some die instantly from the fall. But not all their victims are The Faceless. In the chaos, a few land on the chained women, causing injuries or even death, blood staining not only The Faceless but also the sheets covering the women.

Those closest to the fallen jumped scared in shock. Some desperately try to stay silent, pressing back into their chains, while others lie motionless, their fates uncertain amidst the chaos.

Whenever a Faceless gets too close to the Preliators, they're met with bone-crushing shoulder checks, slamming them into the ground with brutal force. The impact causes violent whiplash, leaving many of the attackers dazed. Those who manage to stand are swiftly dispatched—specialists 1113 and 0774 step in, raising their shotguns to deliver flawless headshots. Each shot is precise, the sound of skulls shattering filling the chaotic air before they quickly move to the next target.

Amid the chaos, three women remain under the protection of the Preliators. April, who has endured captivity the longest, is unconscious, her body limp and unaware of the unfolding carnage. The other two women stand trembling, their eyes squeezed shut, arms raised in surrender as they cower from the violence surrounding them. Every thud of The Faceless bodies hitting the floor, every crack of gunfire, heightens their terror. In their minds, they desperately search for any hope of escape, trying to imagine a way out of this hellish nightmare.

As fewer of The Faceless jump from the ceiling, 3009

quickly realizes their numbers are dwindling. He raises his voice above the chaos, "Everyone, head slowly toward the main doors!"

Following his command, the group begins to move toward the doorway, weapons still at the ready. As they advance, 0021's attention shifts to the chained women scattered among the bodies. Some lie dead, their covered eyes staring at nothing. Others remain motionless out of sheer terror, pretending nothing happened, while a few struggle in panic, desperately trying to free themselves.

Caught in the moment, 0021's focus lingers on them, his thoughts swirling. That split second of distraction almost costs him—3009 spots a Faceless rushing toward 0021 from behind. With precise timing, 3009 fires a shot, dropping the attacker just in time.

"Move it! We need to get going before more show up!" 3009 barks, urgency in his voice.

"What about the others?" 0021 snaps back, pointing to the remaining captives, their faces etched with fear.

"Our orders are to save these three! That's all that matters!" 3009 reminds him firmly, his tone leaving no room for argument.

0021 grumbles under his breath, frustration boiling inside him. He knew The Faceless were no match for them; he wanted to stay, to take them all out and end this once and for all. The thought of being the last man standing, freeing everyone, gnawed at him. But another thought quickly surfaced—he could come back later, better trained, and save them all. For now, he had no choice but to follow orders.

Reluctantly, 0021 fell in line, his eyes lingering on the women for one last moment before turning toward the door.

When they reached the door, the team briefly broke formation. Preliators 0444 and 1113 slipped out first, followed by the women, while the rest of the group moved in sequence, with 0021 and 0774 guarding the rear. Once back in the upper hallways of the mall, they quickly reformed their protective circle—but more of The Faceless men were already there, waiting, hissing in anticipation.

0444 and 1113 exchanged a glance, spotting the broken escalator they had used earlier. They took point once again, moving cautiously down the corridor, one step at a time, with the others following close behind. As they neared the escalator, they saw about a dozen of The Faceless men scattered across it, as if waiting to ambush them.

Without hesitation, 0444 and 1113 knew what needed to be done. Leaving the group behind at the edge of the escalator, they holstered their guns and drew their knives—better suited for close-quarters combat. The two Preliators rushed forward with precision and lethal intent, ready to take on the fight head-on.

The Faceless men carried makeshift weapons—jagged shards, broken pipes, and heavy clubs—but they were no match for the precision and training of the Preliators. 0444 and 1113 moved with grace and deadly efficiency, jumping from one side of the escalator to the other, their knives gleaming in the dim light. Every motion was precise, a showcase of their brutal mastery of close combat.

With each Faceless man they felled, they quickly shoved the bodies aside, sending them tumbling down the escalator to the cold, frozen ground below. They remained focused, eyes locked on the next target, their movements fluid and unrelenting as they cleared the path for the group.

Back on the second floor, The Faceless men rush at the Preliators, armed with crude, homemade weapons. Their reckless charges make them easy targets, as if the Preliators were back in basic training. Some of the attackers try to dive into the protective circle, aiming to break through and seize the women. Instead, they are shot in mid-air or quickly stabbed and slammed to the ground. Every attempt to breach the Preliators' defense ends in brutal failure.

A few of the smarter Faceless soon realize that their blind charges aren't working. Hanging back with metal pipes and other makeshift weapons, they hope the constant attacks will wear the Preliators down. They bide their time, waiting for a chance to strike when exhaustion takes hold.

But the Preliators never get tired. They remain sharp, relentless, and efficient, turning the battle into a massacre where only The Faceless men suffer. Each wave of attackers is met with cold, calculated violence—gunshots, knife slashes, and the sickening thud of bodies hitting the ground. The smarter Faceless, still waiting for their moment, begin to understand too late that it will never come.

3578 quickly scans the escalator and spots 0444 and 1113, who have cleared a path for the group.

"Alright, it's time to leave. Let's head home," 3578 shouts, his voice cutting through the chaos.

1983 ensures April is secure on his shoulder, her unconscious body steady as he leads the way toward the escalator. Pam and Kimberley rush down the steps, desperate to reach 0444 and 1113. One by one, the Preliators follow, maintaining their defensive formation as they descend.

0021 was the last one to leave, as usual. He kept firing until he was sure no more Faceless would show up, watching for any movement in the shadows. Just as he was about to head down the steps, something familiar caught his eye. He paused, using his visor to zoom in. His heart sank. Lying on the ground was the naked woman who had been raped and then fled. Her lifeless body was twisted on the cold floor, with a section of her left arm torn off.

A wave of shame washed over 0021. He had focused too much on the mission, on following orders, and had failed to protect her when she needed it most.

"There's nothing you can do about it now," Pedia's voice chimed in, calm but cold. "The only way to ease this is to save the three women we were assigned to protect."

0021 clenched his fists. The truth of Pedia's words stung, but the guilt lingered.

"0021, let's go! Now!" shouted 2288 from below, urgency in his voice.

0021 took one last look at the woman, her tragic end burning into his memory, before sprinting down the stairs to join 2288. As they reached the others waiting at the bottom, anger bubbled up inside him. Most of The Faceless had been dealt with, but there were still more guarding the main doors.

The group began to gather, preparing to huddle and hear Pedia's next plan. But all eyes turned to 2288, already knowing what the next move would be.

"Well, everyone, stay here. Let me do what I do best," 2288 said confidently, striding toward the main doors alone.

As he approached, 2288 calmly holstered his rifle, securing it to his upper back. From his lower back, he pulled out a small metal box, the familiar sound of clicking mechanisms filling the air. With swift, practiced movements, he manipulated the box, transforming it into the VDY-90—a deadly weapon designed for moments like this.

"Pedia, set my vision to target mode," 2288 requested, his voice calm yet commanding.

"Target mode is now activated," Pedia replied instantly.

Outside the mall, a group of The Faceless men had just finished feasting on the remains of one of their own. The sound of distant gunfire from inside made them pause. Some stood still, uncertain, while others inched forward, heads tilted as if debating whether to investigate or remain where they were.

Suddenly, the doors burst open, and 2288 stormed out, gripping the VDY-90, its long chain of bullets almost dragging down to the ground. The Faceless eyed him warily, hissing and barking, trying to intimidate him as they moved closer. Their animalistic sounds grew louder, but they were unaware of the true power they were facing.

Unfazed, 2288 stopped a few feet from the crowd and activated target mode. Instantly, his vision prioritized each of The Faceless, marking them for elimination. He squeezed the trigger, and the VDY-90 roared to life. Bullets tore through the air, ripping into The Faceless with brutal precision. Skin shredded, bones snapped, and the air filled with the metallic scent of blood.

2288 moved fluidly, his weapon spitting out round after round, cutting through every one of The Faceless that crossed his path. There was no hesitation in his actions—each shot was deliberate, each target felled with brutal efficiency. The horde had no chance to react. Bodies collapsed where they stood, torn apart by the relentless barrage.

In mere moments, the ground was littered with the dead. Not a single Faceless remained standing outside the mall.

Silence descended as 2288 lowered his weapon, surveying the carnage with a cold, calculating gaze.

2288 scanned the area one last time, ensuring there were no lingering threats. Satisfied, he quickly reloaded his weapon, the mechanical click of the fresh rounds sliding into place breaking the eerie silence.

"There are no more threats here. You can move ahead. I'll inform the others," Pedia's calm voice echoed in his ear.

The Preliators received the message and, without delay, rushed out of the mall. As they reached the outdoors, Kimberly and Pam were hit by a biting chill that seeped into their bones. After being trapped inside for so long, the cold was a shock to their system. Even April, slung over 1983's shoulder, began to stir, the harsh winter breeze slowly pulling her back to consciousness.

The Preliators maintained their protective formation, their eyes scanning for any signs of danger as they led the group away from the city. Along the path, they passed the results of 2288's grim work. Spent bullet casings littered the ground, gleaming faintly in the snow. The aftermath was brutal— bodies of The Faceless lay strewn across the bloodstained snow, limbs twisted at unnatural angles, eyes frozen in death.

Kimberly and Pam struggled to keep pace, their breath quickening as they navigated through the gruesome scene. The reality of the situation began to weigh on them. The Faceless were dead, but at what cost? As they passed body after body, doubt crept into their minds. Were they truly escaping one group of monsters, only to find themselves under the protection of another?

Each step was more difficult than the last, not only because of the blood-soaked snow but because the weight of their thoughts grew heavier. Kimberly shivered, glancing at Pam, who shared the same unspoken fear. The Preliators had saved them, but the cold brutality of 2288's handiwork made them question what kind of men they had been rescued by.

This time, there was no sneaking from block to block or hiding in the shadows. They ran straight down the center of the road, following the red trail highlighted in their visors as directed by Pedia. The route left them exposed, vulnerable to the trucks guarding the community. 2288 took point, 0074 close behind, as the rumble of a truck grew louder in the distance.

It wasn't long before the truck appeared, carrying four Faceless men—two inside, two clinging to the cab. One of the men squinted at the figures on the road, his eyes widening when he recognized the Preliators and the women. He pounded frantically on the roof and yelled at the driver, "Go faster! Run them over!"

The truck surged forward, its engine roaring. The headlights cut through the darkness, their glare reflecting off the snow, and the women's fear spiked once again. They froze, staring wide-eyed at the oncoming vehicle. The Preliators remained calm, ensuring none of the women bolted in panic. 0074, however, continued walking toward the truck, daring it to charge him.

He calmly secured his assault rifle at his side and reached into his pocket. With precision, he retrieved two grenade rounds from his right hip pocket and loaded them into his weapon. Without breaking stride, he continued his approach, eyes locked on the speeding truck, patiently waiting for the perfect moment to strike.

The Faceless men screamed in a frenzy, urging the driver

to ram the group. The truck thundered closer, full speed now, headlights cutting through the dark and casting long, frantic shadows.

But 0074 remained calm. He waited for the perfect moment, calculating the distance in his head. Just as the truck seemed like it would flatten him, he fired.

The grenade hit the driver's side wheel dead on, triggering a massive explosion. The force of the blast was so intense that it lifted the entire truck off the ground. Shrapnel and debris filled the air, the twisted remains of the vehicle flipping mid-air before slamming back down onto the road in a fiery wreck.

The truck was obliterated, leaving a smoking crater in its wake.

Everyone halted, instinctively shielding themselves as debris rained down around them, the flaming wreckage of the truck soaring past. The two Faceless men who had been perched atop the vehicle were thrown even higher, their screams echoing in the air until they disappeared from view. The truck crashed onto its hood with a deafening thud.

0074 took a moment to assess the chaos before firing his VFV launcher again, igniting the wreckage in a fierce blaze that illuminated the night. Flames danced, consuming the twisted metal as they scanned the area for further threats. Pedia's scans revealed no more trucks or Faceless men nearby. Satisfied, they resumed their flight, eager to escape the cursed city limits.

As they about to leave the city of Brand behind, some of the Preliators looked back, absorbing the smoke and ruin they'd left behind. To these few, the hardest part of the Trial was finally over. But for others, something different stirred—a sense of pride, as if the ease of this victory confirmed what people always said about the Preliators: that they were superior in every way. Feeling invincible, they now believed that nothing could stand in their way. If this was truly the worst they'd face, then everything ahead would be nothing more than child's play.

After about thirty minutes of relentless running, they finally reached the outskirts of Brand and made their way toward the riverbank, retracing their steps back to the farm. April, now almost fully conscious, fluttered her eyelids open and took in her surroundings. The familiar chill of the snowy prairies was a stark contrast to the chaos of the city, but her body felt heavy, her energy drained.

She wanted to scream, to lash out like before, but the words escaped her. Instead, she murmured to herself, "We've entered the monster's world now. There will be nowhere to hide. Nowhere to hide but to die." Her voice was barely a whisper, lost in the howling wind. No one heard her—not even 1983, who was too focused on the distant glow of headlights piercing through the darkness.

"More company!" he shouted, his voice slicing through the tension as he pointed toward the approaching truck.

Everyone stopped, instinctively turning to see the oncoming headlights of another truck barreling toward them.

"Stay here!" 0021 shouted, urgency lacing his voice. He started rushing toward the vehicle, determination etched on his face. "I'll stop them. Everyone else, keep going and finish the mission. I'll catch up when I'm done."

"Remember, nothing personal," 3009 ordered, his tone firm but not unkind. "Finish the job as fast as you can and get back to the group."

0021 nodded quickly, the weight of responsibility pressing

down on him. He locked his gaze on the approaching lights, feeling the adrenaline surge through him as he sprinted forward, ready to face whatever threat awaited him.

Meanwhile, the rest of the group continued toward the riverbank, hearts pounding as they hoped to blend into the darkness. No matter how cold the air of the winter night felt, they pushed on, determined to make the rest of their journey easier, relying on the cover of night to shield them from danger.

The Faceless truck bore a striking resemblance to the previous one, with four men inside behaving like crazed lunatics, banging against the rusted metal and following the Preliators' tracks. They seemed to have no coherent plan, oblivious to what had become of their comrades. Their instincts kicked in, and they pursued the tracks like hungry predators on the scent of prey.

Inside the cab, the most unhinged of the four was the driver. He bounced up and down in his seat, emitting a cacophony of bizarre animal noises, his excitement palpable as he smacked the steering wheel with reckless abandon. The fresh tracks fueled his eagerness; he was starved for action and desperate to catch his quarry.

As the truck careened forward, the passenger light flickered and went dark, but the driver remained blissfully unaware, keeping the pedal to the metal. Suddenly, the headlights sputtered out completely, plunging them into darkness. The driver's jubilant bouncing ceased as confusion set in.

"What the—?" he mumbled, glancing around, trying to make sense of the failing lights when, out of nowhere, a gunshot rang through the night.

Before he could locate the source of the shot, a bullet

struck him squarely in the neck. Instinctively, he clutched his throat, blood seeping through his fingers, which sent the steering wheel veering wildly. The truck swerved sharply to the left, hurtling forward at breakneck speed until it crashed into a massive, unseen obstruction buried beneath the snow.

The impact was violent, tipping the truck onto its driver's side, the screech of metal grinding against metal piercing the night air.

With the truck now lying on its side, the driver struggled to breathe, bleeding profusely as he searched for an escape. A sharp piece of metal had pierced his rib cage, and with a dawning realization of his grim fate, he ceased his labored breathing, succumbing to death's grip.

The other three Faceless men were violently thrown from the wreckage, tumbling onto the hard, compact snow. Though disoriented and dazed, they fought to their feet, their bodies unsteady as they stumbled toward the overturned truck. Just as they attempted to regain their bearings, footsteps echoed through the night.

It was 0021.

He dropped his XDIV sniper rifle into the snow, its weight no longer needed. He unsheathed his two knives, the blades gleaming under the pale light. The red glow of his helmet's eyes lit up the night, making him look even more intimidating. With a deliberate and measured pace, he advanced toward the struggling men. Each of The Faceless tried to rise but continually fell back to the ground, their movements sluggish and uncoordinated.

A dark smile crept across 0021's face as he surveyed the scene. *This is where the fun begins*, he thought, savoring the moment before the chaos that was about to unfold.

0021 approached the nearest Faceless man, who remained blissfully unaware of the impending danger. With a swift motion, he tripped the man from behind, sending him sprawling into the snow. As The Faceless fell hard, 0021 drew his knife and severed the man's right foot in one fluid motion. A scream of anguish erupted from The Faceless, who rolled in the snow, clutching his mangled leg. Without hesitation, 0021 followed up by slicing off the man's left hand, leaving him writhing in agony, blood spraying like a grotesque fountain, desperate for a quick death that 0021 had no intention of granting.

"Please, just finish them off and head back to the group," Pedia urged, her voice laced with concern.

But 0021 dismissed the warning and shifted his focus to the second man, who had regained his balance and was now intent on rushing the Preliator. 0021 drew his pistol and fired twice into the man's right leg, then once more into the left. The Faceless fell, whimpering and rolling in the snow like his companion, a pitiful sight.

Walking past the moaning figure, 0021 was a stone-cold killer, fixated on the last remaining Faceless man, who clutched his neck in a panic, as if something was lodged there, begging to be released. This one, he decided, would suffer even more.

"Please, make it stop!" The Faceless man pleaded, his voice a mixture of desperation and terror.

0021 had no idea what the man was referring to, nor did he care. He seized The Faceless by the back of the head, slamming it into the bottom of the truck with brutal force. The man gasped, releasing his grip on his neck. Without mercy, 0021 slammed him again, harder this time, until he fell to his knees in the snow, dazed and disoriented.

"I'm not here to make it quick for you," 0021 said, his voice cold and unyielding. "I'll stop when I feel like stopping."

"You're taking this way too personally. This is not part of the Preliator Code," Pedia pleaded, her voice echoing through the tension.

The Faceless man, spiraling into panic, seemed oblivious to 0021's words. He spun around on his knees, terror etched across his features as he screamed, "The noise! So loud! I can feel it all over!"

Without a second thought, 0021 kneed him in the face, shattering his nose and sending him crashing onto his back. Climbing on top of him, 0021 unleashed a flurry of punches, each one landing with brutal precision. He struck until The Faceless man lay still, breathing only enough to indicate he was alive, a fragile rhythm against the chaos.

In a final act of contempt, 0021 removed the bag covering the man's face, wanting him to behold the menacing red eyes of his helmet one last time before the end.

But as he stared down at the man, he froze. The lights in his helmet shifted from red to yellow, illuminating The Faceless man's pale features. Yet, instead of the expected fear, he was met with eyes as bright and blue as April's. A shockwave of confusion coursed through 0021 as he released the man and laid him down in the snow, captivated by the haunting resemblance.

He continued to watch, the world around him fading as he pondered the connection between them. The vibrant blue eyes, once full of fear, gradually dulled as the man's breath slowed and finally ceased. The life drained from him right there in the snow, leaving 0021 with an unsettling sense of emptiness.

"Pedia, describe to me why their eyes are like that. Has this ever happened before?" 0021 demanded, his voice laced with urgency.

He could hear Pedia's response, but it was muffled and distorted, as if the world around him had dulled. A sharp pain pierced his neck unexpectedly, like a snake bite piercing into his skin. Instinctively, he reached back to assess the source of the pain, his fingers brushing against a small, hard object embedded in his flesh. Wincing, he yanked it out and inspected it—a tiny dart, foreign and sinister in its design.

His visor scanned the object, but the display flickered back an unsettling message: *Unknown*.

"Pedia, tell me what this object is!" he barked, frustration surging through him.

But this time, Pedia remained silent.

Something ominous began to seep into his bloodstream, a creeping sensation that sent waves of dizziness crashing over him. An overwhelming electrical hum filled his ears, a cacophony of noise that spiraled into chaos. Desperation clawed at him as he stumbled, circling around, trying to escape the maddening sound.

It became too much. He fell to his knees, instinctively removing his helmet in a futile attempt to regain control.

Despite the biting cold, sweat drenched his brow, and nausea roiled in his stomach. His hands tingled and went numb. When he looked down, panic gripped him. He glanced at the broken window nearby and caught sight of his reflection. What he saw sent a chill down his spine— his pupils were turning a vivid blue, mirroring those of The Faceless man and April.

For the first time in years, 0021 felt utterly helpless, lost in a torrent of confusion and fear. The lines of his identity began to blur, leaving him uncertain of what he should do next.

Then, from the darkness, a familiar voice echoed through the cold night. "Is this how you answer for your crimes? By punishing others for the wrongs, they've committed. Does that ease your mistake?"

0021's head snapped up, his heart racing. The electrical noise in his ears vanished, the dizziness dissipated, and the numbness in his hands faded away. With his now all-blue eyes, he squinted into the distance, searching for the source of the voice. Out of the shadows, a figure emerged—Pre-Elite 2245. He walked slowly, deliberately, until he stood right in front of 0021. His appearance was exactly as 0021 remembered: the same Pre-Elite training suit, still marked with the scrapes and bruises from their last fight.

"How did you get here? You're dead! I killed you!" 0021 shouted, his voice trembling with confusion and a surge of emotions he hadn't felt in years.

2245 regarded him with a calm, almost pitying expression. "Dead?" he replied softly. "Or perhaps I'm the part of you that you can't kill. The part that reminds you of your failure." His voice was haunting, cutting through the silence like a knife, speaking directly to 0021's deepest fears.

0021's mind raced, battling between the logical and the impossible. He had ended 2245, left him for dead. Yet here he was, a ghost from his past, demanding answers to questions that struck at the core of his guilt.

"What do you want from me?" 0021 demanded, clenching his fists despite the lingering numbness. His voice was strained, teetering between anger and fear. "I can't change what I've done!"

2245 took a step closer, the air between them thick with tension. "You can't change the past, but you can choose how to confront it. Will you continue this cycle of violence, or will you find a way to atone?"

0021 didn't give an answer. As 2245 just simply stared into 0021's blue eyes, as if searching for something buried deep within. Finally, he said, "What I want... is for you to remember. To understand that the monsters we fight are not the ones out there. They are the ones within us."

"The ones within us?" 0021 muttered, grappling with the weight of 2245's words. As he blinked, the cold prairie night vanished. He was no longer outside; instead, he found himself in the very room where he had killed 2245 two years ago. The familiar matted floors, the same Pre-Elite outfit he had worn back then—it was all the same. His mind reeled. Was this real, or was he hallucinating?

2245 stood in front of him, just as he had on that fateful day. The two Preliators flanked the door, silent and unmoving, while the five shadowy figures loomed overhead, watching, just like before. 0021's heart raced. He felt trapped, as though time had rewound, forcing him to relive that moment of horror.

2245 stepped forward and slapped 0021 hard across the face. The sharp sting jolted him; the pain was real. This was real.

"The monster within us—this is it," 2245 said, his voice eerily calm. "The day you lose sleep over. The day you always wished you could change. Well, this is your second chance. Fix what has been haunting you."

2245 lay down on the mat, completely defenseless, making no move to fight. "Come on," he continued. "Not many people get a second chance to fix their mistakes."

0021 stared down at him, stunned by how much 2245 seemed to understand. He had spent years thinking about this moment, imagining what he would do differently. Now, Pedia appeared beside him, her voice cold and mechanical. "Step two of your challenge begins now. You have three minutes to finish. The clock is ticking."

All those sleepless nights, all that regret—this was his chance to fix everything. Yet, all 0021 could do was stand there, frozen. "I can't," he whispered, his voice barely audible.

2245 urged him again. "What are you waiting for? This is what you wanted—a second chance. Take it before it's too late."

"You now have one minute left to finish the challenge," Pedia's voice echoed in his head.

0021's eyes flicked toward one of the Preliators guarding the door. The guard noticed his hesitation and stepped forward, raising the VFV assault rifle to his chest. 0021 froze, unable to move, his trembling hands at his sides. Tears filled his eyes, threatening to spill over. He was no longer the cold-hearted killer from Regret—just a scared, lost child, his voice breaking as he muttered to himself, "I can't."

Pedia's countdown continued. "Ten... Nine... Eight... Seven..."

The Preliator didn't flinch, but 0021 couldn't move. As he continued to sob, staring down at 2245, he choked out, "I'm sorry."

Pedia finished the countdown, but the Preliator didn't fire his weapon. Instead, 0021 felt a sharp, searing pain in his chest. He looked down and saw two massive blades piercing his body, the cold metal coated in his blood. He gasped as the blades withdrew, and blood poured from his wounds. He collapsed to his knees, knowing his time was up.

Blinking again, he found himself back in the snowy winter prairies. Blood stained the snow all around him. His breaths came in shallow gasps, and his vision blurred. A massive, dark shadow loomed over him. Desperately, he fought to see who had done this to him, but before he could make sense of anything, his breath faltered, and he collapsed onto his side, dead.

Standing over 0021's lifeless body, the creature from the barn loomed like a dark specter in the night. It quietly sheathed its futuristic two-bladed spear, the metallic sound echoing through the now-desolate snow-covered landscape. The creature's orange eyes glinted as it stared down at the fallen Preliator, its expression unreadable.

Then, in a voice that seemed to carry the weight of death itself—slow and haunting—it spoke: "Always too personal."

With that chilling remark, the creature vanished into the night, blending into the shadows as if it had never been there at all. The area around the wrecked truck fell eerily silent, no signs of life remaining. Only the wind stirred, carrying the memory of the battle into the cold, unforgiving darkness.

CHAPTER 10
ALL OF THIS FOR A KISS

April's voice sliced through the icy night air, her words laced with venom and despair. "There's no point in saving me if you can't even save yourselves!" she shouted from atop 1983's shoulders. The Preliator remained stoically silent, his determination to ignore her evident, but her relentless tirade was clearly starting to wear him down.

"Why bother with the beast trailing us?" April continued, her voice dripping with cynicism. "Just kill me now. It'll be quick, and you won't have to endure my voice any longer." Her gaze wandered up to the dark sky, her words a taunt to the stars. "Oh, gods, after all you've done to me, just let me die. Let me see my loved ones one last time before you cast me into some dark corner of the sky."

The hours stretched on, and 1983's patience wore thin under the relentless weight of April's morbid ramblings. Finally, with a sudden, sharp movement, he halted and threw her to the ground. His helmet's red lights flared with barely contained fury. The harsh snow beneath April's body was biting, but she, numb from years of abuse, barely reacted.

"How dare you speak to my gods like that?" 1983's roar shattered the cold silence. April's response was a twisted smile, her defiance unshaken. "Someone else can carry her. I'm done with her non-stop negativity chatter."

0444 stepped forward, placing a steadying hand on 1983's shoulder. "We're only a few hours from the farm," he said in a calm, measured tone. "Soon, we'll be home, and the government will handle her."

1983 sighed, frustration etched into every line of his face. "Can't we at least drug her again? Just to keep her quiet until we get there?"

"No," 0444 said firmly, shaking his head. "Administering more of that chemical risks an overdose. We need her alive to return to the Wall, not as a corpse."

April's voice cut through the discussion; her tone laced with a dark sort of glee. "I like that idea! Better double the dosage, just to be sure." The notion of a quick, painless death seemed like a welcome escape for her.

1983's eyes, glowing red through his helmet, locked onto her with a piercing intensity. For a fleeting moment, the idea of ending her suffering—and their own—seemed almost tempting. After all, they only needed one captive alive.

"No," 0444 snapped, his voice a steely command. "We are not doing that. This is not the Preliator way. We will bring all three back alive and well. Do you understand?"

1983's frustration boiled over as he brushed off 0444's hand. "If you think a couple of hours with her isn't so bad, then I guess you've just volunteered to carry her the rest of the way."

"If that's what it takes, fine. I'll do it," 0444 replied

resolutely. As 1983 walked away, the red glow in his helmet dimmed, fading back into the darkness.

As 0444 moved to lift April onto his shoulders, 3009 approached, a new message crackling through his helmet. Pedia reported that the other two women were in dire condition—exhausted, terrified, and shivering from the cold.

"How about we all take a fifteen-minute break?" 3009 suggested. "Let's give these women a chance to rest and eat. We're ahead of schedule, and the main threat is gone. It'll also give 0021 time to catch up with us."

The Preliators agreed it was a sensible plan. They found a snow-covered rock for Pam and Kimberly to sit on. 0774 and 1113 carefully brushed off the snow and laid down small towels before guiding the women to sit. Blankets from Brand were still draped over them, offering some semblance of warmth.

Reaching into their pockets, the Preliators produced small, cookie-like crackers and placed them gently in the women's hands. Pam and Kimberly, their lips trembling from the cold, looked up with silent gratitude, their eyes pleading for permission.

"Go ahead and eat," 1113 said softly. "You need all the energy you can get."

The women exchanged a quick, silent glance before devouring the crackers with the urgency of those who had been starved.

April remained seated defiantly on the frozen ground, refusing the small blanket 1983 offered—the same small one he'd had carrying her. But when her eyes landed on the food, her expression changed. She snatched the crackers from his hand, her hunger overpowering her pride, and began eating with desperate speed. 1983, patience at its limit, turned and walked away in disgust, the sound of her frantic chewing echoing in his ears.

April's eyes glinted with a dark amusement as she turned to 0444. "Do you think your companion is still alive?" she asked, her voice a mix of curiosity and malice.

"Can you be quiet for just one moment?" 0444 snapped, trying to keep his composure. "We're almost at our destination. Focus on what you'll say to the government during your parole."

April's gaze was unrelenting. "You didn't answer my question. Do you think he's alive?"

"Yes," 0444 replied with a trace of confidence. "I believe he is. We're trained for this. If you weren't so out of it, you would've seen how we handled The Faceless. He'll be back with us soon."

April scoffed, her tone dripping with disdain. "Who cares about the mindless Faceless?" Her words seemed to resonate with a deeper understanding of the Preliators' struggles. "I'm talking about the monster that runs Regret. If your companion encountered it, he's as good as dead. But the real question is whether he dies quickly, like a true warrior, or slowly and painfully, revealing the cowardice that most men hide."

0444's patience snapped. "Okay, that's it! No more talk about this monster. Just finish eating, and we'll get moving."

April's smile widened as she stuffed the last of the cookie crackers into her mouth. 0444 waited for her to finish, his frustration palpable.

She swallowed and continued with chilling calmness, "I don't know how long it's been in Regret or why it stays there. But I know it's watching us right now, in the dark, deciding how to attack. It's probably thought of a thousand ways to get us, just deciding whether to take it easy or have fun."

· "Have you even seen this 'Monster'? Or is this just a story to keep you from running away when you were trapped in Brand?" 0444 asked, his skepticism barely concealed.

"Yes, I've seen it!" April's response was sharp, her seriousness evident. The conversation hushed as the Preliators listened intently, except for 1983, who climbed up the hill from the riverbank to scan for 0021.

April continued; her voice laced with a grim satisfaction. "I've seen it because this isn't the first time you Preliators tried to save me."

"You mean another group came before?" 2288 asked, curiosity piqued.

"Yes, another group!" April confirmed. "I don't know exactly when, but the snow hadn't covered the ground yet. There were ten of them, young men like you. They went into Brand, but instead of killing everyone like you did, they were making a deal with The Faceless. They agreed to The Faceless' demands and took only me. We were about this far back to their drop-off when the monster appeared and killed them all, one by one."

"Why did it kill them and keep you alive?" 3009 asked, his tone skeptical.

April's sharp look was a clear sign that she wasn't to be underestimated. "I don't know. I never asked it. When the monster appeared, it went after one of them. One Preliator started acting crazy, screaming in fear before the monster killed him. Then it went after another. Next thing I knew, I woke up back in the same place again."

"What do you mean by 'going crazy'? Preliators are trained

to control their emotions during missions," 3578 interjected.

"The monster has a way of dragging you into your worst nightmare," April explained, her voice hollow. "It tortures you with your own mind before killing you. After seeing it for the first time, I had recurring nightmares of The Faceless eating my baby in front of me. It's a memory I couldn't block out until I saw that creature. It's only a matter of time until it shows up and kills us all. When it does, I hope I'm part of it. I have nothing to live for anymore."

April buried her head in her knees, covering herself with her arms as if seeking solace in isolation. The Preliators fell into uneasy silence, scanning the surrounding darkness for any sign of the monster, though they saw nothing but shadows.

"There is no monster," 3009 said firmly, his skepticism evident. "It's just a tale to scare people. If anything like that existed in Regret, Pedia would have it in the archives. Isn't that right, Pedia?"

Pedia's voice crackled through the helmet's speaker. "There is no information about anything resembling what April described. It's nothing more than a folk tale."

"You see?" 3009 addressed the group. "No more talk about this. Ten more minutes, then we keep moving, with or without 0021."

3009 climbed to the top of the bank, joining 1983 in the search. He lay down beside him, his night vision visor sweeping the area. The landscape was a blur of blowing snow and undulating prairie grass, the cold wind carrying a haunting stillness.

"I assume you haven't found him yet?" 3009 asked, breaking the silence.

"My guess is he's probably already at the farm waiting for

us," 1983 replied, his eyes never leaving the visor's display. They continued their vigil, the quiet only punctuated by the occasional gust of wind.

"It's so quiet, there aren't even any monsters around," 3009 said with a forced lightness. His attempt at humor seemed out of place in the chilling stillness.

1983 paused his scanning and turned to him, a look of disbelief in his eyes. "I thought you were the serious and logical one in the group."

"I am," 3009 said with a shrug. "But I'm also human. Dealing with someone like April can drive anyone to distraction. Just remember one thing."

"What's that?" 1983 asked, his curiosity piqued despite his fatigue.

"After this, we've got ten more years of this," 3009 said, his tone sobering. "There will be even crazier ones in Regret than her. So, we better get used to it."

They fell back into silence, the weight of 3009's words hanging between them. 1983 grimaced at the thought of facing worse challenges than April, but as he mulled it over, he realized the truth in 3009's statement. The harsh reality of their duty was undeniable, and despite his resistance, he knew he had to accept it. The road ahead would be filled with Trials far beyond their current struggle.

Down on the frozen river ice, a tangible chill lingered in the air, mirroring the distance the Preliators kept from April and her relentless negativity. Most of the group huddled together, while they waited for the women to finish their meager rations and warm up under the blankets. The cold was biting, but the promise of the final push to the farm kept them focused.

0444 made his way over to Pam, who was holding Kimberly close for shared warmth. He set down his assault rifle and sat on the edge of the rock beside them, the snow crunching softly beneath him.

"It's been a lot of hard days and nights for you," 0444 said, his voice carrying a rare note of empathy. Pam glanced up, her face pale from the cold, as he continued, "Especially today. So much blood and violence. Most people would have never-ending nightmares."

Pam's lips were tinged blue, and she shivered despite the warmth of Kimberly's body pressed against her. "Every day has been crazy. So many that I've lost count," she mumbled, her voice barely more than a whisper.

"Have you been part of their experiments?" 0444 asked carefully, searching for a less painful term than "rape."

Pam hesitated, her eyes revealing a flicker of distress. After a moment, she spoke quietly, "They tried using me for their experiments a couple of times. No baby for them."

"I'm sorry to hear that," 0444 said sincerely, trying to convey genuine sympathy. "No one deserves that, no matter what crime they committed. How do you know there's no baby yet?"

"Back home, I had two children. I got fixed before I was sentenced to Regret," Pam explained, her gaze steady despite the frost clinging to her eyelashes.

"So, they haven't figured out that you can't get pregnant," 0444 said, a trace of relief in his voice. "If they knew, you'd have been used as a food source right away."

"Lucky for me you arrived when you did, I guess," Pam said with a hint of sarcasm. "I wasn't there long enough for them to find out. They're not that smart, but they would've figured it out eventually, probably in a few weeks."

"I'm glad we got you out of that place in time," 0444 said, feeling a surge of pride. His gaze softened as he looked at Pam, recognizing the gravity of what they had managed to achieve.

"If you wanted to say that." Pam's sarcasm cut through 0444's confidence, leaving him momentarily stunned.

He blinked, trying to grasp the weight of her words. "Why do you say that? Don't you want to go back home, not worry about getting eaten alive, and see your kids again?"

Pam's gaze was distant, her voice tinged with a weariness that belied her calm demeanor. "You just don't get it. It's not going to be as easy as you think," she said. "Of course, it would be great to see my kids again. But it's been almost two years. What will they think when they see their mother, an ex-Regret criminal? Plus, I'll be forced to go back to the job where I broke the Code. The reason I broke it is that the labor was too hard for me. I'm too weak for heavy construction, and as I get older, it only gets worse. I'd probably end up back here in no time, because I'd break the rules again."

She paused, her gaze dropping to the snow-covered ground. "And then there's my husband. He's also in Regret for trying to take my place at that job. Who knows if he's still alive? If he is, maybe we could start becoming a family again, even if it's just for a short time. It's better than nothing. That's my only hope if I get out of this place."

0444 started searching the archives for information about Pam's husband, his eyes flickering with the silent communication he maintained with Pedia. The system hummed as data scrolled past, but before he could get any concrete information, Kimberly's voice cut through the cold silence.

"I just wanted to kiss him!" Kimberly's voice broke, sharp and raw, her frustration mixed with a deep sadness. A few Preliators turned to look, drawn by her sudden outburst.

Shivering, she pressed on, her words spilling out in a rush of emotion. "There was a boy named Matt. I've known him my whole life. I was always drawn to him, trying to talk to him whenever I could. When I finally thought I was old enough to date, he was the one I wanted. But my parents told me I had to marry the neighbor's son instead. They said it was because he and I had 'easy jobs selected,' while Matt did not. My parents and the neighbor's parents arranged everything, deciding it would make life simpler for our families. And just like that, when we were old enough, the wedding happened. No one ever asked me what I wanted."

Her voice softened, but the pain was still there. "I wanted Matt. I was willing to risk the hardship of his job just to be with him. I felt like I had to know...to feel what 'true love' was like, to experience something I wanted for once, not what everyone else wanted. I thought we were somewhere safe, somewhere no one would find us, and all I wanted was to kiss him. But then you Preliators showed up. And for that, you sentenced us both to Regret."

The Preliators listened in silence. Their training had prepared them for combat, discipline, and survival—yet beneath their armor, they were still teenagers, shielded from the complexities of ordinary human emotions. They'd spent most of their lives under the guidance of Pedias, trainers, generals, and Telos staffers, with little exposure to the lives of people like Kimberly. For some, Kimberly's story stirred a rare flicker of empathy, an uncomfortable reminder that beyond the missions and directives, there existed choices and desires they'd never been free to consider.

Kimberly's voice broke slightly as she continued, "Even if I get out of this place, would Matt still be alive? Would my family see me as Kimberly, or as the 'whore' of the family, the outcast they might try to send back here? All because I needed to know what a stupid kiss felt like."

Kimberly's tears began to fall, her sobs breaking through the cold air. Pam, who had been through similar struggles, gently rubbed her back in an attempt to offer comfort.

0444, sensing the gravity of the moment, turned to Pedia and asked, "Can you check on Matt's status for me?"

Pedia responded gently, "Certainly. Please hold on a moment." After a brief pause, her voice returned, subdued but precise. "I'm sorry, but Pam's husband died in the northwest region of Regret about four months ago. Reports from the Preliators who found him indicate he was killed by The Collectors, likely from a stabbing incident that led to fatal blood loss.

As for Kimberly's Matt, his chip stopped transmitting on his first day in Regret. There's no information on what happened. He's officially listed as missing, but it's assumed he's deceased."

0444 absorbed the news, his gaze shifting to Pam and Kimberly, who were huddled together for warmth, both visibly shivering. He faced a tough decision: whether to reveal the harsh truth to both women, adding to their grief, or to keep the information to himself to avoid causing them further pain.

0444 made his decision. With a determined stride, he approached Pam and Kimberly, who were huddled together on the cold ground. He stopped in front of them, his expression resolute.

Looking directly at Pam, he said, "I have some news from Pedia. Your husband is alive and well, he is waiting for you in Telos as we speak. If you cooperate with us, I can guarantee you'll see him again."

Pam's eyes widened with disbelief and hope. She stopped rubbing Kimberly's back, her face brightening as she asked, "You're saying he's alive and well?"

"Absolutely," 0444 replied with conviction. Pam's smile was hesitant but growing, as she thought about the possibility of reuniting with her husband.

0444 turned to Kimberly, his voice steady yet kind. "I haven't been a Preliator for long," he said, "but I've seen people in your situation. When someone returns from Regret, their family and friends are just relieved—overjoyed, even—to see them alive. They don't ask questions or hold grudges. They welcome them back, no judgment, no shame. And I promise you, no one will ever think to call you that word – 'whore'."

Kimberly, still wiping her tears, looked up at him. "And... I'll really be treated that way?"

"You will," 0444 assured her. "And Matt is alive. He'll be out of Regret in no time."

Just then, Pedia's voice crackled in 0444's ear, "I never provided you with that information. Why did you tell them that?"

Pam and Kimberly exchanged glances, their faces showing the first signs of relief and hope. Pam took 0444's hand and stood up, pulling Kimberly with her. They clasped each other's hands, their resolve to return home strengthened.

0444 responded to Pedia, "That's why I said it. We need to

do whatever it takes to complete this mission. We'll handle the rest when we're done."

Pedia's tone softened, her voice almost gentle. "Today, you have fully embraced what it means to be a true Preliator—not only by following the Code, but by doing whatever it takes to see the Trial through, even if it means hiding certain truths to get it done. I'll let the rest of the team know it's time to move out."

As Pedia relayed updates to the team, 0444 wrestled with a gnawing discomfort. For the first time in his life, he had knowingly spun a web of lies, and the weight of it was stifling, like his very soul was contracting to the size of a pinky finger. He fought to push these thoughts away, focusing instead on the task at hand.

"I think I see someone coming!" shouted 1983, jolting 0444 from his turbulent thoughts. He and the rest of the Preliators scrambled up the snowy hill towards 1983 and 3009. When they reached the top, they peered through their night vision visors, scanning the darkness.

"I don't see anyone!" 2288 said, squinting through his visor, zooming in to get a better look. "Where exactly did you spot them?"

"I saw a figure in the northeast," 1983 replied, pointing in that direction. "They were too distant to identify, but they were definitely there, and now they're gone."

"I saw the same figure, but further southeast," 3009 added, his visor tracking the area. "It looked like they moved between locations almost instantaneously."

2890 furrowed his brow in confusion. "What do you mean, 'jumping from one location to another'?"

Down on the icy river, Kimberly's scream shattered the

silence, drawing the Preliators' attention. Panic gripped the scene as she and Pam huddled together, both frozen in terror. April stood nearby; her demeanor strangely calm compared to the others. The Preliators helmets' eyes turned red in unison. Beside her loomed a seven-foot figure, clad in all-black, futuristic samurai-like armor. Despite its imposing appearance, the figure moved with unsettling grace and precision. Its gloved hand encircled April's neck, holding her in a vice-like grip.

"You talk too much for too long... revealing secrets that should remain hidden..." the figure intoned, its voice a slow, deep growl that resonated like a demonic whisper. "Because of this, your nightmare will end, but no one will be awaiting for you in another life."

The creature drew a small, gleaming blade and pressed it to April's throat. Pam and Kimberly stumbled backward; their faces contorted with horror. April's eyes fluttered open, meeting her fate with a resigned calmness that seemed almost surreal.

The figure's voice continued, each word dripping with menace, "Your children are calling for you... But it will not be the reunion you hope for."

With a sudden, brutal motion, the figure slashed April's throat. Her blue eyes widened in shock as blood spurted from the wound, staining her clothes and the ice below. She gasped for breath, her life slipping away as she slumped to the ground. The figure then flung her lifeless body against the frozen hill, causing an anguished scream from Pam and Kimberly.

The Preliators, stunned by the horrific scene, sprang into action. Half of them rushed to shield Pam and Kimberly, while the rest aimed their weapons at the figure. Just as they prepared to fire, the creature vanished into thin air. They halted abruptly, their eyes wide with disbelief at the empty space where it had been.

"Pedia, what did we just witness?" 3009 asked, his voice tinged with urgency.

"I didn't get a good scan," Pedia responded. "The details of what we saw are still unclear."

"Did that thing just disappear?" 2288 asked, his gaze darting around frantically.

"No technology from this world can do that, right?" 3578 inquired, a note of uncertainty in his voice.

"Who said it's from this world?" suggested 0774.

3578 turned to 0774, alarmed. "Not from this planet?"

The group looked at 0774, their skepticism giving way to concern. He moved closer to April's body, noting the lack of footprints and the stark contrast of her blood against the ice. The others began to consider the possibility he proposed.

"So, what do we do now?" 2288 asked, his voice trembling.

"I say we keep moving," 3578 replied firmly.

"Keep moving? After what just happened? Are you serious?" 2288 shot back, struggling to contain his fear.

"It's better than standing here and doing nothing," 3578 insisted.

"I agree with 3578," Pedia interjected. "We have no information on this creature. The best course of action is to continue toward our destination."

"What about 0021?" 2890 asked, glancing around. "Are we just going to abandon him?"

"We're facing an unknown threat," 0774 said, gesturing toward April's body. "We've given him enough time. If he's alive, he's on his own now."

"What do you think?" 2890 asked 3009 but received no answer.

2890 scanned the area and realized 3009 was missing. The Preliators quickly began searching and calling out for him through their visors, but all they received was eerie silence. Suddenly, 1983's voice cut through the quiet. "Everyone, up there!"

The team turned their attention to the opposite side of riverbank, where they saw 3009 standing alone, his weapon nowhere in sight. He was breathing heavily, and behind him loomed the monstrous figure, gripping a long, sharp pole. With a cruel twist, the monster drove the pole into 3009's lower back, twisting it with sadistic force.

The creature spoke with a chilling hiss, each word dripping with malice. "Out of everyone here, you're supposed to be the serious one. Instead, I know the truth. The truth is, you're nothing but a fraud, always acting tough. Deep down, you're just covering up the coward who you really are."

3009 moaned in agony as the monster twisted the pole further, but the Preliators were too far away to get a clear shot. The scene was chaos, the team immobilized by shock and fear.

"The problem with cowards, is that you need to loosen up," the monster continued, a sinister tone in its voice. It clicked a button on the pole, which began to emit a rhythmic beeping, like a ticking time bomb. The beeping escalated until, with a deafening pop, blood and mangled pieces of 3009 erupted into the air.

The gruesome display showered the riverbank, and the women screamed in horror as fragments of 3009 landed on them. The Preliators were paralyzed with shock, their training and composure shattered by the brutality they had just witnessed. They stood frozen, their minds racing but unable to decide how to confront or escape the terror that had just been unleashed upon them.

CHAPTER 11
WHEN FIRE MEETS WATER

As the final pieces of 3009 hit the ground, scattering across the snowy terrain. The Preliators stood frozen for a moment, awe-struck by the sheer power of this well-advanced monster before them. But only for a moment. They quickly regained their focus and opened fire with everything they had. Most wielded VFV assault rifles, except for 2288, who brandished a VDY minigun. The air filled with the deafening roar of gunfire as they pulled their triggers, hoping to land a shot that would bring down this beast from hell.

The Monster of Regret stood its ground, absorbing the barrage of bullets. It began to step backward, not out of defeat but seemingly to put some distance between itself and the relentless gunfire. Yet, it remained unyielding. The Preliators refused to let up; they advanced, closing in as they kept firing. When their rifles ran dry, they reloaded with swift, practiced motions, resuming the attack without hesitation. The fact that the creature was still standing unnerved them.

2288 screamed in fury, swinging his minigun left and

right, unleashing a storm of bullets that sent snow flying in every direction. But still, the monster stood.

"There is no effect on the target," came Pedia's calm voice over the comms. "I suggest saving ammo and using something with a bigger impact."

The Preliators with assault rifles paused and quickly switched the part of the gun to grenade launchers. The following explosions rocked the battlefield, sending fire and snow into the air. For a moment, it was impossible to see anything through the thick cloud of smoke and debris.

When the smoke began to clear, the monster lay face-down in the snow, completely still. The Preliators stared, waiting for any sign of movement. A few sighed in relief, daring to hope that it was finally over. But then, 2288's eyes went wide with shock.

"It's moving!" he shouted.

The creature's arms twitched, and slowly, it began to push itself up. The Preliators watched in stunned silence. Nothing on Earth should have survived that blast.

With an eerie calm, the creature stood tall once more, its body appearing unscathed. It turned its glowing orange eyes toward the Preliators, raising one arm as if pointing at a specific target in their midst. It was a silent, chilling challenge.

And then, in an instant, the creature vanished, leaving only the churned-up dirt and snow as evidence of its presence.

"Tell me that didn't just happen!" 1983 exclaimed, his voice filled with disbelief.

"That thing *pointed* at me!" shouted 2288, his eyes wide with terror. He clutched his minigun, scanning the faces of the others, fear etched across his features. "You saw what we did to it! Nothing on this world could survive that! And you saw what it did to 3009. That crazy woman was right—it's going to hunt us down, one by one. And now it's chosen *me*!"

Panic gripped him, and before anyone could intervene, he started firing his minigun wildly into the air, spraying bullets in every direction. Pam and Kimberley huddled together on the ground, covering their ears, their faces pale with fear. The other Preliators yelled at him, desperate to get him to stop, but he was lost in his frenzy.

As his gun finally clicked empty, 0444 stepped in, grabbed the minigun, and forced it down to the ground. He stared into 2288's helmet, holding his gaze until he finally let go of the trigger.

"It's gone! Try to stay calm!" 0444 commanded.

"How do you know it's gone?" 2288 shot back, his voice trembling. "It could be right behind you, watching us! It knows exactly what we're going to do, while we're stumbling around in the dark!"

"Panicking won't help!" 1983 barked. "We're Preliators! We have two frightened women to get home. That's our mission, and that's what we're going to do!"

Pedia stepped forward, her voice calm but firm. "Agreed. If we want to survive this, we need to work together and move quickly. We've seen that a few of us can't take that thing down alone. Our best option is to run, get back, and report to the generals."

2288 let out a shaky breath, dropping his gun onto the ice. He tried to calm himself, taking slow, deep breaths. 1983 and 0444 kept a close watch on him, ready to intervene if he lost control again. When he finally seemed to steady, they turned to the rest of the group, who stood, eyes wide, filled with uncertainty.

1983 pointed to the west. "If we sprint in that direction for a few more hours, we'll complete this Trial. A few more hours, and we're done. Standing here is a death sentence, and I'm not ready to die tonight. What about the rest of you?"

"What about the monster?" 3578 asked, his voice barely above a whisper. "It could still be out there, watching us. Like April said, it could pick us off one by one."

"Let it watch," 0444 snapped. "Pedia's right—we need to move. If it comes at us again on our way back to the farm, we fight it with everything we've got. Now, grab what you can, and let's *go*."

"Pedia, keep an eye out for anything unusual while we get ready," ordered 0774, his eyes scanning the surrounding darkness.

"Watch mode is on," Pedia replied coolly. "I'll alert you if I notice anything unusual."

The Preliators moved quickly, double-checking their gear. They focused on their weapons, stripping down to the essentials, leaving blankets and other small items behind. They needed to travel light, and every extra ounce could slow them down. In dire situations like this, the Preliators clung to positive thinking, knowing that every step forward brought them closer to the end of this grueling Trial.

Before setting out, a few of them took one last look around the riverbank, even though Pedia was already on watch. The monster's disappearance still haunted them, and they wanted to be sure it hadn't returned since 3009's death. With a flick of a blink, they activated their night vision and swept the area, their hearts pounding in the tense silence.

3578 and 0774 approached Kimberly and Pam, who remained huddled on the ground, clinging to each other.

They crouched down, speaking softly to the two women.

"We'll do our best to get you both out of here alive," 3578 said, his voice firm yet gentle. "Stick with us, and it'll be over soon."

Kimberly, still trembling with fear, didn't respond. Pam, however, managed a small nod and helped Kimberly to her feet, steadying her for the journey ahead.

With everyone in place, they began to move. Their helmet eyes switched to stealth mode, though it might not make much difference. They formed a single file, just as they had when they left Brand. 0444 took the lead, his assault rifle sweeping the path ahead. Kimberly and Pam stayed safely in the middle of the line, guarded on all sides, while 2288 brought up the rear. He struggled with every step, his breath coming in ragged gasps as he fought to keep calm. Sweat dripped down his face despite the cold, each stride worsening his nerves.

0444 glanced back occasionally, keeping an eye on the group. He could see the tension in everyone's posture, especially in 2288, whose hands trembled as he clutched his minigun. They moved quickly, each step echoing in the silence of the night. Despite the fear gnawing at them, they pressed on, driven by the hope that they might outrun whatever horrors the monster had in store.

2288's pace slowed as his legs grew heavy, and a wave of dizziness washed over him. He glanced back, half-expecting to see the monster lurking in the shadows, but there was only the unyielding darkness of Regret. With millions of questions swarmed in his mind: *Where is the monster? Why hasn't it shown up? Is it running with us? Did it only want 3009?* The relentless spiral of fear and doubt made it hard to concentrate, each thought blurring into the next.

Desperately, he pushed himself to keep running, his eyes darting backward every few minutes. An hour dragged by, and despite his efforts, he fell further and further behind. Through his night vision, he could barely make out the distant forms of his comrades ahead. His attention wavered; he was more preoccupied with scanning for the monster than keeping pace with the group.

"We're falling behind," Pedia's voice crackled in his ear. "If this pace continues, you'll be out of range. I can signal the others to slow down so you can catch up."

2288 didn't respond. His heart pounded, not just from the physical strain but from fear that gripped his mind. He was becoming the weak link of the team, but no one had noticed yet—they were all too focused on the path ahead and the ever-present threat of the monster.

The group reached the end of the riverbank, beginning the ascent up a snowy hill that would lead them back to the frozen prairies. They paused to help Kimberly and Pam over the slippery terrain, and that's when they realized 2288 was lagging far behind.

2890 paged him, irritation clear in his voice, "This is not the time to fall behind. Get a move on."

"I'm coming!" 2288 panted, his chest heaving. "You better not leave me!"

"If you don't hustle, we will," 2890 shot back. "We're here to finish a job, not wander around."

"I'm not wandering..." 2288 began to reply, but his words faltered.

A sudden, sharp sting jabbed the back of his neck—quick and unexpected, like an insect bite. Instinctively, he dropped to his knees, more from shock than pain. His minigun slipped from his grasp, tumbling into the air, though that quickly became the least of his concerns. His hands shot to his neck, frantically searching for the source of the sting. But before he could comprehend what had happened, a cold numbness began spreading through his body, draining his strength with alarming speed.

His vision blurred, and the cold around him felt distant, disconnected. *What just happened?* he wondered, panic rising as he tried to stay upright. But his limbs felt leaden, and he slumped forward, his hands clawing at the snow as darkness closed in around him.

"2288, what are you doing? Get back up, or we will leave you behind!" 2890 shouted, his voice laced with confusion and urgency. He watched as 2288 crumpled to the ground. "Can you understand me?"

"I can't move!" 2288 gasped, his eyes wide with panic. "It feels like lightning is inside me!"

The group skidded to a halt, turning their full attention toward 2288. There he was, in the middle of the frozen river, on his knees, hands gripping his head as if trying to contain an unbearable pain. His body convulsed, twisting in ways that made the others cringe.

"That sound! My gods, please make it stop!" 2288 screamed, his voice raw with agony.

He groaned and yanked off his helmet, hoping it would relieve the electric sensation and the piercing ringing in his ears. But it only made things worse. He clawed at the back of his neck, pulling out a small dart similar to the one 0021 had been struck with earlier. For a moment, he stared at it, eyes wide with a mix of terror and confusion, before hurling it away. His hands shot up to cover his ears, his scream echoing across the frozen landscape.

The rest of the Preliators, except for 1113 and 3578, who stayed behind to protect Kimberly and Pam, bolted down the snowy bank toward 2288, desperate to reach him in time.

2288's eyes suddenly turned a brilliant blue, identical to April's. The world around him slowed to a crawl. He saw his companions running toward him, their movements sluggish and distorted, as if they were wading through water. The ringing in his ears grew louder, so overwhelming that it drowned out every other sound. He opened his mouth to scream, but no noise escaped.

Then, just as abruptly as it had begun, the noise stopped. A jarring silence enveloped him, the world around him becoming eerily quiet. His body slowly regained feeling, the numbness retreating, leaving only his heavy, ragged breaths. The Preliators were still moving toward him, now appearing to return to normal speed, but 2288 was too dazed to understand what had just happened.

He tried to stand, his mind racing to make sense of the situation, when a sharp, searing pain shot through his right hand. His body jerked in response, his eyes snapping down to look at his hand.

A metal chain spear, cold and unforgiving, pierced through 2288's right palm. The pain shot up his arm, white-hot and blinding. He saw the chain extending from the ice itself, a dark, twisted tether linking him to the frozen river. Before he could even process the agony, another chain lashed out, spearing through his left hand. Blood flowed freely from both wounds as the chains tightened, binding him to the icy surface.

He screamed, thrashing in a desperate attempt to break free, but the chains only grew tighter, their grip unyielding.

"Someone, please, help me!" he begged, his voice filled with raw terror.

A third chain snaked its way around his chest, coiling tightly and yanking him to the ground. He struggled, but it was no use—the chains had him pinned to the ice, and he lay there, utterly helpless.

1983 and 2890 reached him first. Their eyes widened as they saw the eerie blue glow in 2288's eyes, instantly recognizing the monster's influence. They scanned the darkness around them but saw nothing unusual. Their only option was to focus on their comrade.

Moments later, 0774 and 0444 arrived. While 0774 joined the others in trying to help 2288, 0444 noticed the dart lying on the ice. He quickly picked it up and turned to Pedia. "Analyze this, now," he demanded. The remaining Preliators and the two women stood at a distance, watching anxiously, hoping that 2288 would snap out of it.

The three Preliators looked on in horror as 2288 writhed on the ice, his body twisting and contorting like a fish out of water, struggling against chains that none of them could see.

"What can we do to help?" 2890 asked, his voice strained with urgency.

Through gritted teeth, 2288 gasped, "The chains! Get these chains off me!"

The Preliators exchanged confused glances, seeing nothing binding their friend.

"What chains?" 1983 asked, his tone sharp and baffled.

The fear in 2288's eyes intensified. "Hurry! The chain around my chest—it's tightening! I can barely breathe!" His voice rose in panic, his chest heaving as if he were suffocating.

"There are no chains on you!" 1983 snapped back, trying to break through whatever was happening in 2288's mind.

"That's impossible!" 2288 screamed, his entire body seizing up in pain.

"Pedia, what can we do?" 0774 asked, desperation coloring his words.

Pedia's reply was unsettling. "He seems lost in his mind. I don't know how to snap him out of it."

Invisible to the others, the chains continued to pull 2288 toward the ice. The surface began to crack beneath him, thin fractures spider-webbing outward. He stared at the fissures with horror, realizing he was about to be pulled into the river's icy depths.

"Help me! It's pulling me into the river! Someone, please do something!" he cried out, his voice breaking as his body trembled with fear.

2890's mind raced, trying to find a way to help. He shouted at 2288, "There's nothing there! It's all in your head. You're okay!"

But as if in response, a chilling, disembodied voice drifted through the wind, "What you can't see; he can sure feel."

Everyone except 2288 froze and scanned the area, searching for the source of the voice. The monster stood there on the riverbank, arms crossed, its orange eyes gleaming with malicious intent.

The Preliators aimed their rifles, their emotions so unsettled that their helmets stayed in stealth mode. They were ready to fire, but before they could act, the monster raised one hand, revealing a device that looked like a bomb trigger. It held the Preliators in check, forcing them to stand down. The monster exuded confidence, its posture casual and taunting, knowing it had the upper hand.

"What are you planning?" 0774 shouted, his voice cutting through the tense silence. "Is that trigger meant to kill us all?"

The monster turned its glowing eyes toward him. "No," it replied calmly, its voice dripping with malice. "Something far worse. I'm here to make your companion's worst nightmares come true."

Without hesitation, the monster pressed the button on the device. Immediately, the ice around 2288 shattered with an ear-splitting crack, creating a circular explosion. The Preliators near him staggered backward, shielding their faces from the blast.

In 2288's mind, he was suddenly surrounded by fire. It engulfed the ice around him, blazing fiercely as if it had been soaked in gasoline. He thrashed wildly, trying to put out the flames, but the chains tightened their grip, holding him in place. More chains shot up from the freezing water, coiling around his limbs like constricting serpents.

"This is not how I want it to end!" 2288 screamed, his voice echoing through the frozen landscape. His eyes were wild, filled with terror, as he struggled against his invisible captors.

The other Preliators watched in horror, baffled by what they were witnessing. To them, 2288 seemed to be in the grip of an unseen force, his body twitching violently as he fought against an enemy they couldn't see. The ice beneath him groaned and began to sink, threatening to pull him into the icy river. They raised their guns, tracking the monster, but hesitated to fire, afraid of provoking it further.

As the monster melted into the shadows, its form vanishing into the darkness, 2288's screams pierced the air. "It's all in your mind!" barked 1983, desperately trying to snap him out of it. "You have to fight it!"

But 2288, his voice breaking into gasps and desperate screams as if he were on the brink of death, could only repeat, "Oh gods, this is not how I want to—"

Suddenly, flames roared to life around him, spiraling out of control. In his mind, the ice burned like it had been drenched in oil, the flames licking at his skin. The river yawned open beneath him, and the chains dragged him downward. He felt the icy water crash over him, the flames now replaced with a bone-chilling cold as the river filled his lungs. His struggles grew weaker, his body consumed by both fire and water.

The Preliators stood in stunned silence as 2288 slipped beneath the dark waters of the river, vanishing from sight. They remained frozen, their eyes fixed on the spot where he'd disappeared, waiting for any sign of movement. But all that surfaced were a few bubbles, breaking quietly before fading away. Soon, the river was calm once more, leaving no trace of him behind.

The monster reappeared, standing on the riverbank, illuminated by the pale light of the full moon. Its presence sent a wave of fear through the group, each of them paralyzed except for 0444, who pocketed the dart he had picked up earlier and took his place among his companions.

"This is just a taste of my power," the monster declared, its voice cold and triumphant. "There's nothing you can do to stop it. More of you will fall."

It raised its hand, pointing one by one at each Preliator, its gesture slow and deliberate. "Who will be next?" it taunted, savoring their fear. Its gaze finally settled on Kimberly and Pam, trembling and clutching each other in terror.

A flash of rage swept through the four Preliators. Without a moment's hesitation, they pulled out their guns and opened fire, unleashing a barrage of bullets toward the monster.

As the Preliators fired into the darkness, the monster vanished yet again, leaving only the unsettling echoes of their gunfire in the empty night. The wind carried a chilling, robotic chuckle, mocking their efforts. It was as if they were pawns in some twisted game they didn't understand.

The monster's voice filled the air, cutting through the night. "You think you can kill me?" it sneered. "Many have tried, and all have failed. Your only option is to run. This is my world; this is my hour."

In a blink, it reappeared in a different spot. The Preliators quickly aimed and shot, but just as before, the monster melted back into the shadows, evading their every attempt. Its laughter grew louder, echoing ominously through the snow-covered prairies.

"The clock is ticking," it taunted. "The next has been chosen."

The Preliators spun around, their eyes scanning the endless blackness, hearts pounding with dread. Even Pedia's scans came up empty, providing no comfort. They moved in a circle, keeping their rifles raised, while the monster's voice continued to drift mockingly around them.

"What do we do now?" asked 0774, his voice wavering.

"The only thing we can do is fire everything we've got and hope for the best!" replied 1983, his tone fierce but desperate.

0444 opened his mouth to object, to say that wasting ammo would only make things worse, but it was too late. 1983 began firing wildly at where he imagined the monster might be, his shots lighting up the darkness. The others hesitated, then followed his lead. 2890 and 0774 fired in different directions, their weapons blazing. Feeling he had no other option, 0444 joined in, unleashing bursts of gunfire as they tried to flush out their elusive enemy.

Pam and Kimberly watched, huddled together, their faces pale with fear and confusion. The Preliators' frantic gunfire and the constant laughter of the monster added to the chaos. Behind their helmets, 1113 and 3578 trembled. They had stayed close to the women, but the loss of 2288 had shattered their resolve. Fear gripped them, threatening to break their already fragile nerves.

The monster's laugh echoed, twisted and almost gleeful, pushing 1113 to his breaking point. Heart racing, he turned and sprinted toward the abandoned farm in the distance. "Run!" he shouted, his voice cracking with panic. "We have to get out of here!"

Equally terrified, 3578 followed without hesitation, abandoning the mission and leaving the women and their fellow Preliators behind. In that moment, he thought only of himself, desperate to survive and hoping to see another day.

Pedia's calm voice cut through the chaos. "This isn't the time to run. You must help your comrades. Bringing them back alive is crucial."

But they ignored Pedia's plea, their fear overriding any sense of duty. Their figures disappeared into the darkness, leaving behind only their retreating footsteps in the snow.

Pam and Kimberly stared after them, horror dawning on their faces as they realized they had been abandoned. Panic flooded Kimberly, and she took off after the fleeing men. "They left us! They left us!" she cried, her voice breaking into sobs as she sprinted into the night, following their tracks.

"Kimberly, stop!" Pam shouted desperately, stumbling forward in the snow. "We have to stay together! Slow down so I can catch up!"

But Kimberly didn't hear, or maybe she couldn't. Her fear had taken over, and she vanished into the blackness, repeating her panicked mantra as she ran.

Pam pushed herself up from where she had tripped, her heart hammering in her chest. She didn't want to be left alone, not in this frozen wasteland with that thing out there. She started running, hoping to catch up to Kimberly, unaware that the other Preliators were still too absorbed in their futile assault to notice the two women had fled.

In the darkness, the monster's laughter grew fainter but no less haunting, like a specter stalking their every step. The Preliators continued firing blindly, unaware that their situation had just grown far more dire. They were no longer six; they were now only four, standing alone against the horror that awaited them.

CHAPTER 12
THINGS COULDN'T GET ANY WORSE

The Preliators stood in the chaotic aftermath of their onslaught, eyes scanning the shredded landscape. What was once a snow-covered prairie now lay in ruins, marked by craters and scorch marks. A thick silence replaced the eerie laughter, making the scene all the more unsettling.

"Please turn around. The two we need to finish the Trial are gone! We must find them! Please turn around now!" Pedia's urgent voice crackled through their helmet comms, snapping them back to reality.

2890's heart sank as he quickly scanned the area where Kimberly, Pam, 1113, and 3578 had been. They were gone, their tracks barely visible in the churned-up snow and dirt. "Stop! Stop shooting!" he shouted; his voice strained with urgency.

1983 and 0774, caught up in their barrage, fired their final grenades before finally processing his command. The last explosions echoed into the night, sending plumes of snow and debris into the air. As the smoke cleared, they all turned to face 0444, who pointed toward the empty spot where the others had stood moments ago.

Realization hit them like a punch to the gut. The women and the two Preliators had disappeared into the darkness, leaving the four of them standing in the cold, empty battlefield. An eerie calm settled over the scene as they listened, trying to catch any sign of their missing teammates.

"Do you guys hear that?" 2890 asked, his voice tense.

0774 paused, holding his breath. "Hear what?"

"Exactly," 2890 replied. "The laughing. It stopped."

0774's face twisted in confusion. "So, what are you saying? That the monster has chosen its next victim?"

"Exactly," 2890 answered, his eyes scanning the horizon.

1983, now gripping his empty assault rife with no more grenades left, added, "Who will it be?"

0444 stepped forward, holding out the dart he had retrieved earlier. He passed it around, and each Preliator took a moment to scan it with their helmet visors, watching the readings as Pedia analyzed the substance.

"This device is unknown to anyone on Earth," Pedia began. "It seems to contain a strange chemical that causes people to act out of character, giving this unknown beast an advantage."

0444 nodded, grimly agreeing. "I think the monster is using this dart to inject that chemical. It forces us to face our worst fears, paralyzing us when we're most vulnerable. It's picking us off one by one, starting with the weakest and moving toward the strongest. Those who ran... they're the next targets."

A heavy silence fell upon the group as they digested his words. Each Preliator looked out into the dark expanse where their companions had vanished, trying to make sense of the nightmare they were trapped in. It wasn't just about the monster anymore; it was about fighting against their own minds, staying together, and not giving in to the fear that was threatening to tear them apart.

"So, what now?" 0774 asked, his voice a mixture of frustration and fear.

"We find them," 2890 stated firmly. "Before it's too late. We stick together this time, no matter what."

1983 gritted his teeth, gripping his weapon tightly despite its emptiness. "If it's going after the weakest first, then we need to find Kimberly, Pam, and those cowards before it does."

0444 holstered the dart, locking eyes with his companions. "Then we move. We follow their tracks, stay alert, and prepare for anything. This creature feeds on our fear. We won't give it the satisfaction."

With their resolve hardened, the four Preliators set off, retracing the faint footprints left in the snow. They moved cautiously, staying close, their senses on high alert. They knew the clock was ticking, and that any misstep could mean the difference between survival and becoming the monster's next victim.

Everyone agreed with 0444 and quickly began their investigation. With their night vision active, they spotted fresh footprints on the ground. Low on ammunition, they dropped their assault rifles and drew their XEI handguns instead. Following the trail left by the four who had run off, they sprinted, hoping to catch up before it was too late.

1983 took off at full speed, racing ahead without a second thought. 0444's frustration simmered—his closest friend had promised only moments ago that they'd stick together.

Gritting his teeth, he called out for 1983 to slow down, but it was too late. 1983 had already disappeared into the thickening fog, leaving the others behind.

Meanwhile, 1113 was running as fast as his legs could carry him. He was drenched in sweat, exhausted, but pushed forward by sheer fear. His eyes flickered to the screen on his visor, desperately scanning the horizon for any sign of the helicopter lights as he neared the farm, still about two miles away. Pedia's voice crackled in his ear, trying to reach him.

"This is not the Preliator way. We must finish the Trial. Returning empty-handed will be seen as Trial of Failure by the U.W.E.G.," Pedia urged.

But 1113 didn't listen; survival was his only concern. Then, he felt a sudden pinch in the back of his left leg. He stumbled but managed to keep running. However, after about twenty more steps, he stopped, sensing something was terribly wrong.

Pain surged up his leg, and as he reached down to touch his calf, an electric current shot through his body. The screams of the previous Preliators filled his ears, echoing through his mind.

1113 struggled to push forward, grinding his teeth as he forced himself to move toward the farm. The noise in his ears grew unbearable, like nails on a chalkboard, making him feel as if his eardrums were about to burst. Desperately, he checked his visor, hoping for some reassurance.

"Pedia, how much farther to the destination?" he demanded, his voice strained with pain.

Silence. For the first time, Pedia didn't respond. Panic surged through him as he glanced at the visor's display. His eyes widened—he was moving away from the farm, not closer.

"Pedia, what is happening to me?" he shouted, his heartbeat

thundering in his chest. Still, there was no reply. He took a few more steps, but the distance to the farm kept decreasing.

Frustrated, he tried to sprint, but it was like running against a powerful current. Every step seemed to drag him farther from his goal.

"Pedia! I order you to answer me! Now!" he screamed.

The electronic noise grew louder, buzzing in his head until it felt like it would split his skull. In a fit of agony and rage, he tore off his helmet and threw it to the ground, hoping to stop the relentless sound. Dropping to his knees, he covered his ears, teeth clenched, eyes squeezed shut.

And then, just as he thought the noise would consume him entirely—it stopped. Silence fell around him like a heavy blanket.

1113 opened his eyes, scanning his surroundings. The sky above was pitch black, and snow covered the prairie grass stretching out around him. He could see his breath in the icy air. Realizing he was alone, he sighed in relief and lowered his hands. For a moment, he thought the worst was over.

But then, something felt off in his right hand. Slowly, he looked down. His eyes widened in horror—it was his own right ear, resting in his palm. A chill ran down his spine as his eyes turned a pale blue.

"How can this be possible?" he whispered to himself, frozen in shock.

He dropped the ear into the snow and hesitantly reached up to touch the side of his head. His fingers pressed against wet, soft tissue. Pain surged through him, confirming his fear: his ear was truly gone. His heart pounded as he pulled his hand back, now covered in blood.

"My gods! What is happening to me?" he cried out, his

voice trembling.

His face began to itch, a maddening sensation crawling across his skin. He hesitated, terrified to touch his face, fearing more pieces of him might fall apart. Clenching his eyes shut, he fought the urge to scratch, but the itch only grew more intense.

"Please, I don't want to be next!" he shouted into the emptiness.

He knew this was the monster's doing, yet he saw no one around. The itching became unbearable, clawing at his sanity. He started to scratch, lightly at first, but that only made it worse. Panic gripped him, his heartbeat racing in his chest.

"Please, gods, no! I don't want this!" he screamed, his voice breaking.

But he was losing control. His hands moved on their own, scratching harder and faster. His skin began to tear away, revealing raw, red muscle tissue underneath. The pain seared through him, and he let out a blood-curdling scream, helpless against the horror unfolding within his own body.

1113 collapsed to the ground, scratching frantically as he rolled in the snow. Blood poured from his exposed flesh; his face now almost entirely stripped to raw muscle. His bulging blue eyes filled with tears, his cries of agony echoing through the darkness.

The itching spread, crawling over his entire body. He twisted and thrashed, desperate for relief. Then, suddenly, 3578 appeared, sprinting so fast that he sped past 1113 without even noticing him. He was so blinded by the terror of the beast, and so focused on what was chasing him, that he blocked out the screams of his suffering comrade.

In the darkness, the monster emerged. When 3578 caught

sight of it, his eyes widened in pure panic. Without hesitation, he turned and sprinted in the opposite direction. Each time the monster appeared, a dark, creepy laugh followed, echoing through the night.

"You think you can escape from me? No one has ever escaped and lived to tell about it," the monster whispered, its voice carried by the wind.

3578 didn't respond. He kept running, his breath ragged, every nerve screaming at him to survive. The monster suddenly materialized in front of him, and he stumbled to the ground. Scrambling to his feet, he dashed in another direction, only to hear the monster's laughter again.

"If you're running from me, then all you'll see is me!" the monster taunted.

Terrified and exhausted, 3578 kept running, his chest heaving as he gasped for breath. A sharp pinch struck the side of his neck—another dart. Stunned, he staggered and fell to the ground. An electronic ringing filled his ears, growing louder until it was all he could hear. Clutching his head, he pounded the snow-covered earth, screaming as electric shocks surged through his body. He rolled in the snow, writhing in agony while the monster watched, unmoved.

Then, just as abruptly as it began, the ringing stopped. 3578 opened his eyes, now glowing an eerie blue. The monster stood over him, arms crossed, its presence ominous and unyielding.

"You are too weak to face anything dangerous unless you finish me off," the monster warned, its voice a low, menacing growl.

3578 stared up at the creature, repeating, "No... no..." in a trembling whisper. The fog began to creep in, swirling around them, obscuring everything in a dense, icy mist. The monster's eyes blazed bright orange, its laughter ringing out like a demon from the underworld, filling 3578's heart with despair.

Shivering from the cold, Kimberley sprinted through the darkness, desperately trying to find the footprints left by one of the Preliators. Her legs felt numb, each step growing heavier, and her breath came in ragged gasps. Tears streamed down her face—not just from exhaustion, but from the crushing weight of fear and stress.

"Where are you, Kimberley?" Pam's voice echoed nearby, but Kimberley didn't respond. She was too focused on her task, scanning the ground for any signs of the others. Then, she noticed a fog starting to roll in, swirling ominously around her feet. From within the thickening mist, she heard a man moaning, a sound that sent chills up her spine.

Without thinking, she moved toward the noise, each step making the moaning grow louder. "Is someone out there?" Kimberley panted, her voice shaky and breathless.

Silence. No answer—only more moaning. Pam emerged from the fog; her eyes wide with worry when she spotted Kimberley standing still. Relief washed over her as she rushed forward. Just as she was about to embrace her friend, Pam too heard the moaning and paused, thinking it might be one of the Preliators.

"I promise I won't hurt you. Just tell me who you are. Maybe we can help each other?" Kimberley called out; her voice filled with a fragile hope.

Still, there was no response. The moaning stopped, replaced by a faint whimper: "I never wanted this to happen." Then, silence. The stillness in the air made Kimberley's heart race.

Pam, now standing right behind Kimberley, reached out

and gently touched her shoulder. Kimberley jumped with a startled yelp, her nerves on edge. But when she turned and saw it was Pam, she exhaled in relief, momentarily forgetting the eerie moaning that had drawn her in.

Suddenly, 1113 lunged out of the fog, appearing right beside Kimberley. He grabbed her back, and she screamed, leaping into the air. When she turned, her heart nearly stopped. His face was a ghastly mess, raw muscle exposed where skin had peeled away. Blood dripped down, soaking what remained of his armor, which hung in tatters. Patches of his skin were missing, revealing torn flesh underneath.

"Please, kill me! I can't take this anymore! The itching won't stop!" 1113 begged, his voice a tortured rasp.

Kimberley recoiled, trying to back away, but he latched onto her with a death grip, using the last of his strength. She struggled, desperately clawing at his hands, but he held on, gripping the collar of her worn-out jacket with shaking fingers. His eyes, wild and blue with agony, locked onto hers.

"It won't stop itching!" he sobbed, his voice cracking. "I'd rather be dead than scratch for another second! Kill me, please!"

"I can't! Please, let me go!" Kimberley cried, panic flooding her eyes.

1113's screams grew louder, his face contorting in unbearable pain. "It's getting worse! For the love of the gods, you're the only one who can help! I need it to stop!"

Pam, watching Kimberley struggle, rushed forward to help. But 1113 shoved her away with a burst of strength, sending her sprawling to the ground. As she scrambled to her feet, she spotted a large rock half-buried in the snow. Without hesitation, she grabbed it and swung, striking 1113 on the side of his head.

The impact stunned him, making him release his grip on Kimberley, though it didn't knock him out. Pam dropped the rock and seized Kimberley's arm, yanking her away.

"We have to move now!" Pam shouted, her voice sharp with urgency. "There's nothing we can do for him—it's up to us now to look out for each other."

Kimberly nodded, though her legs felt unsteady as she stumbled forward. She and Pam broke into a sprint, fear etched across her face. "Do you... do you know where we're going?" she mumbled, barely able to keep her voice steady.

Pam turned to face her, eyes burning with urgency. "Anywhere but here! Now, let's go!"

They sprinted into the fog, vanishing from sight. Behind them, 1113 collapsed to his knees. He clawed at the snow, crawling after them with blood-soaked hands raised, his voice a pitiful whisper.

"Please," he whimpered, hoping they'd return to put an end to his suffering. But the fog swallowed him whole, leaving him alone in the darkness.

As they stumbled through the darkness, with no clear direction or visible footprints, Kimberley glanced at Pam, desperation in her eyes.

"What's the plan? Where are we going?" Kimberley panted, her voice tight with fear.

Pam scanned their surroundings, trying to get her bearings. "I don't know. We keep running until we find any kind of shelter. We'll stay there until we figure out our next move."

Kimberley's face showed her growing anxiety. "What if we run into the bad ones again?"

Pam faltered, her mind scrambling for an answer. But

before she could speak, a familiar, commanding robotic voice pierced through the fog, steady and unmistakable.

"Halt in the name of the Code!"

Both women stopped abruptly, their breaths visible in the cold air as they searched the fog for the source of the voice. Footsteps crunched closer through the snow, their hearts racing with the fear that the beast had finally caught up to them.

Suddenly, 3578 emerged from the mist, his helmet's eyes glowing a menacing red. He was poised for a fight, his pistols drawn and aimed.

"You killed my whole team. Now, there are two of you," 3578 said, his voice a mixture of rage and accusation.

Pam and Kimberley exchanged bewildered glances. "What are you talking about? Some of your team is still alive," Pam shouted back, her voice laced with confusion and desperation.

"Liars!" 3578 roared. "I saw you kill them one by one. I may have escaped, but now I'm back to finish both of you off, so you'll never do this to another Preliator again!"

3578 advanced, his steps deliberate and menacing, forcing Pam and Kimberley to backpedal. Pam, trying to defuse the situation, pleaded with him.

"Please, you have to believe us. We're the two women you're trying to save. The monster you're hunting is making you think we're it."

But 3578's perception was clouded by fury and fear. To him, the two women before him appeared as monstrous threats, their words twisted into a sinister promise: "You're back so we can finish the job. We promise your death will be slow and painful."

"Then let's get started!" 3578 roared, his voice echoing

with vengeance.

Without warning, 1983, who had been ahead of the group and somehow got lucky finding them, burst from the fog and tackled 3578 from the side. He grabbed 3578's wrist, wrenching the gun away from Kimberley and Pam. Startled, 3578 fired, but the bullets scattered harmlessly into the snow. In a swift move, 1983 slapped the gun out of 3578's grip, sending it skidding away.

Dazed, 3578 looked up to see 1983, his fellow Preliator, intervening. Hesitation flickered in his eyes as 1983 grappled with him, trying to break through his fog of confusion.

To 3578, the world was a blur of shifting threats. 1983 appeared as yet another menacing creature. Panic surged through him—now there seemed to be three dangers instead of just one.

"It's me!" 1983 shouted, grasping 3578's helmet to force him to focus. "Please, tell me you're alright! You are Preliator 3578, a Preliator of Telos."

But in 3578's ears, all he could hear was the growling of a beast: "Like I said, a slow and painful death."

Fueled by rage and fear, 3578 shouted back, "If I die, then all three of you will die with me!" In a frenzied burst of energy, he lunged at 1983, tackling him to the snow. They tumbled across the icy ground, struggling for dominance.

3578 drew a knife from his belt, his eyes blazing with resolve. He tried to pin 1983 down and plunge the blade into him. 1983, his grip unyielding, caught 3578's wrist just in time, keeping the blade a hair's breadth from his throat. The two Preliators wrestled in the snow, their breaths coming in ragged gasps, as the night and the fog closed in around their desperate struggle.

Seeing 3578 about to overpower 1983, Kimberley acted on instinct. She darted forward and grasped 3578's hand, struggling to wrench the knife from his grip. Despite her desperate efforts, 3578's strength was overwhelming. With a brutal shove, he sent her sprawling. Kimberley stumbled backward, tripping over a snow-covered rock. She twisted her ankle and hit the ground hard, a cry of pain escaping her lips.

The distraction gave 1983 the opening he needed. He scrambled to his feet, pulling out his own knife. The two men faced off, circling each other warily. Pam, seeing Kimberley's plight, rushed to her side, helping her up.

"Please, don't make me do this!" 1983 pleaded, his voice strained with desperation.

But inside of 3578's mind, 1983's words sounded like a cold threat: "The more you fight us, the worse the pain will be. We will not be stopped. We will finish you off the way we want to."

With a guttural scream of defiance, 3578 charged at 1983 once more. The clash of their knives was immediate and fierce, a brutal dance of steel and skill. Each man's movements were a deadly blur, their familiarity with each other's techniques evident in their quick, precise strikes and parries. The snow around them was stained with their struggle, the night air charged with the intensity of their fight.

Meanwhile, 0444, 0774, and 2890 were closing in on 1983. Despite knowing they were close, the dense fog made it difficult for their visors to track him accurately. The grunts and clashes of a fierce battle reached their ears, and they stopped, pistols ready, assuming 1983 was engaged in a fight with the monster.

The sounds of the struggle grew louder, then abruptly stopped, replaced by the sound of heavy breathing. The

Preliators edged forward cautiously, trying to pinpoint the source of the noise.

Suddenly, 1113 staggered into view, his hand clamped onto 2890's right shoulder. His face was a ghastly sight, with his jawbone exposed through gruesome self-inflicted scratches. He tried to speak but only managed a raspy, incomprehensible whisper. Weak from blood loss, 1113 was easily shrugged off by 2890.

The three Preliators stared at 1113, who now resembled a half-dead, bleeding corpse rather than a fellow soldier. Realizing the grim necessity, 2890 took aim and fired two shots into 1113's head. The impact sent 1113 sprawling onto his back, blood pooling beneath him as his body slowly shut down. His blue eyes, filled with a mix of pain and resignation, stared up at them.

After ensuring 1113 was no longer alive, 2890 and the others shared a solemn look. They understood the necessity of ending his suffering, knowing they would have done the same in his place.

Just then, a female scream pierced the air, coming from a direction only a few yards away. The Preliators rushed toward the sound and soon saw two women running straight at them. Recognizing the Preliators, the women let out terrified screams.

In a swift reaction, 2890 and 0774 covered the women's mouths, trying to calm them down. After a few tense moments, the women realized the men were not a threat and began to settle. Slowly, 0774 and 2890 removed their hands.

"What is happening?" 0774 asked Pam, his voice urgent.

Pam, struggling to keep her composure, mumbled, "Both of them are trying to kill each other!"

"Who is trying to kill each other?" 0774 pressed.

Pam didn't answer directly but instead pointed toward the direction of the noise. Even through the fog, the sounds of the ongoing fight between two Preliators were unmistakable.

0444, recognizing the urgency, turned to 2890 and said, "Take these women to the destination now! It's just over there."

Without hesitation, 2890 nodded and began guiding the women away from the chaotic scene, while 0444 and 0774 prepared to head towards the source of the fight, determined to put an end to the madness.

0444 pointed northwest. 2890 scanned the foggy expanse and calculated the distance—about four kilometers. Without hesitation, he nodded to 0444, then hoisted both women onto his shoulders. He started towards the farm, determined to get them to safety.

Once 2890 and the women disappeared into the fog, 0774 and 0444 turned their attention back to the fight. Both drew their pistols and moved forward cautiously.

Suddenly, out of the dense fog, the two fighting Preliators came barreling toward 0774. He backpedaled instinctively as both men, their helmets removed and faces smeared with blood, crashed into the snow. 1983 stumbled but slowly got to his feet. 3578, his eyes glowing with an eerie blue light, charged at 1983 again, brandishing a pistol weapon. The force of the charge made 0774 and 0444 leap aside momentarily.

As they repositioned, 0774 and 0444 tried to find a clear shot. The chaotic melee made aiming nearly impossible. 1983, spotting his two companions, shouted, "What are you waiting for? Shoot him now!"

The two men continued their brutal struggle in the snow, each movement a blur of violence. 0774 and 0444 remained silent, waiting for an opportunity to shoot without endangering 1983.

In the midst of the fight, 3578 fired three shots. 1983 dodged the first two but was hit by the third in his ankle. He screamed in agony, his grip on 3578 loosening. Seizing the moment, 3578 prepared to pull the trigger.

Before he could fire, multiple shots rang out, hitting 3578 squarely in the chest. He was thrown backward, crashing onto the snow with a thud. Although not dead, he dropped his gun and struggled to rise.

0774 hurried over and aimed his pistol at 3578's face. Without hesitation, he fired two shots, ensuring 3578 was dead. He held his aim for a moment, confirming the kill, before turning to check on 1983.

Meanwhile, 0444 was already at 1983's side, working to stop the bleeding. He applied a sealing glue from his armor suit to 1983's wounded ankle. 1983 winced in pain as the glue hardened, but he bore the discomfort.

"Can you stand and walk?" 0444 asked, concern evident in his voice.

"I can stand, but I might need help walking," 1983 replied, his voice strained as he tried to mask the pain.

As 1983 tried to stand, he collapsed once more. 0444 rushed to catch him, already thinking things couldn't get worse. But then, a sharp sting pierced his neck. He froze, pulling out the dart and realizing it was from the monster. Panic surged through him as he grappled with what to do next.

CHAPTER 13
THE TRUTH ALWAYS HURTS

"Get everyone out of here, now!" 0444 commanded, ripping a dart from his neck and holding it up for the others to see. 1983 and 0774 exchanged looks, their shoulders slumping in dismay—it is happening again, and now 0444 is the next target.

Before he could say anything more, a sharp electronic ringing pierced his ears and spread through his skull like wildfire. His teeth clenched as the pain shot down his spine and into his legs. Stumbling, he dropped to one knee, hands gripping his helmet while still clutching his pistols. 0774 rushed over, helping him steady himself, watching the torment on his comrade's face. They both knew they were close to the farm, but abandoning 0444 wasn't an option.

"We're not leaving you here!" 0774 insisted.

Pedia's voice echoed in 0444's mind, speaking directly to him. *"This wasn't supposed to happen. Why did you intervene? This wasn't part of the plan."*

0444 opened his mouth to respond, but realized no one

else could hear her. The ringing intensified, each wave of pain pulling him deeper. He waved them off, fighting the overwhelming noise in his head. "Yes, you are leaving! You've got enough to deal with. Help him, and make sure the Trial is a success."

The noise surged, spreading like poison through his entire body. His fingers twitched, and his grip on the pistols slackened. Dropping them into the snow, he tore off his helmet, revealing his eyes—now an all-unnatural blue.

"Go, now, before you end up like this!" he shouted, pointing to his face with urgency. He shoved 0774 away, his actions underscoring his seriousness. "The mission matters more than me. If I'm going to die, I'll die for something. Now move!"

0774 hesitated only for a second. "What's your plan?"

0444 retrieved his pistols from the snow, raising them high. "I'll stall it. Buy you enough time to finish the Trial and escape. No more arguing. That's an order!"

Seeing the resolve in 0444's eyes, 0774 knew he was right. Wasting any more time could mean losing everything. He checked on 1983, making sure he could walk at a steady pace, ready to lead the group. There was so much he wanted to say—*good luck, thank you*—but they both knew words would cost them precious seconds.

With a final glance back, 0774 and 1983 exchanged a silent understanding before turning to sprint after 2890 and the two women. The icy wind whipped around them as they left 0444 behind, alone in the snow.

The last of the Preliators and the women moved quickly into the fog, nearly speed-walking. 0444 didn't turn to check if they disappeared—his mind was too consumed by the ringing in his ears and the searing pain running through his body. He held one pistol pointed forward, the other ready at his shoulder, forcing himself to focus.

But Pedia's words echoed in his mind: "*Not part of the plan.*" The noise in his head transformed into bright, disorienting flashes, making it hard to stay upright. Memories from his time as a Pre-Elite surged forward—so many of them tied to Pedia. He remembered how she'd motivated him through brutal training sessions, promising it would all be worth it in the end.

"That's enough!" he shouted, his voice hoarse and desperate.

Suddenly, the electronic ringing stopped, leaving a heavy silence. The images of Pedia vanished, and 0444 blinked, trying to clear his thoughts. His eyes shifted—glowing fully blue.

Something stirred in the fog ahead.

He raised both pistols, bracing himself. As a figure emerged, slow and deliberate, its orange eyes gleamed through the mist, and the distinct shape of a samurai-like helmet became clear. Without hesitation, 0444 squeezed the trigger on his XEI with his right hand. The bullets flew wide, missing their mark. He emptied the magazine, cursed under his breath, and immediately switched to his left pistol, counting every shot carefully.

The creature drew closer, seemingly unfazed by the onslaught. 0444 kept firing, his shots still missing. He saved his last bullet for when the figure was right in front of him, but just as he prepared to pull the trigger, the creature vanished into the fog like a phantom.

0444 stood alone, panting, as silence closed in around him. His entire body was going numb. *Is this it? Am I dead?* The question echoed through his mind, and a wave of helplessness washed over him. He hadn't bought them much time, and the bitter thought crept in—*Was it all for nothing?*

"Why the sad face?" a familiar voice asked, soft and teasing.

0444 spun around, instinctively raising his pistol. *It couldn't be...* He had no idea where his helmet was, yet the voice was unmistakable—it was Pedia. Her familiar purple glow broke through the swirling fog, and she stepped forward, dressed in that classic 1950s blue-and-white plaid dress she always wore in his quarters. Her smile was warm, almost affectionate, as if she were genuinely happy to see him, the way she looked at him bringing an unexpected comfort.

0444 narrowed his eyes, keeping both hands on his gun, aimed directly at her. His mind screamed not to trust what he saw, but something held him back from pulling the trigger. How could she be here, in the middle of Regret, of all places? Pedia raised her right hand, a gesture of peace, but he didn't lower the weapon.

"I'm not here to hurt you," Pedia said calmly. "You can put the gun down. I've come to tell you the good news."

0444's heart raced, emotions swirling in confusion and disbelief. "Why should I believe you?" he demanded, his voice tense. "There's no way you could actually be here. This is impossible."

Pedia's expression softened, her voice almost a whisper. "Deep down, I know you want me here. You want to go home. We can go back—to our mornings together, our evenings. Don't you miss that? Doesn't that sound good?"

A strange sense of comfort tugged at 0444. He could picture it—the quiet moments, the routine. For a fleeting second, he wanted to believe her. But no... this couldn't be real. He shook his head hard, trying to clear his mind, fighting to hold onto reality.

"You're just saying what I want to hear!" he barked, his voice cracking, filled with doubt. It all sounded too good to be true.

Pedia kept walking toward him, her gaze fixed on his face. As she drew closer, she noticed the pure blue eyes glowing, and the exhaustion etched into his features. "Ahh... look what's become of my sweet boy. This day has not been kind to you."

She was now standing right beside him, and 0444 felt his resolve weakening. Slowly, he lowered his gun, allowing her presence to wash over him. He couldn't resist as she gently reached out, her fingers brushing the side of his face. The moment her hand touched him, 0444's eyes fluttered shut, and for the first time in hours, he felt something other than pain. A tear of joy slid down Pedia's cheek as she whispered, "You have no idea how long I've wanted to do this."

He could feel the steady rhythm of her heartbeat, so real and vivid that it made it harder for him to believe this was just a dream. He wondered what was going through her mind—perhaps she thought this was what heaven truly felt like.

0444 didn't flinch at the word when she touched him. It felt so right. After everything that had happened, being here with her—seeing her smile—gave him a sense of peace he hadn't felt all day. For the first time on this cursed day, he allowed himself to smile. He leaned into her warmth, wrapping his arms around her in a tight embrace, the kind of hug a child might give his mother.

Pedia's hug was strong and comforting, and for a brief moment, everything felt like it would be okay. But then, a subtle nagging feeling crept into the back of his mind, a whisper of doubt that he couldn't ignore. As comforting as this moment was, there was something he needed to know—something he could no longer keep to himself.

"Since you're here," 0444 began, his voice strained, "tell me one thing. How did all of this happen? We trained to be the best, to last for decades. But in one night, I watched the people I trained with for years die... painfully. Now, I'm next." He hesitated, searching Pedia's eyes for answers. "I thought I was going to be part of something special. Was that a lie?"

Pedia's expression softened, her gaze never leaving his. "No, that was no lie at all," she replied, her voice gentle but firm. "I believed then, and I still believe now, that you will be part of something special. What happened to you—was simply being in the wrong place at the wrong time."

0444's brow furrowed in confusion. "The wrong place at the wrong time? What does that even mean? Did you know this was going to happen? Or is there something else you're not telling me?"

His words hung in the air, and for a brief moment, the warmth of her embrace felt distant. He searched her face for any sign of the truth, but her smile remained unchanged, as though she held an answer just beyond his reach.

"If I had known this was going to happen," Pedia began calmly, "that dart was meant for Preliator 1983. His injury would have been permanent—below Preliator standards. We couldn't allow that. But you... you stepped in front of the target. You were chosen to survive. The Preliator program has been doing this for decades. Everything that's happened... was essentially planned all along."

Her words hit him like a physical blow. 0444 stumbled

back, breaking free from her embrace, his eyes wide with disbelief. "What do you mean it was all planned out? Who gets to decide who survives or dies? That... thing? The monster gets to decide?" His voice shook, anger and fear mixing as he continued. "There's something out there—something not human—killing us like animals. And you knew about it?"

Pedia's gaze didn't falter. "That 'thing' has a name. We call them the Harbingers of Regret. But you don't need to worry about that now."

"Harbingers?" 0444 repeated, his confusion deepening. "The government created them? Another program?"

Pedia's smile faltered, a hint of sadness flickering in her eyes as she tried to deflect. "Time isn't on your side," she said softly. "There's so much I wish I could explain, but... it's too late for that now."

"No!" 0444 snapped, his voice filled with anger as he cut her off. His sudden outburst startled her, and she took a step back. "The time is now," he insisted, his tone unyielding. "No more secrets. Tell me the truth!"

The silence that followed was heavy, the tension between them palpable. 0444's frustration burned in his eyes as he stood there, waiting for the answers that had been kept from him for far too long.

Pedia stood silently, her eyes locked onto 0444's glowing blue ones. "If I tell you the truth, be prepared," she warned, her voice low. "It's not something you want to hear."

0444's expression hardened; his voice unwavering. "After all these years... if you truly care about me—and if I'm about to be gone forever—I *need* to know why."

Pedia sighed, her voice weighted with the burden of truth. "From the start of the one true government, the first group of Preliators struggled. After the 'Great Six Week Cleanse,' many questioned whether their actions were right or wrong. Because of this, the program had to be revised. But only a select few know about a darker, secret program.

This program takes young, outcast Pre-Elites and transforms them into Harbingers—agents who are better trained, better equipped, and incapable of making mistakes. What they endure... most would call inhumane. The people behind this program will stop at nothing to make them indestructible. Here in Regret, their role is to oversee and test new Preliators, evaluating whether you're truly capable. They remain silent, no matter how dire the circumstances, and aim to mold Preliators to be just like them—emotionless.

In the end, it's all about ensuring you're worthy to serve the U.W.E.G."

0444 processed her words, the pieces slowly falling into place. But a deep unease twisted inside him. "That doesn't explain everything. These 'Harbingers'... they're different. We've shot at them, and it's like firing at air—bullets just pass right through. They don't even flinch. It's as if they're not human at all, like they're something... godlike."

Pedia met his gaze steadily. "When you first put on the armor with the helmet, you felt a pinch, right?" She paused as he nodded slowly. "That pinch was from a chemical we call compound ME2. It's designed to create illusions—make you see or hear things that aren't really there. Like how the Harbinger seems to take damage when you shoot at it, but it's never actually present. Or how the fog can appear and vanish at will. These are just a few effects of what a little bit of compound ME2 can do."

"ME2? What does that mean?" asked 0444, his brow

furrowed in confusion.

Pedia quickly responded, her tone calm and clinical. "'Mind Effective.' It's a drug series with five levels, each designed to affect the mind in different ways."

0444 stood frozen, the truth sinking in. Everything he'd seen, everything he thought he'd fought—it was all a carefully crafted illusion. A chill crept up his spine as the full scope of the manipulation became clear.

0444 lashed out, his voice sharp and full of fury. "You injected a chemical into us? What happens to them when the Trial is finished? This sounds insane!"

Pedia tried to reach for his hands, but he recoiled, brushing her off with a scowl. "Don't touch me!" he snapped. She paused, lowering her head in shame, then took a couple of steps back, giving him space as the tension thickened between them.

"It's just a small dosage," Pedia explained, her voice quieter, as if she were trying to calm him down. "Enough for all of you to see things differently. It keeps Preliators cautious—always alert, always inspecting everything. When Preliators return from their Trials, we inject them with a temporary antidote. It helps them sleep, keeps the nightmares at bay."

"Temporary!" 0444 burst out, his voice cracking with frustration. His mind raced, piecing together the twisted logic. "So the Harbingers pick off the Preliators they think are weakest and inject them with more of that... poison? It messes with the mind, makes us see things that aren't there, drives us mad." He clenched his fists, anger radiating off him. "But why lie? Why keep us in the dark? We trusted you! We deserved to know the truth from the start!"

"You know why we never tell the truth," Pedia replied, her

tone unyielding, but her eyes softened just enough to show the weight of her words. "The truth is a wound that doesn't heal. The truth always hurts. Do you think if we told you what this program truly demands, you'd all simply accept it? And as for the parents, do you think they'd willingly hand over their sons to become hollowed-out, chemically-controlled servants for the government, discarded in exchange for order? No, most would resist. They'd reject this system entirely. And without the Preliator program, everything falls apart—both worlds left vulnerable and exposed."

0444's eyes narrowed, his frustration clear. "You always told us to be honest, especially with you. To find the weakness and turn it into a strength."

Pedia's eyes flashed as she retorted, "So, you're the innocent one who's never lied?" Her expression hardened, a challenging glint in her gaze. "Is that what you told those two young, terrified women just a few hours ago? Reassuring them that everyone they love is alive and waiting for them?"

0444 froze, the weight of her words hitting him harder than he expected. He replayed the moment in his head, remembering how easily the comforting lie had slipped from his lips. He had reassured those women, even though he knew deep down their chances were slim. His mind searched for justification, but none came.

Pedia didn't wait for his response, her tone shifting to something more measured, though no less forceful. "And that's okay. You did what you had to do to get the job done. If you'd told them the truth, it would've made everything harder—maybe even impossible—to finish the Trial. Just like we keep secrets from you to make you the best. It doesn't matter whether you're from the old world or the new one.

People always lie to get things done. And that's the reason why the Harbinger wanted to keep you alive in this Trial."

She took a step closer, her words striking deeper. "Without those lies, there'd be complete chaos. The truth often brings out the worst in people. But sometimes, it has to be twisted, shaped, and wielded to make them better."

0444 clenched his jaw as Pedia's words sank in. She had lied to all of them, and he had watched his brothers—men he had trained with, fought alongside for years—die like it was all just some twisted game. It felt like a sick reality show, the kind the old world might have watched for entertainment. Their sacrifices, their deaths, all seemed meaningless now.

As much as he hated to admit it, 0444 knew she was right. Lies had become essential to survival, a tool they all used to navigate this brutal world. They had been playing this twisted game for longer than he cared to acknowledge. Now, with everything falling apart, there was only one more question he needed answered.

"What you told me before the Trial... you said I could come visit you afterward. That was never going to happen, was it?"

Pedia simply shook her head, her silence confirming the truth.

0444 closed his eyes, tears streaming down his face. Though he had known, deep down, the truth hit him harder than he expected. Seeing it reflected in her expression was enough to crush him. The truth left a bitter taste, twisting the ideals he had once held into something much darker. Lies, survival, betrayal—everything had become tangled together, forming a cruel reality that felt impossible to escape.

Pedia stepped closer to 0444, gently taking the pistol

from his trembling hands. Her voice softened as she tried to reassure him, "Hey, it's going to be okay." She raised the gun slowly, bringing it up to the side of his head. His eyes locked onto hers, a mixture of confusion and dread flooding his expression. "But I do have some good news," she continued, her voice calm, though charged with an unspoken weight.

He looked at her, waiting, heart racing.

She spoke steadily, her tone calm and unshaken. "We have two choices here. We can keep talking, but it won't change a thing. Even if you find a way out, you'll still end up like the rest of your brothers—just another number, a soulless machine that the people of the U.W.E.G. fear. Or..."

Her hand softly guided his finger to the trigger, deliberate and firm, as though steering him toward a decision. "You can pull this trigger, and everything will be as we always imagined. The pain, the nightmares, the horrible memories—they'll all fade away. From then on, it'll be nothing but peace and good memories."

She stepped back, leaving him grappling with the weight of her words. His hand shook uncontrollably, the cold barrel pressing against his skin. He closed his eyes, recalling simpler times with Pedia—how she had always been there to help him chase his dreams. But doubt crept in, coiling tightly around his heart. "I don't know if I can do this," he admitted, his voice barely a whisper.

Pedia's encouragement cut through his uncertainty. "After all these years of never being able to touch you, of never experiencing the things we've always wanted… now we have that chance. I can finally feel your heartbeat. But will it beat for me? If you pull that trigger, I'll know we were meant to be."

He loved the sound of her words, but his hand trembled, a storm of thoughts swirling in his mind. Gripping her hands gently by her face, he hoped for clarity, for the right decision to surface. But the longer he looked into her eyes, the more he sensed something was off. In a sudden surge of instinct, he pointed the gun at her and pulled the trigger before she could react.

The bullet struck her right shoulder, and shock flickered across her face. She grabbed her wound, fury igniting in her eyes as she glared at him. "This can't happen to me! It's never happened like this!"

With a furious scream, she lunged at him. Caught off guard, 0444 froze as her hand clamped around his throat. Her eyes burned with rage as she hurled him to the ground with incredible strength. Struggling to get back up, he watched in shock as her form began to shift, twisting into something unrecognizable. The horrifying realization hit him: Pedia was never there. It had been the Harbinger all along.

Believing he had a chance, 0444 surged forward, thinking the creature was wounded. But his eyes had deceived him; his last bullet had merely grazed its armored shoulder. The Harbinger anticipated his move, countering with a brutal backhand that sent him sprawling.

"You dare to come after me!" the Harbinger bellowed, its voice echoing with a chilling intensity as it struck him down.

The impact sent 0444 flying nearly ten feet, crashing hard onto the frozen ground. His pistol vanished into the swirling darkness of the fog. The Harbinger loomed over him, watching intently for his next move.

0444 struggled to get back on his feet, rolling onto his stomach before pushing himself upright. He raised his fists, ready to fight, even though he knew they were no match for the creature. Still, he refused to show any fear. The Harbinger smirked, clearly amused. "Most people would be terrified by now," it said mockingly.

0444 said nothing, steadying himself as the creature circled him.

"No one has ever broken free from compound ME5 before," the Harbinger continued, a mocking tone lacing its voice. "You truly are special, just as your dear Pedia said. You could have been a great Preliator. What a shame it's all for nothing."

With a determined glare, 0444 shot back, "So why are you telling me this? What happens next?"

The Harbinger came to a halt, pulling something from behind its back with both hands—a modern mace attached to a thick chain. 0444's blue eyes widened at the sight of the massive weapon, unsure if the chemicals coursing through him were distorting his vision. With a casual flick, the Harbinger tossed one end of the mace near 0444's feet.

Cautiously, he approached it, realizing the compound ME5 was influencing the weapon's form. The Harbinger watched intently as 0444 picked it up, never breaking eye contact.

"I'm going to give you something only a true warrior would ask for," the Harbinger taunted.

As 0444 lifted the mace, feeling its weight settle in his grip, he dropped into a fighting stance. The Harbinger removed the facepiece of its samurai-style helmet, letting it clatter to the ground. Fear surged through 0444, and he instinctively backpedaled a few steps. The Harbinger advanced, spinning the mace effortlessly in the air, its face a void of inky blackness.

"And then what happens next?... You won't be alive to tell

anyone about this 'Trial of Truth!'" the Harbinger declared, its voice echoing with ominous finality.

The Harbinger swung the mace at 0444, who barely dodged the lethal arc. The weapon crashed into the frozen ground, leaving a deep dent and sending snow flying in all directions. The Harbinger swiftly retrieved the mace, spinning it once more with effortless grace. 0444 struggled to control his own mace, feeling its weight more acutely than the creature.

The effects of the dart warped his perception, transforming the Harbinger into a seven-foot monster, a terrifying behemoth with the strength of a hundred men. Its face was a black void, devoid of a soul. In reality, it was a normal six-foot man, pale and hollow-eyed, resembling a zombie—a stark contrast to 0444's vibrant blue eyes.

"She said you would be special. Now prove it!" the Harbinger scowled.

With a wild, dizzying flourish, the Harbinger spun its mace. 0444 felt a surge of overwhelm, torn between the instincts to attack or defend. The Harbinger's mace collided with his own, embedding them in the ground and entangling their weapons. Panic gripped 0444 as the Harbinger twisted its wrist, yanking his mace from his grip with brutal force.

Realizing he was now defenseless, 0444 braced himself for the inevitable blow. The spiked ball of the Harbinger's mace smashed into his chest armor; the impact brutal enough to send him flying. He hit the ground with a cry, blood spilling from his mouth as his chest plate crumpled under the assault.

Struggling to roll onto his stomach, more blood trickled out as he gasped for breath. He knew he had to act quickly or face death. With his left arm protecting his chest, he managed to retrieve his mace and rise to his feet. The Harbinger could have finished him off, but it allowed him a moment to recover, eager for another round.

A chilling laugh echoed from the Harbinger's soulless face, taunting him as it waited to see what he would do next. 0444 launched an offensive, but his movements were sluggish compared to the Harbinger's agility. Each strike was deftly dodged, the creature's laughter ringing out as it toyed with him.

Spinning its mace rapidly, the Harbinger struck again. 0444 anticipated the attack and ducked, but the Harbinger was quick, catching one of his legs with the chain. With a powerful pull, it sent 0444 crashing to the ground once more. He struggled to rise, slower this time, while the Harbinger laughed mockingly. "This is too easy!"

Frustration simmered in 0444 as he stared at the Harbinger in disbelief, grappling with the daunting challenge before him. How could he possibly defeat this creature? He braced himself, waiting to see what the Harbinger would do next.

With a casual toss, the Harbinger flung its mace aside and began walking toward him, cracking its knuckles menacingly. "You won't die tonight from weapons alone. I will destroy you with my own fists!" it bellowed, charging at 0444.

In a desperate attempt to defend himself, 0444 swung his mace with all his might, but the Harbinger sidestepped effortlessly, shoving him hard to the ground. The mace flew into the darkness, lost to the night.

Realizing the Harbinger was deadly serious, 0444 sprang to his feet, determination surging through him. He launched a flurry of punches and kicks, but the Harbinger blocked each one as if anticipating his every move. The thought of striking that black void where a face should be terrified 0444;

he feared being consumed by its emptiness.

"Show me your best!" the Harbinger taunted.

Undeterred, 0444 kept attacking, yet every strike was met with a counter. In a swift motion, the Harbinger caught 0444's fist mid-air and twisted it painfully. 0444 dropped to one knee, eyes clenched in agony, struggling against the creature's overwhelming strength.

"You had your chance," the Harbinger sneered. "Now, let me show you what I can do."

The Harbinger released 0444's hand and shoved him away. As 0444 turned to face his foe, the Harbinger unleashed a flurry of punches and kicks with blinding speed and precision. 0444 struggled to defend himself; each blow landed with brutal accuracy. The Harbinger, seemingly tireless, laughed maniacally as he pummeled 0444, transforming his face into a bloody mask, eyes swollen and bruised.

The relentless onslaught left 0444 staggering: his arms too weak to shield his face. With a fluid motion, the Harbinger stepped back and unleashed a powerful spinning back kick, sending 0444 sprawling to the ground. Dazed and disoriented, he struggled to get up, blood pouring from his mouth and smearing across most of his face.

Realizing he was outmatched, 0444 turned to flee. The Harbinger's laughter echoed behind him, mocking as he watched 0444 stumble away like a wounded animal.

"Maybe I was wrong about you," the Harbinger said, his voice laced with cold disappointment. "I thought you might be the Preliator capable of upholding the Code. But even a Harbinger can make a mistake sometimes."

Ignoring the chilling voice, 0444 collapsed to the ground. Out of the corner of his eye, he spotted one of his pistols nearby, and doubt crept in—had he miscounted his bullets? Crawling on his knees to reach it, he sensed the Harbinger hovering just behind him, toying with his desperation.

"All you wanted was the truth," the Harbinger said. As it prepared to finish him off, it revealed the same futuristic double-bladed spear it had used to kill 0021.

"The truth is I'm stronger, faster, smarter, and more experienced. I know exactly what it takes to be the best. You might be a skilled musician in an orchestra, but I'm the conductor. I set the tempo, and without me, you're just fumbling in the dark."

As 0444 dragged himself toward the gun, the Harbinger's boot came down on his ankle, crushing it with merciless force. A sharp, searing pain ripped through his body, halting his progress.

The Harbinger raised the spear high above its head, ready to strike. The agony compelled 0444 to roll onto his back. Gasping for air, he looked up at the towering figure. With his strength fading, he lifted his right hand; a desperate, silent plea for mercy.

The Harbinger's gaze was cold and unyielding. "I was wrong about you. No Preliator begs for his life. Tell me, what did you learn from your years of training?"

"You should have crushed me completely when you had the chance," 0444 retorted, defiance igniting in his voice.

Confused by his words, the Harbinger hesitated for a split second. That moment was all 0444 needed. With a swift motion, he revealed a hidden one-shot gun from his wrist. The Harbinger's eyes widened in shock; he believed that device was still in development, and he had underestimated 0444.

Before the Harbinger could react, 0444 twisted his wrist and fired. The gunshot echoed through the foggy night, hitting the Harbinger square in its featureless face. The spear slipped from its grip, falling to the ground.

To anyone watching, it looked as though part of the Harbinger's skull had been blown away, with blood gushing out like a fountain. For a brief moment, the creature stood frozen. Then, its body twitched, malfunctioned, and finally collapsed into the snow, lifeless.

Silence enveloped the scene, broken only by 0444's labored breaths. He lay on the ground, staring up at the fog-laden sky, questioning whether he had made the right choice. Had it all been a lie, or would he die with honor? The distinction felt meaningless now. The cold wind seeped into his bones, a grim reminder of his impending death. In those final moments, he closed his eyes, focusing on each slow breath, seeking a fleeting solace amid the horrors of Regret.

CHAPTER 14
WHAT COMES NEXT

0444 lay severely wounded on the frozen ground, staring up at the night sky. He took a deep breath, holding it for a moment, wondering if it would be his last. Not yet, he thought, releasing it slowly and drawing in another. Snowflakes began to fall, their delicate beauty a stark contrast to the harsh world around him. The cold bit deeper with each passing second.

Another breath. His mind wandered to the thoughts that troubled him most. He thought of Pedia, of their past. He wished he could ask her about what the Harbinger had revealed—whether she had known the outcome of his First Trial, if he would live or die. He wanted to ask her about their religion, about its significance. *Was there even a true religion?* Or was he just another puppet, strung along by the government?

The cold crept through his body, his fingertips numb and unresponsive. He wished the Harbinger had never spoken at all. He wished the creature had just killed him, allowing him to embrace the night of the two gods, to become another star in the endless sky. But it had all been a lie.

And now, as the snow fell heavier, he was left alone with that truth.

Complaining was pointless now; there was no one left to hear him. 0444 closed his eyes, surrendering to his fate, letting the snow and cold consume him. He accepted it—this frozen hell would be his end. Perhaps, after death, he would finally know where he belonged.

As his eyes remained shut, something shifted in the darkness—a faint light. *Am I dead?* he wondered. Then a familiar sound broke through the silence: the unmistakable whirring of helicopter blades. His eyes snapped open, and through the swirling snow, he saw a helicopter descending nearby, its rotors kicking up a storm of ice and wind. But after everything—the pain, the torment from the Harbinger—this was nothing. All he could think about was how they had found him.

As the helicopter's blades slowed and its side door opened, two Telos medics, Richard and Scott, stepped out. Richard carried a stretcher, and Scott held a tablet, its screen glowing in the dim light. The tablet beeped steadily, leading them to 0444's exact position. When they reached him, their eyes widened in disbelief.

"By the gods, it's true. He survived the encounter," Richard muttered, kneeling beside 0444 as he extended the stretcher.

"I've never seen anyone survive in this condition," Scott muttered, as he shined a flashlight into 0444's unresponsive eyes. "Harbingers don't operate like this—they either choose a Preliator to survive or finish them off completely. Leaving someone in a state like this... it's unheard of."

"Maybe this is what the Harbinger wanted," Richard

suggested grimly. "A slow, frozen death alone in Regret."

Scott paused, considering the idea. "Maybe." But as he examined 0444's eyes, his concern deepened. They were completely blue—a telltale sign of a full dosage of the Harbinger's fear-inducing drug. A cold chill ran down his spine. Something had gone horribly wrong.

"Richard, call for backup," Scott said sharply, his voice tense. "We have another body to pick up."

"What do you mean?" Richard asked, confused as he prepared to lift 0444 onto the stretcher.

Scott's face hardened as he stood up. "We have a Harbinger's body to take back with us."

Richard's skepticism was palpable. "Impossible, only one has ever defeated a Harbinger..."

But Scott wasn't paying attention to Richard's doubts. His foot had nudged something solid beneath the snow. At first, he thought it was a rock or a chunk of ice, but when he shined his flashlight down, he realized it was something far more ominous.

"Richard!" Scott shouted, the urgency in his voice cutting through the cold night air. "I found the Harbinger!"

Richard, still doubtful, approached to see for himself. As soon as he laid eyes on it, his disbelief shattered. His jaw dropped, and he stood frozen, staring at the figure in the snow, making sure it really was the Harbinger.

Without hesitation, Scott barked, "Call the helicopter. We need another stretcher out here. Now."

Richard immediately radioed for another team, knowing they couldn't leave without both bodies. The Harbinger's death raised countless questions, and they needed to find out how 0444 had survived an encounter no one was meant to survive.

By the time the second Telos team arrived, they efficiently began strapping the Harbinger onto a stretcher, while the first team carefully lifted 0444, whose life was hanging by a thread. With both bodies secured, the teams headed back to the helicopter, burdened with the weight of what they had just uncovered.

With an oxygen mask over his face, 0444's eyes fluttered open. For a moment, he thought he was dead. But as the cold air bit his skin and the ache in his body remained, he realized he was still alive. Strapped to a stretcher, he couldn't move, but for the first time since entering Regret, a sense of safety washed over him. He believed his surviving companions had returned for him. He had so much to tell them, about the Harbinger, the lies, everything.

As they loaded him into the helicopter, he tried to turn his head, searching for familiar faces. His heart sank when he saw none of his fellow Preliators—none of the team that had entered the Trial with him. He quickly deduced that this was a second rescue team, not his companions.

The engines roared to life, the vibrations rattling through the stretcher. Unease gnawed at him, his blue eyes darting around as a creeping realization set in. Then, they placed a second stretcher beside him. His gaze locked onto it—on the body bag containing the Harbinger. Panic surged through him. He wanted to scream, to warn them. The Harbinger couldn't be trusted, even in death.

Before he could react, Scott clamped a hand firmly over his mask, preventing him from removing it. At the same moment, Richard jabbed a syringe into his left shoulder, injecting a mysterious substance. 0444's vision began to blur, and his body grew heavy and unresponsive. His mind screamed at him to fight, to resist, but the drug's effects were overwhelming. As his eyelids drooped, his last conscious thought was a chilling wave of dread.

The helicopter blades whirred at full speed, drowning out the world as they lifted into the air, leaving the frozen wasteland of Regret behind. As 0444 drifted into unconsciousness, he remained unaware of the true intentions of the men escorting him. This was only the beginning of what awaited him at Telos.

Back at Telos, in a small, sterile room where everything was blindingly white—the floors, walls, and ceiling—the atmosphere felt heavy, despite its spotless appearance. The U.W.E.G. called this place the *Review Room*, where every Preliator went after completing a Trial. In the center of the room stood a single chair, the only thing breaking the stark emptiness. Sitting in that chair was Preliator 2890.

He sat still, waiting, the only sign of life being the slow transformation of his eyes as they turned a little spotty blue—a symptom of the compound injected into him days ago, now quietly altering him from within. His gaze was locked on the small camera mounted on the far wall, knowing someone was watching but not knowing when they would appear.

The silence stretched on, every second feeling like an hour. Then, without warning, the straps on the chair snapped into place, constricting his wrists and ankles. Panic surged through him as he tried to pull free, but the restraints held him tightly, immobilizing him completely. The more he fought, the tighter they seemed to squeeze.

Suddenly, the room brightened, and out of the corner of his eye, something shifted. A figure materialized—a different version of Pedia, yet unmistakably her. This version had an eerie blue glow, her form almost luminous against the stark whiteness of the room. She wore what looked like a lab coat, the kind you'd expect from someone working in a sterile laboratory. Her disturbingly cheerful expression clashed with the cold steel restraints holding him captive, making the moment feel even more unsettling.

"Welcome back, Preliator 2890," Pedia said cheerfully. 2890 didn't know how to respond, so he simply nodded.

Pedia continued, "Today, we're here to discuss your first completed Trial. I want to know how it went from your perspective."

She waited expectantly while 2890 took a moment to gather his thoughts. Finally, he said, "Well, we completed the mission as requested, but..."

"But what?" Pedia asked, feigning ignorance, though she already knew.

"A lot of good men didn't make it," 2890 replied, his voice heavy with emotion. "Honestly, I don't know how I survived. I guess you could call it luck."

Pedia began to pace around the chair, her movements confident and practiced, as if she had done this countless times before. "Why do you think you were lucky to be here, alive and well?"

2890 hesitated, unsure whether to share what he had experienced. He feared she wouldn't believe him, but he felt he had no choice. "Something was out there, hunting us down."

"Oh, you mean some other group, like 'The Collectors,' or maybe a rival group you crossed paths with?" Pedia asked, her tone casual.

2890 shook his head firmly. "No."

"Well, then what?" Pedia pressed, her curiosity piqued.

2890 began to sweat. "I don't really know what it was. We started calling it a monster, something I believe wasn't from here. It had one purpose: to hunt us down, one after another."

Pedia feigned ignorance. "A monster in Regret? According to my data, there are over four million prisoners there, many of whom are called monsters."

"This thing is no human," 2890 replied quickly. "We had multiple chances to kill it, but it just kept coming after us."

Silence hung in the air as Pedia seemed to process this information, continuing her slow circuit around the room. Meanwhile, a robotic arm silently descended from the ceiling behind 2890, holding a needle poised just behind his neck, though he remained oblivious to its presence.

"Based on your body language, I believe you're telling the truth," Pedia said, her tone steady. "The question is, will you keep this quiet and pretend this never happened?"

"Never happened?" 2890 exclaimed, his voice rising in disbelief. "How can you expect me to forget something like that? This will haunt my dreams for as long as I live! I have to tell someone—warn them—before someone else ends up suffering the same fate!"

"I have my ways to keep things quiet," Pedia said, her gaze fixed on the robotic arm. Without hesitation, the arm swiftly injected a chemical into 2890's neck. He flinched at the unexpected sting, but before he could react further, the needle had already done its job and retracted.

"Just let the substance work its magic," Pedia reassured him. "Trust me, you'll feel a lot better."

2890's body convulsed briefly as he struggled against

the effects, his eyes widening and his mouth falling open in shock. Then, suddenly, his body went still, overcome by a wave of profound relaxation unlike anything he had ever felt. It was as though a heavy weight had been lifted from him. The horrifying memories of the monster—the fear, the chaos—began to dissipate, slipping away into the void as if they had never existed.

"I see someone is enjoying himself," Pedia observed, her voice almost playful.

2890 didn't respond; instead, he closed his eyes, surrendering to the sensation as the pain and horrific memories began to fade into oblivion.

Pedia continued, "No more monsters lurking in your mind. It will stay this way for days." A smile crept across 2890's face as he embraced the idea.

"I hope you're enjoying this," she said, watching as 2890 visibly relaxed, his body surrendering completely to the euphoric high. Her tone was calm, almost soothing, but carried an unmistakable edge. "This is what Preliators receive after completing a Trial—a reward, if you will. But there's a catch."

She leaned in slightly, her glowing presence casting an eerie blue hue over his face. "If you want more of this bliss, you'll need to follow some rules. First, you keep your mouth shut about everything you've seen out there. No exceptions. The only time you're honest is here, in this room, and nowhere else. Break this rule, and I promise you..."

Her expression darkened, the cheerful facade slipping just enough to reveal the threat beneath. "That monster? It will return. Not just in your dreams, but in every waking moment. Do you understand?"

2890 nodded slowly. "I understand."

"So, is there any 'monster' roaming around Regret?" Pedia asked, her eyes keenly fixed on him.

"There are no monsters in Regret," 2890 said firmly, shaking his head slowly, refusing to believe it.

"Good," Pedia said, her smile widening. She knew that Preliator 2890 had now joined the ranks of the silent soldiers, ready to comply with whatever the U.W.E.G demanded of him.

As she observed him basking in the effects of the drug, she made a mental note to wait until he was fully immersed in his newfound tranquility. Once he was settled, she would discreetly exit and pay a visit to Preliator 0774 in the next room, ensuring the same conditioning took place.

Outside the Preliator airstrip in Telos, a group of weary individuals stands in a long line, shivering in the biting cold. This line leads into a smaller tunnel, a stark contrast to the one that had taken them into Regret. Here, they wait for the removal of their chips, a step toward returning to the New World.

The people in line look exhausted, their faces drawn and pale from the harsh conditions. As they shuffle forward, Pedia's familiar voice crackles over the speakers, repeating a scripted message designed to reassure them.

"Welcome back to the New World of the U.W.E.G. Please stay patient and calm until it is your turn to move up the line. The chip will be removed, and you will receive a hot shower and fresh clothing before you enter. First, a member of Telos will answer all your questions. Then, you'll be able to contact the closest member of your family. When you re-enter, please be kind and follow the rules of the Ian Royale Code of Law.

Thank you and have yourself a great day."

In the midst of the crowd, Kimberly and Pam huddle together under a thin, cheap blanket that offers little warmth. Kimberly has her eyes closed, lost in thoughts of the quick, hot shower that awaits her—the first since she was thrust into the nightmare of Regret. The prospect of warmth fuels her hope, even as the cold bites at her skin.

Pam glances at her friend, noticing the serene look on Kimberly's face. "It'll be worth it," she whispers, trying to offer a bit of comfort as they wait, longing for the warmth and safety of home.

While Pam tried to contain her excitement, she recalled what Preliator 0444 had told her: her husband was waiting for her. The thought of seeing his smile and holding him again made all the hardships they had faced worthwhile.

As the line inched forward, Pam noticed a member of Telos asking questions to someone ahead. She patted Kimberly's shoulder, signaling that they were getting closer. Just when they were about to get excited, the sound of a helicopter filled the air, drawing Pam's attention.

Turning to her right, she watched as the helicopter landed, its blades still spinning. The back door swung open, and several Telos medical personnel rushed out, two stretchers in tow—one carrying a body bag and the other holding a Preliator. Pam's heart raced as she considered the possibility that the Preliator on the stretcher could be 0444, and that he might have survived after all.

As the line shuffled forward, it was finally Kimberly's turn to answer a few questions. Pam, momentarily lost in her thoughts, smiled as she watched the stretcher until it disappeared from view. She silently hoped that if it was

0444, he would recover quickly, so she could thank him for everything he had said and the sacrifice he made for her.

Pam longed to see him one more time, not just to express her gratitude but to ensure he was okay. She wanted to show him that not all Preliators were heartless soldiers. She believed that some, like him, were genuinely good. Despite her questions about certain laws, she understood that Preliators aimed to uphold their beliefs and often told the truth.

Suddenly, an angry voice broke through her reverie. "I don't understand! I was told my family would be here waiting for me. I was told Matt was alive and well!" Kimberly's outburst jolted Pam back to the present, pulling her attention back to the line.

The Telos officer remained calm as he replied, "The person you're describing, Matt Huffman, has been dead for months. Who told you he was alive?"

"One of your special Preliators told me!" Kimberly snapped back; her voice tinged with frustration. "He promised me that Matt is alive and waiting for me here, with the rest of my family."

The Telos staffer glanced at his tablet and frowned. "I'm sorry, but at first, his chip stopped working, and he was declared missing. Then, Matt Huffman was found dead by the Preliators just moments ago in the northern part of Regret. Here are the pictures they took."

He turned the tablet toward Kimberly. She peered at the screen for a few seconds, enough time to catch a glimpse of a body that resembled Matt's. Quickly, she pushed the tablet away, shaking her head in denial. "You're lying. Preliator 0444 told me that he is alive! He wouldn't dare lie about something like that to me. You had to be there to understand!"

The Telos staffer, needing to keep the line moving, pressed a button on his tablet. Within moments, two Preliators appeared, armed with assault rifles and their eyes glowing yellow. "Whether you believe me or not, you need to keep moving and contact your family to make arrangements to get back home. If you refuse to cooperate, we can put you back in Regret."

Kimberly looked at Pam, tears streaming down her face, heartbroken. She felt ashamed for having believed in 0444, but she had no choice but to comply. With a heavy heart and tears pouring down her face, she whispered, "Matt, I'm sorry for making you fall for me. This is all my fault!"

As Pam processed Kimberly's words, she realized the truth behind 0444's earlier assurances. He had said those things just to motivate them to move, prioritizing his mission over their well-being. Watching Kimberly walk away, Pam felt a growing sense of dread as it became her turn to speak with the Telos staffer. She looked at him, anxiety tightening her chest, fearing she would receive the same devastating news as Kimberly. Her eyes began to water as uncertainty loomed over her.

In a dimly lit, spacious room, Preliator 0444 lay motionless on a bed, restrained by straps. An oxygen mask covered his face, and a feeding tube was attached to keep him alive. His body was dressed in white, sheet-like clothing, with bandages wrapped around the cuts and bruises left by the Harbinger. He was kept in a deep, drug-induced sleep.

The quiet room echoed with the sound of footsteps as three doctors entered—Dr. Brown, Dr. Wingstead, and Dr. Patel. Dr. Brown and Dr. Patel carried tablets, while Dr. Wingstead held a small glass container filled with a green chemical.

Dr. Wingstead approached 0444's bedside, removing an empty glass container and replacing it with the fresh one. The green chemical inside began to transform into gas as soon as it connected with the machine, slowly being released into the air in 0444's mask. He began to inhale the gas.

The doctors watched in silence as the chemical gas entered his system. Gradually, 0444's eyes fluttered open, his pupils now a deep, glowing blue. His mouth opened, as though he wanted to speak, but his gaze was distant—his mind clearly somewhere far away.

In Preliator 0444's mind, he stood alone in a vast desert under a starless night sky. The air was still, but with each step he took, the ground shifted beneath him like quicksand, threatening to pull him under. Panic crept in as he glanced around, desperate to find a way out. High above, a blinding light pierced the darkness, catching his attention. He raised his hand to shield his eyes, squinting to make out what it was.

Back in the room, Dr. Brown stood over him, shining a flashlight directly into his face. The doctor studied 0444's reactions carefully, satisfied that the drug was taking effect. He leaned closer and spoke firmly. "Preliator 0444, can you hear me?"

In the desert of his mind, 0444 knew he was trapped in another U.W.E.G. mind game, perhaps orchestrated by a Harbinger or someone else pulling the strings. The darkness echoed the voice again, this time louder. "Preliator 0444, can you hear me?"

Feeling the weight of the situation, 0444 had no choice but to respond. He gazed up into the blinding light and shouted, "Yes, I can hear you!"

The voice responded calmly, "Good. We don't want you to

be afraid. We just have a couple of questions to ask."

0444 took a few steps forward, trying to get closer to the voice, but with each movement, he sank deeper into the desert sand. The ground felt like quicksand, pulling him in. He stopped, looking around, analyzing the situation. This wasn't real—just another twisted mind game, like when the Harbinger had morphed into Pedia. He knew he was drugged again.

Suddenly, a laugh escaped him, breaking the eerie silence. He looked up at the light, defiant. "You think this is going to scare me into telling you what you want to know?" he yelled. "I've beaten the Harbinger's mind games, and now you think Compound ME5—or whatever this drug is—will make me break?"

In the observation room, the three doctors exchanged stunned glances. No one had ever called out the drugs before. Most Preliators, under the influence, would be terrified, spilling everything they knew. Dr. Brown leaned in closer to 0444, intrigued. "So, the Harbinger told you about the process for all Preliators?"

0444 smirked. "He told me everything—all the lies we were fed, the fake beliefs forced on us. It was all designed to turn us into your emotionless servants. And the more I think about it, the more I realize: the ME drug wasn't just used on Preliators. It's probably been used on others too—ex-con Regret citizens, maybe even people in the new world." He paused, his eyes fixed on the glowing light. "I could go on, but I think you get the idea."

The three doctors exchanged uneasy glances, clearly alarmed that 0444 had uncovered their secrets.

"Why do you think the Harbinger told you everything?"

asked the voice from the light, its tone calm but questioning.

0444 paused for a moment, then replied, "The Harbinger thought it was going to finish me off right then and there. It wanted to toy with my mind a bit longer, drag out the suffering. It had plenty of chances to kill me. I guess I just got lucky."

"So, what will you do with this new information?" the light questioned, its presence growing more intense as 0444 continued sinking into the quicksand, though the sensation didn't bother him anymore.

He thought for a moment, weighing his options as the sand dragged him deeper. "There are only two choices," he said. "I can expose everything and tell the truth. Or... you can do what the Harbinger couldn't—finish me off and keep this all going."

The light responded without hesitation, "There are always more than two choices, especially in the position you're in."

By now, 0444 was sinking even further, though he stood still. He clenched his fists, recognizing the psychological trap they were trying to spring. His voice grew angrier, more defiant. "I've already beaten your first two attempts. Do you really think a third, or a fourth, or dozens more will break me? You won't change me. The easiest way is to end me now! No matter what you try, I won't stay silent, I won't be controlled, and I'll make sure everyone knows the truth about what goes on here."

Back in the room, 0444 shouted, "Your only choice is the truth, or finish me off! I won't break from anything you throw at me! So go ahead. I'm waiting to see the disappointment on your face when you fail again. Fail, and fail some more." His voice rang out, full of defiance and unshakable resolve.

Suddenly, Supreme Commander Douglas Sr. entered the room. The father of the current Supreme Commander Douglas, his presence exuded far more authority and intimidation than his son's. Though in his fifties, decades of leadership had hardened him, making him appear unshakable. Standing in the background, he took in the scene, a faint smirk barely hidden beneath his thick mustache.

With an air of cold confidence, he strode forward, stopping beside the doctors. Turning to Dr. Wingstead, who was closest to 0444, he issued a sharp command: "Put him back to sleep. Now."

Dr. Wingstead snapped into action, his hands trembling slightly as he removed the old chemical container. He fumbled with the new one, knowing the Supreme Commander's eyes were on him, scrutinizing his every move. After a few tense moments, the new container clicked into place, and he quickly pressed the button. The gas began to flow through the tube into 0444's mask.

Unaware of what was happening, 0444 inhaled deeply, still shouting, but his words began to slow. "Finish... me... off..." His voice trailed off as the sedative took effect. His eyes fluttered, struggling to stay open, before finally closing as he drifted into unconsciousness.

Dr. Wingstead exhaled, relieved to have satisfied the Supreme Commander's order. Silence filled the room once again, the tension broken only by the steady hiss of the gas.

The Supreme Commander turned to face the three doctors, his expression darkening. "Well, you know what comes next. Take Preliator 0444 to Level Six. Keep him sedated until his body is fully recovered. Once he's stable, begin testing under *Operation Restore* immediately."

The room fell silent, the weight of the order settling heavily on the doctors. None of them dared to question him, but the sadness in their eyes was unmistakable. Satisfied with their compliance, the Supreme Commander nodded. "Good," he muttered, turning to leave the room.

But just as he was about to step out, Dr. Brown's voice broke the uneasy silence. "Why him, for *Operation Restore*? Ever since Dr. Miller disappeared six years ago, everyone who tried to take over his work has failed. If it fails again, Preliator 0444 will be lost. I feel—"

The Supreme Commander abruptly stopped in his tracks, turning around slowly. His eyes bore into Dr. Brown as he cut him off. "That name—Dr. Miller—will never be spoken again. Do you understand?"

Dr. Brown swallowed hard, nodding as he shrank under the Supreme Commander's imposing presence. In a society that claimed equality, it was clear who truly held power—especially in this part of the world. "I understand, but—"

The Supreme Commander interrupted him. "I hear you have a young son now. A perfect little family—your wife, your daughter, and your new baby boy."

Dr. Brown nodded hesitantly. "Yes, that's right."

The Supreme Commander's smile was icy and deliberate. "We wouldn't want anything disturbing their perfect lives, would we? Perhaps a reassignment to a harsher job—like working on an ocean oil rig, or even something far worse. Surely, we want a better, easier future for them, don't we?"

Dr. Brown's face turned pale. "No, no… I understand. I won't mention that name again," he stammered, his voice trembling. The other two doctors exchanged uneasy glances, their wide eyes betraying their fear at the not-so-subtle threat.

The Supreme Commander smirked, his voice chilling. "You know Preliator 0444 is only the second ever to kill a Harbinger. The first one knew how to keep his mouth shut. But this one? He says he won't, which makes him the perfect first human subject for 'Operation Restore.'"

Dr. Patel hesitated before asking, "And if 0444 fails 'Operation Restore,' what happens to him?"

The Commander gave a casual shrug. "Then you'll get your wish. Kill him. And we'll wait for a new volunteer to emerge." With a satisfied grin, he turned and exited the room.

The three doctors stood in silence, staring at 0444, who was deep in sleep. Dr. Patel sighed, "Well, let's get started."

COMING SOON

THE WORLD OF REGRET
THE CHAOTIC ROADS

When you enter the world without rules, you either die or lose yourself to madness. Escaping the madness is difficult, but once you step onto the *Chaotic Roads*, getting your insanity back becomes nearly impossible.